Luke tilted his head back to stare at the ceiling, and Claire saw the weariness claim his body.

"For the first time in a long, long time, you've got me wanting what I can't have," he said when he finally looked at her again. "Claire, a week from now I'll be back behind bars, and I won't be getting out for a lot of years."

"It doesn't have to be that way," she told him, unconsciously wringing her slender hands.

"Yes, it does. For me, it does. Not for you, though. Look at you," he said, a tender smile lifting the corners of his mouth in spite of the grim resolve still in his eyes. "You're young, and smart, and beautiful. You deserve the very best from life."

"What if I said *you're* the best for me?"

His answer was quiet. "Then you'd be as wrong as you've ever been...."

Dear Reader,

We've got one of our most irresistible lineups ever for you this month, and you'll know why as soon as I start talking about the very first book. With *The Return of Rafe MacKade*, *New York Times* bestseller Nora Roberts begins a new miniseries, The MacKade Brothers, that will move back and forth between Intimate Moments and Special Edition. Rafe is also our Heartbreaker for the month, so don't get your heart broken by missing this very special book!

Romantic Traditions continues with Patricia Coughlin's *Love in the First Degree*, a compelling spin on the "wrongly convicted" story line. For fans of our Spellbound titles, there's *Out-Of-This-World Marriage* by Maggie Shayne, a marriage-of-convenience story with a star-crossed—and I mean that literally!— twist. Finish the month with new titles from popular authors Terese Ramin with *A Certain Slant of Light*, Alexandra Sellers with *Dearest Enemy*, as well as *An Innocent Man* by an exciting new writer, Margaret Watson.

This month, and every month, when you're looking for exciting romantic reading, come to Silhouette Intimate Moments—and enjoy!

Yours,

Leslie J. Wainger
Senior Editor and Editorial Coordinator

Please address questions and book requests to:
Silhouette Reader Service
U.S.: 3010 Walden Ave., P.O. Box 1325, Buffalo, NY 14269
Canadian: P.O. Box 609, Fort Erie, Ont. L2A 5X3

LOVE IN THE FIRST DEGREE

PATRICIA COUGHLIN

Published by Silhouette Books
America's Publisher of Contemporary Romance

If you purchased this book without a cover you should be aware that this book is stolen property. It was reported as "unsold and destroyed" to the publisher, and neither the author nor the publisher has received any payment for this "stripped book."

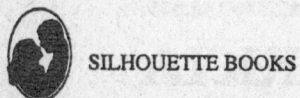 SILHOUETTE BOOKS

ISBN 0-373-07632-0

LOVE IN THE FIRST DEGREE

Copyright © 1995 by Patricia Madden Coughlin

All rights reserved. Except for use in any review, the reproduction or utilization of this work in whole or in part in any form by any electronic, mechanical or other means, now known or hereafter invented, including xerography, photocopying and recording, or in any information storage or retrieval system, is forbidden without the written permission of the editorial office, Silhouette Books, 300 East 42nd Street, New York, NY 10017 U.S.A.

All characters in this book have no existence outside the imagination of the author and have no relation whatsoever to anyone bearing the same name or names. They are not even distantly inspired by any individual known or unknown to the author, and all incidents are pure invention.

This edition published by arrangement with Harlequin Enterprises B.V.

® and TM are trademarks of Harlequin Enterprises B.V., used under license. Trademarks indicated with ® are registered in the United States Patent and Trademark Office, the Canadian Trade Marks Office and in other countries.

Printed in U.S.A.

Books by Patricia Coughlin

Silhouette Intimate Moments

Love in the First Degree #632

Silhouette Special Edition

Shady Lady #438
The Bargain #485
Some Like It Hot #523
The Spirit Is Willing #602
Her Brother's Keeper #726
Gypsy Summer #786
The Awakening #804
My Sweet Baby #837
When Stars Collide #867
Mail Order Cowboy #919

Silhouette Books

Love Child

Silhouette Summer Sizzlers 1990
"Easy Come..."

PATRICIA COUGHLIN

is also known to romance fans as Liz Grady and lives in Rhode Island with her husband and two sons. A former schoolteacher, she says she started writing to fill her hours at home after her second son was born. Having always read romances, she decided to try penning her own. Though she was duly astounded by the difficulty of her new hobby, her hard work paid off, and she accomplished the rare feat of having her very first manuscript published. For now, writing has replaced quilting, embroidery and other pastimes, and with more than a dozen published novels under her belt, the author hopes to be happily writing romances for a long time to come.

Prologue

Already the room smelled like blood.

Luke Cabrio felt the skin at the back of his neck prickle as he stared down at the body on the floor at his feet. Nick Addison looked pretty dead, all right. He also looked... stunned, Luke decided. As if he hadn't expected the bullet that had caught him square in the throat and driven him onto his back between two Queen Anne chairs.

No reason he should have expected it, Luke thought. Seldom is a bully attuned to when his victim has been pushed as far as possible before lashing out in return. As far as Luke was concerned, Nick Addison was a bully of the very worst sort.

The man's blood had splattered across the chair's ivory-brocade seat cushions and made a wide, dark stain on the pale carpet. It spread out on either side of his head, reminding Luke of the ink blots a shrink used. Butterfly wings. The inane association came immediately to mind, and then, just as inanely, he thought about how the hotel's housekeeping staff was going to have their work cut out for them trying to clean up this mess.

Addison was a big man, at least six feet two and two hundred and twenty pounds, and when he fell he'd knocked over a small, oval, cherry-wood table, sending the lamp and clock on it flying. Using the hand not holding the gun, Luke managed to right the table and the lamp. There wasn't much he could do about the clock, however. Its black plastic casing hadn't survived the fall. He replaced it on the table anyway and watched for a moment to see if the time would change. He craved some sign of normality, evidence that outside this room life was going on just as routinely as it had a few minutes ago. The block numbers remained eerily fixed on 9:17, however, and Luke finally looked away.

Chalk up another casualty for this night, he thought grimly, steeling himself for what he knew he had to do. Four years as the security manager for the Delta Queen Hotel and Casino and until now he'd never been the one to check on a corpse. Ironic that his first should be a corpse of his own making.

He went down on one knee and with his free hand carefully felt for a pulse beneath Addison's left ear. He couldn't seem to let go of the damn gun. Addison felt warm and slightly damp and very still. Luke leaned closer, moving his fingertips a quarter inch one way, then another, hoping for he wasn't sure what. A hint of life? Or proof that Addison was out of the way for good? Somehow he managed to get blood on his white shirt and the leg of his pants before convincing himself that he was indeed dead.

Damn, damn, damn, Luke thought. Maybe he ought to feel sorry Addison was gone, but he didn't. He was a lot of things, but a hypocrite wasn't one of them. He was very sorry about how it had come about, and he cursed himself softly.

Damn, he thought again, staring at the gun in his hand, a beauty of a .38 registered to him. This wasn't good.

Should he try to get rid of the gun? Change his clothes? Wipe the room for prints? For a man who dealt with crime, with the unsavory characters who committed them and with police on a fairly regular basis, he suddenly had as much of a notion about what he ought to do next as Mother Teresa would in this situation.

Oh, there's a stretch, Cabrio, he thought disgustedly. This was hardly the moment to compare himself to a woman as close to a saint as he could imagine.

He still couldn't decide what to do, only that he needed time to think. But he wasn't going to get any, he realized, as he heard a sharp rap on the hotel room door.

"Atlantic City Police," called out a rough voice, just seconds before the door was shoved open.

Luke recognized the young officer who was first through the door. Frank Callahan. And his partner, Jim something, a quiet guy with a mustache like a black caterpillar stretched along his top lip. Naturally they recognized Luke, as well.

Callahan glanced from him to the body on the floor and whistled through his teeth. "Looks like you've got yourself a live one, Luke," he exclaimed, guffawing at his own joke.

Ordinarily Luke would respond with an agreeable smile, having come to understand the gallows humor some police officers used to shield themselves from the horror they dealt with on a daily basis. Tonight, however, he was barely conscious of the remark.

"Surprised to find you already here," Callahan continued, putting away the gun he'd drawn before entering.

"Why's that?" Luke asked, his throat dry and scratchy. *From fear,* he thought. Even his damn palms were sweating, making the gun feel slippery. When was the last time that had happened?

"You getting a cold?" Callahan asked, squinting at him.

"Must be," Luke countered. He cleared his throat. "Why are you surprised to find me here?"

"The desk told us they couldn't raise you," he explained. "Said you weren't answering your beeper. Since you were incommunicado, as they say, and it's Brad's night off, we just came on up."

His partner, Jim, gave a nod toward Luke's hand, hanging at his side. "Find that here?"

"Find it here?" Luke echoed, feeling a half step behind the action.

"Yeah," Callahan retorted, "the gun you're holding, the one you've gone and put your greasy prints all over. Heck, Luke, you know better than that." He shook his head disgustedly. "Did the gunman drop it?"

Of course, Luke realized, as it all began coming together for him. Callahan and his partner naturally assumed that he was here for the same reason they were. Someone must have heard the shot and called the front desk. They'd tried beeping him, but of course he'd ignored the calls. Hell, he'd barely been aware of the persistent yapping of the small pager hooked to his belt.

They assumed he was here in his capacity of security manager for the hotel, to investigate the incident. They didn't appear to have any suspicion whatsoever that he might have played a part in what had gone on here. They'd even provided him with a perfect explanation for why his fingerprints were on the gun. He'd made a mistake and touched something at a crime scene. Dumb, yes, but it wasn't the first time someone had made a dumb mistake.

He could play along, he thought, a sudden blast of hope making his heart pound frantically. He could just let them go on assuming the obvious. He could walk out of here and leave this whole mess in the hands of the police. And they, his thoughts continued logically, would promptly launch an all-out investigation into the murder. Immediately his hopes dimmed.

He had a great deal of respect for the Atlantic City Police and he knew they were relentless on unsolved cases.

Love in the First Degree

They would scour this room for fingerprints and other evidence, for hair and fibers, and they would piece together a picture of everyone who had set foot in the room recently, would track their movements. They would open the door on Addison's life and his past. They would discover his reason for being here, would make lists of his known enemies, and all too soon they would finger his killer.

Just the thought of it made him go cold inside. He thought about the waiting and worrying, the constant looking over his shoulder, wondering if this was the day they'd figure out the truth and make an arrest. No, he couldn't stand for that to happen.

There was only one thing he could do to take control over this out of their hands.

"Do you want to give us a statement now?" Callahan was asking him, his tone offhand, "or wait for the homicide guys to get here?"

"Neither," Luke replied, no longer undecided about what he was going to do. "I want a lawyer."

Chapter 1

Claire stood outside the Atlantic City county jail and wondered if she was losing her mind. She had to be, she decided. There wasn't any other plausible explanation for being there.

Last Friday she had won the biggest case of her entire career and what had she done to celebrate? She had walked away from her job with one of the most prestigious law firms in Rhode Island and driven all the way to Atlantic City to help a man she hadn't seen in twelve years. A man who hadn't asked for her help, who in all likelihood didn't even remember her name, and who—for all she really knew—was a cold-blooded murderer.

No, she amended quickly, that last wasn't true. While it was very possible that Luke Cabrio might not remember her name, it was not possible that he had murdered Nick Addison, the man he was accused of shooting. She was so utterly convinced of his innocence that her most pressing concern about meeting him face-to-face was not one of safety, but of recognition. She worried that even after she'd

Love in the First Degree

told him her name, Luke would stare at her blankly, with no idea who she was and absolutely no recollection of the old memories that she had never quite forgotten.

To avoid the possibility of such an ego-bruising moment, Claire had taken the precaution of contacting the state public-defenders office and asking the attorney appointed to represent Luke to relay a message to him. In it, she'd expressed concern for his predicament, mentioned that they had attended high school together and offered to meet with him to see if she could be of any help. The return message had been as blunt and as heedless of polite convention as Luke himself. It had been difficult to tell if the public defender was more amused or embarrassed at having to relay Luke's response to her over the telephone.

"Mr. Cabrio asked me to tell you—and I quote," he added, " 'Thanks, but mind your own business.' "

Of course, Claire thought as she tightened her grip on the handle of her leather briefcase and started for the prison entrance, that's exactly what she ought to do. Mind her own business. Tell herself she'd tried to help and Luke had refused her offer. Then she should get in her car and drive back to her comfortable life, respectable friends and nice safe job. She ought to turn and run.

Unfortunately, she couldn't. Her parents had raised her to be cautious, true, but she had also been taught to pay her debts in full. Right now the situation with Luke had her caught between those two good bits of advice. She owed Luke Cabrio big-time, and she wasn't going home until she'd settled the score.

While she wasn't officially representing Luke, the public defender, Gerald Rancourt, had agreed to arrange with the prison officials for her to meet with him. Claire showed her identification to the uniformed guard at the gate, who checked the approved visitors' list for her name and then directed her inside and through a series of checkpoints.

Another guard led her to a small room set aside for prisoners to confer privately with their attorneys.

It had been years since Claire's stomach had done somersaults at the loud metallic clang of a prison gate swinging shut behind her. Back then, fresh out of law school, she'd been uneasy at the thought of visiting jailed clients, at the prospect of being locked in a cell block with hundreds of prisoners. At the moment, however, it was the thought of being locked in a tiny room with one specific prisoner that was making her palms sweat. Worse, Claire knew she'd be sweating even if her meeting with Luke was to take place in Times Square or a field of daisies. It wasn't the surroundings that had her on edge, it was the man.

The meeting room was predictably small and Spartan, with only a small table and two folding chairs positioned beneath a light fixture mounted flush with the ceiling. Fluorescent, she noted glumly, wondering if there was a more unflattering backdrop than the combination of fluorescent light and institution green walls. Not that it mattered, she took pains to remind herself, even as she smoothed the white silk shell she was wearing under her collarless gray suit and wished she'd thought to choose something with a little more color.

Though it was July, her schedule didn't allow for much time in the sun and her fair skin looked more pale than ever in this light.

She could have at least worn her new linen suit, she thought belatedly. Its turquoise hue would have played up the blond streaks in her light brown hair and made her eyes look even bluer. Not that it mattered, she told herself again. After all, she was here to help Luke, not impress him.

She barely had time to sit and open her briefcase before Luke was led in by a guard, who did a quick inspection of the room before stepping out again.

"You've got thirty minutes," he informed them as he pulled the door shut.

Love in the First Degree

Claire watched, not even breathing, as Luke leaned back against the locked door. At six-one, he was tall enough that his head rested against the small window near the top of the door. He was wearing the standard prison-issue blue jeans and chambray shirt with white, high-top Nikes. Several days worth of whiskers added a decidedly menacing touch to his lean face. Whiskers and prison garb aside, however, he was still, hands down, the most arrogantly handsome man Claire had ever seen.

Gone was the dark brown, shoulder-length mane she remembered from high school, and the passing years had left faint creases on his face that hadn't been there back when he'd been the undisputed bad boy of their small hometown of Oaklawn, Rhode Island. Under the best of circumstances, thirty-two looked different from twenty, and Claire had good reason to suspect that the circumstances of Luke's life had been less than the best. The newspaper photo taken at the time of his arrest had prepared her for the small, inevitable changes in his appearance, but nothing could have prepared her for the way he was looking at her.

His gray eyes were narrow, his gaze coolly assessing. He let it slide from her face, down over her pearl gray designer suit and matching high-heel pumps, and back again. He didn't look pleased.

But, Claire noted in an attempt to reassure herself, at least he wasn't staring at her blankly.

"Hello, Luke," she said, getting to her feet and extending her right hand. "I'm—"

"I know who you are," he said, ignoring her hand and purposefully folding his arms across his chest. "The question is, what the hell are you doing here?"

His deep voice was rough with annoyance, but Claire knew for a fact how that same voice could be silky smooth when he was trying to comfort or reassure.

"I thought my initial message made all that clear," she replied, dropping her arm back to her side and trying to look unconcerned by his less-than-friendly greeting.

"And I thought my return message made my position clear."

"Well, lucky for you I'm not very easily discouraged."

A small smirk curved his lips. "Or very bright, evidently. Whatever misguided impulse brought you here, you're wasting your time. I'm a lost cause, Claire."

If there had been even a speck of uncertainty in Claire's mind that she was doing the right thing, that settled it.

"Don't say that," she admonished.

"Why not? Truth hurt?"

"It just might, if you believe it's the truth. Haven't you ever heard of the power of positive thinking?"

He laughed harshly. "You really believe that what I think will have any effect on the verdict?"

"Yes, I do."

His stare was incredulous. "Where did you go to law school, lady? The University of Oz?"

"No. Harvard."

He whistled and came away from the door. "Just goes to show, nothing's what it's cracked up to be... not even the venerable Ivy League."

Claire smoothed her skirt and sat, her expression unruffled, her stomach doing flip-flops. "Perhaps not. Now, if you're through critiquing my credentials, maybe we can get to work."

"We have no work to do."

"On the contrary, unless you want to spend the rest of your life locked in a room a whole lot less luxurious than the one you're sitting in right now, I'd say we have a great deal of work ahead of us, and no time to waste on posturing."

The reference to being locked in a cell brought an encouraging shadow of concern to his face, but he quickly shrugged it off and narrowed his gaze defensively.

"Is that what you think I'm doing?" he demanded. "Posturing?"

"To tell you the truth, Luke," Claire replied, leaning back in her chair and lacing her fingers together as she contemplated him with a carelessness she was far from feeling, "I don't know what the hell you're doing. Thanks to Gerald Rancourt, though, I do know a little more about your situation than I did when I first contacted you after reading about your arrest in the paper back home."

"Good news travels fast," he commented.

"For instance," Claire continued, "I know that several witnesses overheard you threaten the victim only hours before the shooting occurred. I know the police found you at the scene. I know the murder weapon was a .38-caliber pistol registered to you and that yours were the only prints on it. Any way you look at it, the DA has a good shot at motive, means and opportunity."

"Three strikes, I'm out," he said softly.

"Three strikes? You're giving yourself entirely too much credit. The way I see it, you haven't even swung the bat. Rancourt told me that during your meeting with him you neither denied nor confessed to killing Mr. Addison."

"What else did he tell you?"

"That you're a real pain in the ass."

He grinned. "Did he tell you that before or after you came all the way down here to see me?"

"Before."

That prompted a glint of increased interest in his smoke gray eyes. "And you came, anyway," he said thoughtfully. "I wonder why."

"Because I'm a lawyer," she replied, meeting his gaze levelly. Years of courtroom practice prevented her tone from revealing any of the emotional upheaval inside. "A good one. And, like it or not, you need a good lawyer."

"I've got a lawyer," he said.

"I don't know anything about Gerald Rancourt, other than that, like every other public defender, he has too many cases and too little time. He can't defend you properly against these charges, Luke."

"Then he's perfect for the job. There won't be any defense."

"Are you saying you shot and killed Nick Addison?"

Claire held her breath as he stared at her in silence, the room suddenly feeling even smaller and much too warm.

"I was found alone with the body," he said at last. "It was my gun that killed him and my prints were all over it. That about says it all, doesn't it?"

"No," she exclaimed, exasperated, "that doesn't tell me nearly enough. There are a dozen ways to explain away that kind of evidence and at least a dozen scenarios to establish a justifiable shooting... and a hundred ways a smart prosecutor will be able to arrange the facts to make an innocent man appear guilty as hell unless that man is willing to fight."

"Well, there you go," he said calmly. "I'm not willing."

"What is wrong with you?" she demanded, coming out of her chair and planting her palms flat on the table as she leaned forward, glaring at him. "Do you think this is some kind of game? You against the system, just like back in high school? Because if you do, you're wrong, and you're about to get worked over by a legal system that isn't even going to try to coax you out of your strong, sullen macho routine the way some school guidance counselor might have."

"I can handle it," he said, his tone remaining soft. The only hint that she'd gotten through to him came in the defensive folding of his arms across his chest.

"You think so?" she pressed. "Well, I don't. I checked your record, Luke. There isn't one. You've never even done easy time before. What you've seen so far—a nice cushy holding cell at the county jail—is nothing compared to what's ahead if you're found guilty. You haven't even been formally charged, much less convicted and locked up. Take

Love in the First Degree

my word for it, prison is filled with guys a lot bigger and tougher than you, Cabrio."

"You'd know all about that, huh?"

Claire met his steely gaze head-on. "Yes."

For a few seconds there was silence in the small room. Then, moving very slowly, Luke circled the table to stand beside her, his voice becoming a blend of silk and ice.

"So tell me about it, Ms. Mackenzie," he urged. "Tell me about the last man you defended on a murder-one charge. Was he a lot bigger and tougher than me?"

Claire made a dismissive sound. With him so close it was hard to imagine any man being bigger or more powerful. He was no longer the lean, wiry boy she remembered. He was no longer a boy at all. Claire had an impression of leashed strength and virility that seemed to burn all the air from the tiny room. Her heart pounded in her chest and she suddenly felt a rush of the one thing she told herself she could never possibly feel around Luke: *fear.* Too late it occurred to her that even if she'd been right about him twelve years ago, a man could change a lot in that much time.

"Tell me," he repeated, his soft tone more insistent than a shout.

"Actually," she said, "I've never tried a murder-one case before... not that there's any guarantee that's what the charge against you will ultimately remain. With plea bargaining—"

"Murder two," he interrupted. "Tell me about the last second-degree-murder case you handled."

She shook her head, annoyed by the direct hit to her most vulnerable point.

He nodded, his wide mouth forming into a knowing smile as he once again ran his gaze over her. "That's about what I figured. All right, then, tell me about the last case you handled, period. You *have* handled a case since graduating from Harvard, haven't you?"

"Several," Claire retorted, matching his sarcasm. "As a matter of fact, I just wrapped up a major case in which I defended a prominent bank president. Successfully, I might add."

Luke whistled through his teeth. "Big time. And just what was the prez charged with?"

Claire shrugged. "Fraud...and unfair banking practices," she added over his smug chuckle. "Go ahead and smirk. Those are serious charges and it was a very difficult case to argue, much less win."

Difficult for many reasons she had no intention of revealing to him, she thought stoically.

"I'll bet," he said. "Just the thought of a fraud charge makes me shiver in my boots." He glanced down. "Make that sneakers. I'm shivering just the same. You must be one tough cookie."

"Very funny, but this isn't getting us anywhere."

"Oh, on the contrary," he said in an exaggerated way that left no doubt he was mimicking her, "I feel we're making real progress in resolving this whole question of me needing help from you. Tell me, aside from unfair banking practices, what other sort of work have you done in the last, oh say, six months?"

"Business interruption, embezzlement, corporate mergers—"

"Manslaughter?" he interjected, his expression one of mock hopefulness.

"Yes, actually," she countered, knowing she sounded ridiculously triumphant. "I defended a client on a manslaughter charge sometime last year."

"Tell me about it."

"My client left a bar after having a few drinks at a going-away party for a friend, and while driving off, she hit a pedestrian who—"

He held up his hand to silence her. "Enough."

Love in the First Degree

Before Claire could move, his fingers closed like handcuffs around her wrists. Holding her still, he moved closer until there wasn't enough space between them for her to draw a deep breath without coming into contact with his broad chest. His gaze grew as dark as a sky holding back thunder.

"What are you *really* doing here?" he demanded.

Chapter 2

Claire swallowed hard and lifted her head to meet Luke's hostile gaze directly. "Let me go or I'll scream for the guard."

"Scream."

The silence swelled as he stared at her more than long enough to establish the fact that she wasn't going to scream and risk getting him into more trouble than he was already in.

"I want to know why you're here," he said again.

"I've already told you. I read about what had happened in the paper and thought maybe I could help."

"Bull."

"Think whatever you please," she retorted, trying and failing to free herself.

"What would you think? In the middle of all the crap that's happening to me, some broad I don't even know shows up insisting that we're old school chums and she's here to help me."

"I never said we were friends," she corrected, "simply that we went to the same high school."

"I don't remember you," he told her bluntly. "Did we ever talk?"

"Yes," Claire replied, swallowing the silly lump that a rush of hurt feelings brought to her throat. "As a matter of fact, I tutored you in French for a few weeks. You were a senior and I was a sophomore. Verb phrases."

"That's it?" he pressed, watching her intently. "French lessons?"

Claire nodded, fighting a backwash of heated memories he had obviously forgotten. She wasn't about to remind him. "That's it."

"Well, lady, I don't remember much about high school, I don't remember French verbs, and I sure as hell don't remember you."

"Look, if—"

"Is it money?" he interrupted. "Is that it?"

"I don't know what you mean."

"Maybe you figure I'm desperate enough to pay whatever you ask. Or maybe you just need the work. Lawyers are a dime a dozen and it sure doesn't sound like you're giving old F. Lee Bailey a run for his money. Are you hoping that the publicity surrounding a murder case will give your career a shot in the arm?"

Claire shook her head in disgust. "I assure you, my career is quite successful. I don't need the work... or the money."

"Oh yeah?" he countered, clearly disbelieving. "How much do you expect me to pay for all this help you're offering?"

"My fee is negotiable in this case. This isn't about money."

"And it isn't about school spirit, either," he snapped. "I'd venture to say that I'm not the only graduate of old

Oaklawn High to get himself into a jam in the past decade. How many others have you gone out of your way to help?"

"None," Claire admitted.

"So why me?"

Claire shrugged, knowing there was no way she could tell him the truth. Even she didn't fully understand the mixture of frustration, leftover adolescent longing and adult fantasy that lurked beneath her noble and legitimate reasons for being here. And even if she had understood, his closeness was making it hard to think, much less speak logically.

"Timing," she said simply.

"What the hell does that mean?" he asked.

Her pulse jumped where his thumbs pressed more deeply into her wrists. "It means that there were some things going on back home that made me stop and take a look at my life and realize that I wasn't completely happy with the direction it was taking. I needed a break and this seemed like a good reason to take one."

"What sort of things?"

"Nothing specific," she said, telling herself it wasn't so much a lie as it was none of his business. "It's just that the cases I've handled recently aren't the sort of work I anticipated doing when I dreamed of becoming a lawyer. I went to law school to help people, to make a difference in their lives."

"A real avenging angel," he commented with a scowl.

"Maybe," Claire snapped. "All I know is I'm tired of practicing law that amounts to little more than a high-stakes game of Monopoly."

"So you thought you'd try your hand at something a little more down and dirty, is that it?"

She managed to rake him with a coolly assessing glance. "Yes, I can see how that would be one way of putting it."

"And you just happened to see the news about me in the paper?"

"Exactly. I recognized your picture."

Love in the First Degree

"And decided I'd be the perfect opportunity to get in a little practice on the grittier side of law and order."

"Look, if you're so worried about the quality of the defense I can provide, why don't we agree that I'll take your case *pro bono*. That way you'll be sure to get what you're paying for."

"No, thanks," he said, releasing her wrists as quickly as he'd captured them. "I appreciate the offer, but I still don't want your help."

"You don't want anyone's help, it seems to me."

"I guess you're brighter than I first thought," he retorted, turning toward the door.

"So you plan to just walk into that courtroom and plead guilty—is that it?" Claire called after him.

He turned, his teasing expression gone, and met her exasperated look with one of grim determination. "That's it."

"Even though you're not guilty."

"Who says I'm not?" he demanded, a dangerous glitter in his eyes.

Claire took a deep breath. She'd come this far. She certainly wasn't going to back down now, especially since, for reasons she couldn't explain, much less present in a court of law, she was more convinced than ever that she was right about Luke being innocent.

"I do," she said. "I know you didn't do it."

"How do you know?" he pressed, clearly impatient. "You don't know anything about me."

Oh, but I do, Claire longed to say. *I know that underneath that tough, cynical pose you show the world is the heart of a man whose instinct is to help, not hurt, a man willing to make someone else's trouble his own if need be.*

Instead she shrugged and said, "Call it gut instinct."

Luke laughed out loud. "Very impressive, Counselor, but take my advice and stick with your Monopoly practice."

"Fine," Claire retorted as he turned his back and once more moved toward the door. "You go right ahead and handle this your way."

"Thanks. I intend to."

"So do I."

He slowly turned back to her, his jaw made slightly crooked by the way he was gritting his teeth. "What exactly is that supposed to mean?"

"It means that I know in my heart you didn't kill Nick Addison. That means that whoever did kill him is still out there somewhere and I intend to find him."

His eyes widened, then narrowed as one angry stride carried him back to her. This time Claire was too quick for him to snare her wrists, so he took hold of her by the shoulders, instead. She half expected to be shaken hard, and was fully prepared to scream and let him deal with the repercussions. Since he seemed so determined to self-destruct, why should she stand in his way?

But he only held her tightly enough to draw her toward him and glare down at her.

"Have you lost your mind?" he inquired through still-gritted teeth.

"No. Actually, I feel quite clear about what I'm doing. More clearheaded than I have for a long time."

It was true, she realized as he stared at her in silence, as if trying to make sense of what she was saying.

"Go home, Claire," he said finally. "Atlantic City can be a dangerous place, full of dangerous people."

"I know," she replied, her confidence and determination growing by the second. "I fully expect the man I'm looking for to be dangerous. After all, he killed Nick Addison in cold blood."

Luke winced impatiently. "You don't know that—you don't know anything. Anyway, Addison's killer is the least of your worries, lady. Besides not knowing me, you also don't know this city. You're bound to go wandering into places you don't belong, sticking your nose into things that don't concern you, things that could get you into trouble...or worse." He drew her minutely closer, his gaze boring into her. "Or do you make it a habit to go looking for trouble in all the wrong places, Ms. Mackenzie?"

So maybe he did remember, after all. Claire's breath caught, her pulse racing frantically at the memory of one wrong place she had wandered into, of Luke and her—her blouse ripped open, his eyes hot and hungry—in the midnight-dark parking lot of the Phantom Bar.

"I have no intention of looking for trouble," she said, her tone remarkably calm, considering. "Simply the truth."

"The truth is that you're out of your league," he declared, his hold tightening. "Besides, maybe I don't want you messing around in my life, asking a bunch of questions about things that are none of your business, dragging up stuff that I don't want to have to deal with."

"Then help me," she urged. "Tell me the truth about that night, point me in the right direction to look for answers."

"Home—that's the only right direction for you."

She shook her head.

Luke swore softly. "You're determined to stick your nose into this no matter what, aren't you?"

Claire nodded and he swore again.

"Why won't you let me help you?" she asked quietly.

"Because I want this over and done with," he snapped. "What happened happened. I've accepted that, accepted the fact that the evidence is stacked against me, and I'm ready to pay the price for it. That's all I want, to get started paying, so I can put it behind me."

"It takes a long time to put a murder-one conviction behind you."

He gave her another impatient grimace. "You said yourself the charge won't stay murder one. I fully expect a plea bargain and, eventually, time off for good behavior. Like I said before, I can handle whatever comes in between."

She watched the muscles in his throat constrict as he swallowed hard.

"I just want to get on with it," he said again, the subtle note of desperation in his tone tearing at something inside Claire.

"Are you afraid, Luke? Is that it?"

"What?" he retorted, eyes squinted in disbelief.

"I don't mean afraid of being here or afraid of the other prisoners," she explained hastily, not wanting to put him further on the defensive by seeming to attack his masculinity. "I mean afraid to hope for a better outcome to all this, afraid to fight the charges and lose, because you simply can't bear to be let down?"

He peered at her curiously. "Yeah," he said finally. "That's it exactly. I can't bear to be let down."

Claire reached out to him without thinking, her heart twisting with commiseration, and because of the way he was holding her, her hands ended up pressed against his chest. Even that light contact confirmed that the strength she sensed in him wasn't an illusion. Beneath the cotton shirt his body was hard with muscle.

"I understand," she said softly. "Sometimes it's difficult to keep trying when it seems as if the deck is always stacked against you. I know things weren't easy for you growing up, and I have a hunch that maybe everything hasn't turned out the way you hoped it would. A lifetime of disappointment can take a toll on a person."

"You said it," Luke concurred, nodding, his expression solemn. "A lifetime of disappointment."

"Sometimes it must seem as if it takes more courage than you possess to try one more time, as if the best thing to do is simply go along with whatever you're dealt."

"Exactly. You're uncanny, you know that? That's exactly how I feel. So why don't you—"

"But you don't have to worry," she told him.

Love in the First Degree

He had seemed on the verge of a relieved smile, but it quickly shifted to a look of suspicion. "I don't?"

Claire shook her head, her own smile brilliantly reassuring. "No, because you're not going to be let down or disappointed this time. I'm going to see to it."

"For God's sake, Claire..." He threw his hands in the air and shook his head in exasperation.

"Two weeks," she said to him. "Just give me two weeks to try and turn this around for you. Let me arrange bail and—"

"No," he interjected, shaking his head firmly. "No bail. Every day I sit in here I'm one day closer to getting out."

"But you could be out now. Please, listen to me," Claire pleaded. "Let me arrange for bail and give me two weeks to see what I can do."

"What do you hope to accomplish in two weeks?" he countered, still frowning, but not quite as fiercely.

"A miracle," she retorted. "But even avenging angels sometimes need a little help in that department. That's why I want you someplace where I don't have to drive miles and go through a half-dozen checkpoints every time I need to ask you a question."

"What makes you think I'm willing to help?"

"You have to," she declared, deciding to use what she knew about Luke to her own advantage, "because I'm going to go ahead with or without you. You can't very well make sure I don't go getting into trouble in the wrong kind of places while you're sitting in here and I'm out there, talking to people, asking questions, poking my nose where it doesn't belong."

"Damn you."

"Besides," she continued, energized by the very act of seizing the offensive, "you must have some personal matters you need to clear up before being sentenced."

"I've arranged for a friend to handle all that."

"Well, with two weeks of freedom you can handle it all personally, a much safer approach, and at the same time you can keep me out of trouble."

He frowned, rubbing the dark stubble on his jaw as he thought. "Two weeks?" he asked finally.

She nodded.

"It doesn't mean I've changed my mind about anything."

"Understood."

"And I'm going to want to know every move you make, every piece of information you uncover."

"Of course. Full cooperation between us. How does that sound?"

"Like an offer I can't refuse," he muttered.

"You mean it?"

"As long as you meant what you said... two weeks and then you're out of here. No matter what."

"No matter what," Claire readily agreed, refusing to contemplate the possibility of anything short of total victory. "You won't be sorry, Luke. I came here to save you and I intend to... from yourself, if necessary."

She snapped shut her briefcase and banged on the door to signal the guard outside that they were through. Another time, she might have found Luke's disgruntled scowl unsettling. At the moment, however, she was too exhilarated by the challenge ahead to be bothered by the fact that he didn't appear to be nearly as thrilled to be rescued by her as she had once been to be rescued by him.

Chapter 3

The sun hurt his eyes. And he wasn't even outside, yet. The cramped waiting area near the prison's intake desk wasn't particularly bright or cheerful, but compared to the windowless cell Luke had called home for nearly a week, it was a football stadium. About twenty minutes ago a guard had come for him, leading him to this hallway and a scarred wooden bench that was close to, but not quite, freedom, and had told him to wait.

Luke wasn't sure exactly what he was waiting for, but quick learner that he was, he'd already assimilated the fact that prison guards don't like to be questioned by inmates. His guess was that, since just that morning Claire had made good on her promise to arrange a bail hearing and bail had been granted, he was waiting here for her to finish with the paperwork and come for him. As much as he'd initially resisted the idea of being released on bail, now that freedom was close enough to smell, he was excited.

His excitement was at direct odds with his common sense. He still believed that agreeing to let Claire arrange for his release, even temporarily, had been a major mistake. He simply hadn't had any choice. He couldn't permit her to go running around the city on her own, vigilante-style. The reason he'd gone with a court-appointed attorney in the first place was precisely to avoid such zealous interference. Then Claire had shown up, a hazy figment from his past, full of fiery justice and an absurd conviction that he was innocent. Yep, a real vigilante, he reflected cynically. Pollyanna meets Charles Bronson.

Not that her competence, or lack of it, mattered. Ask enough questions and you're bound to stumble upon a few answers. He couldn't allow that to happen. He also didn't much like the thought of her wandering around Atlantic City alone, maybe getting herself hurt on his behalf, and so he'd agreed to bail and to this crazy two-week quest that Claire had no way of knowing was already doomed to failure.

Fighting his own sudden impatience to be free, he shifted restlessly on the bench and glanced through the glass doors a short distance away. Beyond waited a world of green grass and car horns blaring and a million other everyday pleasures and annoyances that he had once taken for granted. Luke shook his head, struck by how violently he craved the outdoors and fresh air after only a few days inside this hellhole. He didn't want to think about what it would feel like to be locked away for a few years. Or longer.

He didn't want to think about it, but of course he did. The fact was he'd thought of almost nothing else for days now. He didn't have any choice. He released a grim chuckle, drawing a scowl from the guard seated at a desk a few feet away. He didn't have any choice...that one sentence seemed to rule his life all of a sudden. *He didn't have any choice.* Nick Addison had seen to that. The man had deserved to die, and he'd died.

Recalling that night in Addison's hotel room, Luke could once again feel the weight of the gun in his hand and see the

Love in the First Degree 33

gaping hole in Addison's neck leaking blood onto the pale green carpet. He wished with all his heart that things had worked out differently, but they hadn't. Over the years, gambling had taught Luke all about winning and losing and paying up with grace and dignity. He was drawing heavily on those lessons now. Addison was dead and he had to pay the price for it. He really didn't have any choice about that, either, no matter what Ms. Claire Mackenzie wanted to believe.

The thought of Claire suddenly brought him the same tangled rush of emotion it had yesterday, when he'd walked into that interview room and seen her for the first time in twelve years. Now, as then, one overriding feeling pushed to the surface and stayed there—the gut-level awareness that she'd grown up to be one hell of a beautiful woman. Uptight, but beautiful. And sexy in the unexpected and inadvertent way only an uptight woman could be.

Yep, beautiful, uptight and sexy as hell. All in all, Luke mused, she was exactly as he remembered her. The only difference was that twelve years ago her beauty had been unformed, hidden behind bulky clothes and heavy glasses. Back then, a man had to really look closely to appreciate Claire's potential. Luke had looked closely.

He remembered pretending to follow along in his notebook as he sat across from her in the school library, blown away by the sight of her soft-looking mouth forming French verbs. Now, when he was plenty old enough to know better, he was just as mesmerized by the way it dispensed legal jargon. The end result was the same. As ridiculous as it was, he had the same hard-core yen for Claire Mackenzie that he'd had when he was a kid. And now, like then, he couldn't do a damn thing about it.

Making a play for her back then would have been extremely foolish, considering the fact that her old man was a lawyer and a local big shot, and Luke had come as far from the wrong side of the tracks as you could get in the little town of Oaklawn, Rhode Island. But if it had been merely foolish back then, doing anything about it now would be downright dangerous.

Right now, he couldn't afford the luxury of seducing Claire Mackenzie. For the next two weeks, he couldn't afford to let down his guard around her for a minute. Even if she was telling the truth about her motives for coming here being strictly altruistic, he still couldn't trust her. In fact, he thought, smiling at the irony of it, if she really was there to see that justice was done, he could trust her even less.

Not that he bought her avenging-angel routine. In his experience, nobody was that noble, and nobody went out of their way to do something for nothing. There had to be an ulterior motive for the innocent-looking Claire to help him and he intended to find out what it was. At the very least, he suspected that the need to run away from something—or someone—back home had played more of a role in this than she was ready to admit. He'd find out about that, too, he decided, stretching his legs in front of him. After all, they had two weeks' worth of time to kill.

Self-denial didn't come easily to him, however, and deciding that Claire was off-limits didn't make it any easier not to think about her. With the sunlight from the opposite window warming his face, Luke closed his eyes and let himself think about her in detail, finding it a thrilling respite from thoughts of spending the next several thousand days in a world of gray walls, narrow cots and no sunshine.

It was the sound of Claire's voice, with its distinctive, husky thread, that had a way of planting the subliminal suggestion in a man's head—that he was being cajoled even when he knew she meant strictly business—which put an end to his daydream.

He got to his feet and stepped forward eagerly, eyeing her through the bars that separated them, barely aware that she was accompanied by his lawyer of record, Gerald Rancourt. Rancourt, a slick GQ type who obviously had his

Love in the First Degree

sights set on bigger things than the public defender's office, had actually handled the morning's bail hearing. Luke made a mental note to thank him.

"Sit down," the guard at the desk snapped at Luke almost before he was on his feet.

"I'm just—"

"I said sit." The guard's eyes were steely, his hand moving quickly to hover near the collapsible metal baton hanging from his leather belt.

In just a few days, Luke had learned to curb a lifelong defiant streak and not challenge that steely look and hovering hand. But he hadn't come close to learning not to resent it. At that instant, he felt as if he was burning up inside, and the fact that Claire was looking on only made it more humiliating.

"It's all right," she said quickly, before he was forced to either back down or make a fool of himself. "I have Mr. Cabrio's bail forms here, all signed." She handed the papers to the guard through the narrow opening in the bars intended for exactly that purpose. "Please release him."

The guard examined the forms and nodded. "Yes, ma'am."

His smile and manner toward Claire were the antithesis of what Luke had been receiving around here. Having seen some of the garbage the inmates dished out, he could understand the attitude of the guards, but their treatment still grated like sand on sunburned skin. One more reminder of what he'd gotten himself into, and that there was no easy way out.

"You can pick up your things over there," he said to Luke, nodding at the counter on the other side of the locked door as he stood and flipped through his keys until he found the one he wanted. Already the undercurrent of contempt was back in his voice.

Get used to it, Luke warned himself. He'd meant it when he told Claire he could handle doing time, but he also believed she was right when she predicted it was going to get worse before it got better.

The guard unlocked the door, handing Luke his release forms and slamming it shut again behind him.

He was free. The realization brought with it a rush of exhilaration and then, right behind it, grim second thoughts. This felt *too* good. So good that it was going to make it harder than ever to return to a jail cell when his bargain with Claire was finished, harder to do what he knew he had to do.

"If you're all set here, I'm going to take off," Rancourt said, extending his hand to Luke. "Stay out of trouble," he warned in a tone that Luke wasn't sure was entirely joking. Clearly, he didn't share Claire's conviction that Luke was an innocent man. There was no reason he should.

"I'll try," Luke uttered dryly as they shook hands. "And thanks."

"No problemo. Ms. Mackenzie is going to do some preliminary work on your case," the other attorney continued, "which is a huge help, since I'm stretched to the limit, as usual. Just keep me informed of anything major, all right?"

"We will," Claire replied.

Over my dead body, Luke thought, struck by how right Claire and Rancourt looked standing side by side, like models from some glossy magazine.

Rancourt turned to go. "Ciao. I'll be in touch."

Luke glanced at Claire, not even trying to control his sneer. "What do you know? All that charm and bilingual, too."

Her brows arched in surprise. "Don't you like Gerald?"

"Do you?" he countered, interested.

"He seems all right. A little offhand in his approach to your case to suit me, but you can hardly fault him for that when he's taking his cue from you."

"So you do like him."

"I hardly know him. What have you got against him?"

Love in the First Degree

Nothing, Luke thought. Until he'd stared through those bars a few minutes ago and seen Rancourt chatting easily with Claire, he'd had nothing against the man. He had simply considered Rancourt the means to an end of his own choosing.

"Nothing. I don't have anything against him," he told her, in spite of the fact that he was no longer so sure that was true. "Let's just get out of here."

Claire stood beside him as he handed his papers across the counter to another guard, who looked them over and then turned and entered the fifteen-foot wire cage behind him. The cage was lined with shelves. On the shelves were well-worn plastic bins, each marked with a prisoner's number and containing the personal items he'd surrendered upon arrest.

Luke looked on as the guard took his time scanning the rows, searching for the plastic bin with the number corresponding to the one he'd been assigned at intake. He had to clench his teeth to keep from doing what he wanted most to do—turn his head and look at Claire. The desire to stare at her, to gaze at her face with its fragile, perfect features, the graceful line of her throat, her long legs stretching below the short skirt of her blue suit, was nearly overwhelming.

It shouldn't be, he thought irritably. There was no reason he should feel this way. Sure, he was as appreciative of women as the next guy, but after all, six days was still only six days. It wasn't as if he hadn't seen a female or a pair of sexy legs in months or years and was suffering from withdrawal. In fact, what really disturbed him was the fear that he wasn't suffering from withdrawal, at all, but rather intoxication, because it wasn't just any beautiful woman he was longing to look at, but Claire alone.

Thank God the deal they'd struck was for only two weeks. If he expected to handle years of hard time, he ought to be able to handle two weeks of Claire. Of course he could handle it. He just had to practice a little self-control. Starting right now, he told himself, keeping his attention riveted on the beefy, slow-moving guard, who had finally located his bin, so that his gaze wouldn't wander in her direction. If he didn't look, maybe he wouldn't want.

The guard upended the bin, dumping Luke's belongings onto the counter in front of him.

"Says here that your clothes are being held as evidence," he said.

Luke recalled the bloodstains he'd gotten on his shirt and pants, and nodded.

"Return those clothes you're wearing now within ten days, or you'll be charged for them," the guard continued, as if by rote.

Luke reached for his car keys and shoved them into his jeans pocket. Next he picked up his wallet, which had been emptied, the contents now scattered across the dingy, tan Formica. Coins, dollar bills, two tickets to an upcoming performance of a prominent magician, two condoms, the edges of the foil packets well creased, and several photographs that had been clipped or folded to fit inside his wallet.

"Fifty-seven dollars and thirty-two cents" the guard was saying as Luke dropped the money into his pocket and quickly gathered the other items, shoving them haphazardly into the wallet.

As he picked up the condoms, he felt a crazy urge to point out that they'd been tucked inside his wallet for so long he'd forgotten they were even there. When he glanced sideways at Claire, however, she was studying the overhead light with apparent fascination. The last items he picked up were the photographs, taking care to slide them in without bending them. This time when he looked at Claire she was watching him closely. Belatedly, he noted the picture on top and hurriedly flipped his wallet shut.

"All set?" she asked.

Love in the First Degree 39

Luke nodded, relieved by her even tone. Not that there was any reason it should be anything else, he reassured himself as he signed a form stating that he had received everything due him, and they were finally able to walk outside. There was no reason for Claire to feel anything more than a passing interest in the photographs he carried in his pocket. And if he were careful, it would stay that way for the next two weeks.

Overhead, the July sun was like a fire blazing in a sky so blue it made his eyes hurt to look at it. The afternoon heat came off the blacktop below in waves that smelled of city and car exhaust, and Luke loved every bit of it—the heat and the noise and the gritty, familiar smell. It smelled like freedom.

He wanted to remember it all. His arrest had been so sudden and unexpected that he hadn't had time to prepare himself. Now, thanks to Claire, he would have time. He wanted to store up enough memories of the sights and smells and feel of life to last him however long they put him away for.

And he wanted to live every minute he had coming, he thought a little desperately as Claire led the way across the parking lot. For the next two weeks he was going to cram into each day as much living as he could. He was going to do everything he wanted to do. Well, make that *almost* everything, he thought wistfully, as Claire stopped beside a dark blue Volvo sedan and he reluctantly lifted his gaze from the mesmerizing movement of her hips to her face.

"Is this your car?" he asked.

"Yes," she replied as she unlocked the door. She hesitated as she was about to slip behind the wheel. "Is that funny?"

"Is what funny?"

"My car."

Luke shook his head, running a solemn gaze over the vehicle. "Four-door sedan, nice conservative blue that doesn't show the dirt, safest car on the road—nope, nothing funny about that at all."

"Then why did you have that little smirk on your face when I said this was my car?"

"What smirk?"

"The same one you have right now."

He did his best to move his lips into a less-offensive expression. "Better?"

"Not really."

"How about this?" he inquired, trying again.

"Just get in," she snapped.

Luke climbed into the seat beside her. "Look, Claire, I'm sorry."

"Forget it." She reached into her purse for a pair of sunglasses and slid them on. She was a knockout in sunglasses. And her skirt, as she moved around to fasten her seat belt and toss her purse into the rear seat, climbed steadily higher. Hoping he might be truly blessed, Luke looked to see if the car had a manual transmission, already imagining the provocative flexing of thigh muscles as she worked the clutch. It didn't, damn it. Just the same, the drive home from jail promised to be a hell of a lot more enjoyable than his ride there.

"No, I mean it, I am sorry," he said again. "I don't want you to think I was laughing at your car."

"I'm sure you weren't," she retorted. "Not directly, anyway."

"Meaning?"

She turned her head toward him. "I'm sure that what you were really smirking at is me. I'm sure that you find it all very amusing—me, my career, the clothes I wear, the car I drive, the fact that I have my retirement fund invested in blue chips instead of commodities, and that yes, damn it, I like navy blue cars and suits and shoes because they don't show dirt and I always make the practical choice and never take chances. But you know what? I really don't care. You can go right ahead and smirk all you want. Because while I may not be the sort of wild and reckless and ravishingly exciting woman you personally find appealing, I do have what it takes to save your ungrateful butt."

"Feel better?" he asked quietly as she straightened in her seat and started the engine.

"Is there some reason I should?"

"I thought you might, now that you got all that off your chest. Sounds to me like it's been building up there for a long time."

"Since yesterday, to be exact."

"Longer than that, if you ask me."

"I didn't."

"True." He adjusted his seat to make more room for his legs and made himself comfortable. "So why don't you? Take chances, I mean."

"Because I'm too smart."

"Smart?" he queried, watching her face. "Or scared?"

She shot him an irritated glance. "Just fasten your seat belt, okay?"

It took them about fifteen minutes to drive to the Atlantic City waterfront and then twice that long to make their way along tourist-clogged Atlantic Avenue. Ordinarily, Luke had no patience for sitting in traffic, but today he didn't mind at all. He welcomed the opportunity to study familiar landmarks, committing their details to memory. He didn't even mind the silence. In fact, he preferred it. As they inched along, he glanced down the side streets with names familiar to everyone who'd ever played Monopoly—Ohio Avenue, Indiana, Kentucky.

He caught glimpses of the casinos that were the reason for all the tourists and traffic. Caesar's, Bally's, Trump Plaza. At one time or another, he'd played and won at all of them, frequenting their most high-stakes tables and the posh, private rooms reserved for a select clientele. Of course, he'd lost, too, but not often. He'd been lucky and he knew it.

Luck runs in streaks and it always runs out, the old-timers had warned him over and over. They'd been right, even if his luck hadn't run out in the manner they'd expected—over a deck of cards or a pair of dice.

Gambling had always been a game to him, not a passion and certainly not a compulsion, as it became for so many who haunted this seaside resort and who were, in turn, haunted by its slick, neon facade and promises of fortune. By the time Max Feiffer had offered him the job of security manager for the Delta Queen, Atlantic City's newest and grandest hotel and casino, he'd been ready to quit and try something new.

As they passed Tennessee Avenue, the colorful, onion-topped domes of the Taj Mahal came into full view, then the unmistakable riverboat design of the Showboat and finally, the majestic, welcoming sight of the grand lady herself, the Delta Queen. *Home*. Or at least as close to it as Luke could remember.

The hotel and grounds covered a full city block. The front approach was a redbrick, circular drive lined with formal gardens abloom with dozens of different species of all-white flowers. The back, with its wide, multitiered veranda, opened onto the boardwalk for which Atlantic City was famed, affording a spectacular ocean view. Unlike most of the area's hotels and casinos, where glitter and ostentation knew no bounds, the Delta was all clean white lines and dark red tiled roof, a tribute to the easy, gracious living of the South from which it drew its inspiration.

Inside, as well, the architects and designers had opted for elegance over flash, with slow-moving ceiling fans, tropical foliage and hand-painted floor tiles reminiscent of courtyards in the French Quarter of New Orleans. If it was possible for any hotel with a multimillion-dollar casino, eighteen restaurants and bars and over eight-hundred rooms to be called warm and homey, it was the Delta.

"Where are you staying?" Luke thought to ask Claire as she turned onto the one-way street that led to the hotel's drive.

"Here," she replied, looking a bit surprised that he had to ask.

"I suppose I should have guessed that," he said. "Since this is the scene of the crime."

"Among other things. I thought that since we'll be working together, it makes sense for me to be staying as close to your place as possible."

"But I was still in jail when you arrived."

"I knew the judge would agree to bail."

"How did you know *I'd* agree to it?"

She stopped at the entrance to the hotel parking garage to pull a ticket from the automatic dispenser and look straight at Luke. He didn't need to see behind the dark lenses of her sunglasses. Her smug little smile was enough.

"Because," she said, "good lawyers are irresistibly persuasive. And as I told you yesterday, I'm a very good lawyer."

Understanding that his very presence there in her car only added credence to her claim, Luke wisely opted for silence as she located an open space on an upper level and parked.

"What room are you in?" he asked as they headed toward the garage elevator.

"Three-sixteen," she replied, stepping through the doors he held open.

Luke frowned and hit the button for the lobby. "Come with me to the front desk. I want to pick up my mail and take care of a few things." He smiled with grim amusement. "I suppose it might also be a good idea to let them know I'm back, before someone spots me and turns me in as an escapee."

In the short time it took for them to make their way from the elevator to what Claire knew had to be the biggest hotel lobby she had ever seen, she came to understand that the chances of Luke Cabrio being turned in to the police by anyone connected with the Delta Queen were smaller than her chances of walking into the casino and hitting the jackpot with her first pull of a slot-machine handle. Judging from the warm welcome he received from everyone from maintenance men to regular patrons, she guessed the folks here were much more likely to aid and abet him in any escape attempt he might make.

He took time to stop and speak briefly with everyone who greeted him, listening to their expressions of astonishment and disbelief at what had happened and accepting their good wishes. Claire paid close attention to everything that was said, hoping Luke's comments might reveal something new about the night of the shooting or about himself, but while he was a patient listener, he volunteered nothing. By the time they finally reached the reservations desk, she'd learned only that Luke had a lot of friends.

At least ten people were waiting along the velvet ropes to check in, but the instant the tall, willowy blond woman behind the desk caught sight of Luke, she motioned him to a clear space at the end of the counter and hurried to join him.

"Luke, thank heavens," she exclaimed, her cobalt eyes wide and obviously enhanced by colored contact lenses. She was smiling so eagerly that Claire suspected the only thing keeping her out of Luke's arms was the wide counter between them.

"I just knew they'd have to let you go. I've been telling everyone around here exactly that—that if you shot this Addison guy it was because he deserved it, and that it would all be cleared up and you'd be back where you belong."

"Well, I'm not sure how cleared up anything is, but for the time being, I'm back."

"It will all work out," the young woman insisted, dropping her voice as she leaned across the counter and covered Luke's hand with her own. "You'll see."

"Thanks, Lynn. I know you're busy, but—"

"Steve can handle it," she interjected, waving her hand toward the young man standing a short distance away. "What can I do for you, Luke?"

"First I'd like you to page Max and let him know I'm here. Then I'd appreciate it if you would grab my mail and check to see if the room next to mine is available."

"One sec."

The room next to his, Claire mused, not sure whether she was flattered, irritated or alarmed by the fact that he wanted her so close by. She had no doubt that that's why he had inquired about its availability. Well, almost no doubt, just enough of one to make her refrain from commenting on his request and risk making a fool of herself.

Lynn was back so quickly you might think there was a bonus in it for her. Claire thought about what that bonus might be and suppressed a smirk.

"Here's your mail," she said placing a half-inch-high stack of envelopes in front of Luke. "Max said he'll be right down to see you, and yes, the room next to yours is available."

"Good," Luke countered, smiling at her. "Ms. Mackenzie here is currently registered to 316. Could you please arrange to have her switched to the room next to mine?"

Lynn glanced at Claire, as if seeing her for the first time. Claire forced a small smile that was not returned. Instead, the other woman pursed her lips and drummed bright crimson nails on the marble countertop.

"Gee, I don't know, Luke. You know the whole east wing on fifteen is strictly reserved. Max will—"

"I'll clear it with Max," Luke assured her, his smile easy and reassuring. "You just take care of the details for me, okay?"

Claire knew well the power of that smile he flashed and wasn't at all surprised to see Lynn nod and smile back at him, just the way she'd seen teachers in high school smile at Luke, as if they couldn't help themselves. The man did have a way about him that was undeniable. A way with hotel clerks and high school teachers alike. *And with lady lawyers, too,* prodded an inner voice.

"Luke, there's really no need to go to this trouble," Claire said hurriedly. "The room I'm in now is fine."

"You said you thought we should be close," he reminded her.

Claire nodded, wondering if she simply imagined the hint of amusement in his gaze. "True, but as long—"

"Then it's settled," he broke in. "Lynn will handle everything." He turned back to the other woman. "You can send a bellhop to help with her things in about... thirty minutes?" he suggested, looking to Claire for approval.

She nodded.

"Thirty minutes," he said to Lynn with another smile. "Thanks."

They moved away from the desk, Claire still not sure she should allow herself to be maneuvered this way.

"Luke, I'd really rather you hadn't—"

"Luke, there you are."

They both turned toward the man approaching them, a broad smile on his face.

"How's it going, Max?" Luke said, extending his hand.

Claire looked on as the two men clasped hands for a handshake that turned into something more emotional as Max Feiffer, the hotel manager, placed his other hand on Luke's shoulder and squeezed it reassuringly. Feiffer was a distinguished-looking man somewhere in his late fifties or early sixties. His steel gray hair was slicked straight back from a high forehead and his appealing face was dominated by alert brown eyes. As a lawyer, Claire was attuned to body language in and out of the courtroom, and she detected real affection in Max Feiffer's attitude toward Luke.

"It's good to see you back here," he said to Luke. "A couple more days of your stonewalling and I was planning to break into jail to pound some sense into you."

Love in the First Degree

Luke smiled tolerantly. "This lady saved you the trouble," he said, extending his arm to draw Claire into the conversation. "Claire Mackenzie, I'd like you to meet Max Feiffer. Max is the manager and operational genius in residence here at the Delta," he added, something that Claire's research had already revealed, and her own observations confirmed. Max Feiffer looked like a man accustomed to giving orders and seeing that they were carried out.

"Max," Luke continued, "Claire is an attorney from out of state. She's going to be working on my case along with the public defender."

"Now we're getting somewhere," Max exclaimed with obvious excitement as he reached out to grasp Claire's hand in a warm greeting. "Ms. Mackenzie, I'm delighted to meet you, more delighted than you'll ever know, in fact. I talked myself crazy trying to convince this guy he needed to bring in a big gun with more experience than some wet-behind-the-ears PD to get himself out of this mess, but he wouldn't listen. I don't know what heavenly cloud you dropped from, but I welcome you."

Claire smiled, charmed by Max Feiffer's friendly manner as well as his obvious concern for Luke. She recognized a potential ally when she saw one.

"Thank you," she replied. "I'll do everything I can to help Luke."

"Good, good," Max said. "Luke said you're from out of state. I assume that means you'll be staying here with us while you're in town?"

Claire nodded. "Yes, I am. The Delta Queen is a beautiful hotel, Mr. Feiffer."

"Please, call me Max. And thank you," he said, beaming with pride.

"As a matter of fact," Luke said, "I had Claire moved to the room next to mine. I didn't think you'd mind. It will make it easier for us to confer."

"Of course I don't mind. And your stay here is on the house," he added, turning to Claire. "Anything you want, anything you need while you are here—laundry service, room service, whatever." He waved his hand in the air for emphasis. "You just call and it's yours."

"Thank you, but that's really not necessary—"

"It's necessary to me," Max interrupted. He clapped Luke on the back. "Luke is like one of my own family—hell, maybe even closer than that. I can't do for him what you can, but I can do this. Please."

Claire hesitated. Then, prompted by Luke's small, bemused smile and his slight nod urging her to go along with Max, she acquiesced.

"And, of course, I'll help with his case, too," Max assured her. "Any way I can. You need a character witness, you've got one," he declared, thumping his chest. "Hell, I'll get you a hundred of them." As he spoke, he waved his hand around the lobby with its generous presence of uniformed employees.

"Thanks," Claire said. "I may take you up on that offer."

His expression tightened to a worried frown and his voice lowered. "You can help him, can't you, Claire? I mean, you've seen the evidence against him and you think you can mount a successful defense?"

"I need to gather more material before I make any specific decisions, of course...and get some pertinent information directly from Luke," she added pointedly. "But I have every reason to believe that we can prove Luke did not kill Nick Addison."

Claire doubted that Max's sigh of relief would be quite so heartfelt if he knew that, so far, her belief in Luke's innocence was based more on whimsy—her own—than on any hard, cold facts. But that would change, she reassured herself, just as soon as she persuaded Luke to open up to her about what had happened that night.

Love in the First Degree

"Then you have handled cases like this before?" Max asked her. "Tough murder cases, I mean?" He shook his head. "What am I saying? Of course you have. You don't bring in a big gun from out of state unless she's got the right experience, right, Luke?"

"Damn straight, Max," Luke agreed, the note of dry humor in his voice nearly imperceptible.

"So, have you handled any cases I might recognize?" Max asked Claire.

"Several," Luke replied before she was forced to come up with a face-saving reply. "But Claire makes it a practice never to discuss past clients... a consideration that was instrumental in my decision to go with her, I might add."

"Of course," Max agreed. "We want to keep as low a profile as possible on all this, for the sake of the hotel, as well as Luke. Don't want any rumors flying around about a trigger-happy security man." His wide forehead creased. "Not that I think Luke is trigger-happy, or that he shot this fellow without a damn good reason."

"Of course not," Claire agreed.

"It's just that none of us really know much about what happened that night." Max slanted a sheepish look toward Luke. "He's not much of a talker under the best of circumstances, and God knows these are far from being the best."

"Actually," she replied, deciding that since Luke had covered for her, turnabout was fair play, "the less talking Luke and all of us do before the trial, the better."

"Of course, of course. My lips are sealed."

"Great, Max. Now if you'll excuse us," Luke said, "Claire has to get her things together to change rooms, and I see Brad over there. I want to introduce him to Claire, in case she needs him for anything."

"Go right ahead," Max urged. "And, Claire, please remember what I said—whatever you need, just ask. If the front desk or Brad can't help you, call me directly."

Claire thanked him, relieved to have Luke hurry her away. It was a new and not very pleasant experience to be made to feel that her credentials were somehow lacking, and her pride was still smarting slightly. In the six years she'd been practicing law, she'd already made a name for herself in her field. If Max had been looking for a tax attorney or planning a corporate merger, she could have rattled off any number of impressive cases she had handled. Unfortunately, at the moment, that was not the kind of expertise Max needed, and neither did Luke.

"Who's Brad?" she asked Luke as they crossed the lobby.

"Brad Cantrell. He's the tall guy over there by the casino entrance," Luke told her, indicating a young man engrossed in conversation with two uniformed guards.

"Why do you think I might need his help?" she asked.

"He's my assistant." He gave a short laugh. "Correction, make that my replacement."

Surprised, Claire took a closer look at Brad Cantrell. He looked to be somewhere in his late twenties, with high cheekbones and long, straight black hair falling loosely from a center part. His olive suit was fashionably unstructured and worn with a muted, collarless shirt. It projected a vaguely European look that suited him well. He definitely did not resemble any security manager Claire had ever encountered. But then, she reminded herself, Atlantic City wasn't Providence.

"Aren't you being a bit premature in deciding you need a replacement?" she asked Luke.

"No, simply realistic. Something you seem to have a problem with."

"Ha. That's rich."

"What is?"

"Being lectured about reality by a man who chooses to live in what looks like a giant set from *Gone With the Wind,* and spends his days supervising a bunch of perpetual adolescents playing games."

To her amazement, he laughed.

"I never looked at it quite that way, but I suppose you're right. The important thing is that I know when it's a game I'm playing." He stopped and spun her around to meet his gaze. "How about you?"

Chapter 4

Luke's question made Claire think. It was fortunate he didn't demand an answer on the spot, because she didn't really have one. Perhaps running down here to rescue him could be construed as a game of some sort, or at least a childish reaction to matters at home. A way of taking charge in the face of what lately seemed to be an insidious loss of control over her work, her time, even her own personal life.

Graduating from law school and joining Mackenzie and Dwyer, the firm founded and headed by her father and his lifelong friend, John Dwyer, had seemed like a dream come true at the time. The only trouble was that Claire was no longer sure if it was her dream or her father's. More and more lately she had the sensation that she had stepped into a cookie-cutter opening that had been waiting just for her, a role with preordained standards and expectations. Maybe the role had fit once, or maybe in an effort to please her father, she had squeezed herself to make it fit. All she knew was that with each passing day the fit felt tighter and tighter, as if she were being suffocated by her own life.

Love in the First Degree

Last week's win in the Henderson case should have been a professional high point. Instead, the outcome had left her with a bad taste in her mouth that all the congratulations and pats on the back from her colleagues couldn't wash away. She'd hoped that getting away for a while would clear her head, and that working to prove Luke's innocence would help her remember why she'd wanted to be a lawyer in the first place. Now that she was actually here, however, seeing Luke on a daily basis, actually spending time with him, the other, more personal reasons behind her impulsive decision to get involved in his case were not as easily brushed aside as they had been during the flurry of packing and last-minute arrangements back home.

Was she simply playing a game, as Luke's question seemed to suggest? Acting out a fantasy? Using fate and his dire predicament for a chance to revive an old, adolescent daydream? One thing was certain, being around him wasn't doing much to clear her head.

Brad Cantrell proved to be as charming as he was good-looking... which was saying something. It didn't surprise Claire to learn that he had done some modeling in New York before being hired by Luke to assist in overseeing security for the hotel and casino.

"From modeling to security—that's quite a career change," she remarked.

"I never considered modeling a career," Brad explained. "A scout for a modeling agency approached me on the beach one day and it just sort of happened."

"Sounds very exciting."

"*Sounds* being the operative word," Brad drawled. "For two years I did a lot of getting up early and waiting around for photographers and stylists and prop people and everyone else who had an opinion on how a particular shot ought to look. If there's one thing I learned to hate, it's waiting."

Claire chuckled. "So how did you end up at the Delta Queen?"

Brad's sudden discomfit and the flicker of alarm in his eyes made Claire wonder if that's how she had reacted a few minutes ago when Max inquired about her experience in handling murder cases. She had a hunch it was, because once again Luke stepped smoothly into the breach.

"You might say that by hiring me, Max saved me from a life I once thought I wanted," Luke explained easily. "And I simply did the same for Brad."

"I only wish I could return the favor. I mean by helping Luke," Brad added. He looked at Claire. "I'm not denying I wanted to move up the ladder here eventually, but not like this."

"Maybe you can help," Claire told him. "Since you're Luke's assistant, you'd be in a position to know just about everything that goes on around here, right?"

"That's what I'm getting paid for," he replied with a nod.

"What do you know about the night Nick Addison was killed?"

"Nothing," Luke declared before Brad had a chance to reply. "No one at the Delta knows anything about that night... at least not anything that can help."

"I won't know what will help until I hear it," she retorted, firing a warning look Luke's way.

"I know one thing that ought to help," Brad interjected. "I know Luke didn't shoot Addison."

"How?" Claire demanded instantly. "How do you know that?"

"Because I know Luke," Brad countered. "And I know he couldn't have killed anyone."

Claire concealed her disappointment. For a second, she'd thought Brad might be able to offer something in the way of real evidence.

"At least, he couldn't have killed anyone that way," Brad continued, only adding to Claire's disappointment. "I've worked side by side with this guy for almost two years and he's got too damn much control to do something like that.

I've seen him handle drunks and psychos and gamblers so down-and-out they'd kill you for one more stake at craps, and he treats them all as gently as if they were made of blown glass. And I've seen him walk away from trouble plenty of times, just turn his back on insults that would make most other men—me, included—go ballistic. The man's got ice in his veins."

"Maybe so, but several witnesses heard Luke arguing with Addison in the lobby earlier that night. Doesn't the fact that he was somehow driven to arguing and shouting—"

"Shouting?" Brad repeated, his dark brows arching skeptically.

"Well, apparently it was obvious to bystanders that they were arguing. So I assumed—"

"Check it out," Brad interrupted again, shaking his head. "I'm not sure what happened in the lobby that night, but I can't picture Luke losing it in public that way. And as far as I know there was no shouting heard coming from Addison's room later, and no signs of a struggle. The way I figure it, someone just walked in there and blew him away."

"Someone in full control," Claire suggested.

Brad nodded. "You got it."

She sensed Luke's amusement.

"Someone with ice in his veins?" she pressed.

Brad winced at how easily he'd been trapped. "Hey, that's not what I meant at all."

"I know you didn't," Claire told him gently. "But on the witness stand that's how a good prosecutor would twist your testimony."

Brad's brow furrowed. "Do you really think I might be called as a witness?"

"It's possible, if only as a character witness. But I haven't really even begun to think in terms of witnesses." She smiled at him. "And we'd have plenty of time to work on your testimony beforehand."

"Good thing, huh?" Brad countered, returning her smile. "Besides, that was just one scenario of how it could have happened. I've been thinking it's also possible the killer didn't plan on shooting him, at all, but Addison scared him somehow and *bam*... he fired."

Claire nodded, considering his theory. "Interesting."

"Now that would rule Luke out entirely. The man just doesn't lose control like that. And he doesn't scare easy. If Luke *did* kill Addison," Brad concluded earnestly, "he'd have had to have a damn good reason."

"One more question," Claire said hurriedly. Although she'd been studiously avoiding glancing at Luke, so as not to give him a chance to interrupt, she could sense his growing restlessness. "Why do you think Luke would allow the police to think he's guilty if he's not?"

Brad frowned.

"Objection," Luke exclaimed. "The question calls for conjecture on the part of the witness."

"He's not a witness," Claire pointed out, annoyed. "And this isn't a court of law."

"It also isn't the time or place for a lengthy interview of a man who's supposed to be working."

Grudgingly, Claire acknowledged that he was right.

Luke glanced at his watch and then at Brad. "Shouldn't you be doing a monitor check about now?"

"Yes, but what did she mean—"

"In fact, I'd say that check is past due," Luke interjected pointedly.

"Yes, sir, Boss," Brad said, chuckling and shaking his head. He whacked Luke on the shoulder as he turned to leave. "Nice to have you back here cracking the whip...and nice to meet you, Claire."

"Thanks, Brad. We'll talk again."

"Anytime," he agreed, grinning at her and Luke over his shoulder.

Love in the First Degree

"Remind me to keep him busy for the next two weeks," Luke grumbled as they stepped into the elevator.

"Now why would you want to do that?" she asked.

"Because he talks too much. And," he added, "because I'm supposed to be looking after you. Cantrell is hell on women."

"Somehow that doesn't come as a surprise."

"No?"

She shook her head. "The man gives new meaning to the expression drop-dead gorgeous."

"Yeah?" He shrugged carelessly and Claire thought how easily the same descriptions, drop-dead gorgeous and hell on women, could be applied to Luke, as well. "I never really noticed," he added as the elevator continued past her floor. At her quizzical look, he explained, "I thought I'd show you your new room first and then you can go back for your things."

The elevator stopped at the top floor and he trailed her out, continuing their conversation about Brad. "In fact, if you ask me, the kid needs a haircut."

Claire couldn't help chuckling. "Kid? How old is Brad? Twenty-eight? Twenty-nine? All of four or five years younger than you?"

"Around that. But it's not the number of years that count, it's how hard you lived them. Cantrell's still got a lot to learn."

"Then what made you pick him for this job? Why not someone with more experience?"

Luke shrugged again, his gaze on the white magnolias woven into the hallway carpet. "He has to learn somewhere. Besides, he's a damn hard worker and he owed me one. Ambition and loyalty aren't a bad combination in an assistant."

"Not bad at all. Exactly how big a one did he owe you?"

"You ask an awful lot of questions."

"I need an awful lot of answers. And I need them fast. I only have two weeks."

He acknowledged that with a soft chuckle.

"So," she continued, "how big?"

"Not very," he countered, shrugging. "When Brad started raking in big bucks from modeling, he got into the habit of coming down to Atlantic City weekends, playing, hanging out at the casinos."

"Did he win?"

"At first. But even his losses didn't discourage him. Brad's father is a vet out in some dinky Pennsylvania town and Brad has five brothers and sisters, a solid middle-class family. I'm sure the money he was making seemed like a fortune to him at the time." He stopped, his expression rueful, as they reached the end of the corridor and had to turn either left or right.

"You'd be amazed how few spins of a roulette wheel it takes to turn a fortune into pocket change," he went on. "Eventually Brad got in a little over his head and I helped him to... extradite himself. In the process, we got friendly enough for me to know that he'd begun to hate what he was doing, being treated like a piece of prime beef. When I needed someone to be my assistant, I offered him the job."

"Apparently it's worked out," she observed as he turned right and continued along the hallway. The doors and woodwork there were painted creamy white, the wallpaper a subtle pattern of gold, white and moss.

"Better than I expected," he replied. "As I said, Brad works hard and he learns fast." He glanced at her, his mouth twisted wryly. "But he still needs a haircut."

Claire laughed. "My, my, how times change. It seems to me I recall that same comment being made about you a few years ago."

Luke stopped and studied her thoughtfully. "That was more than a few years ago, Claire."

"Twelve, to be exact." She smiled thoughtfully. "It's funny, sometimes high school seems like another lifetime, and sometimes it seems as if it was just yesterday that I was going to classes, seeing friends."

"How does it feel right now?" he asked quietly. "Right this minute. Like yesterday or another lifetime?"

It wasn't so much his question as the way he was looking at her that suddenly made Claire feel as if the air in her lungs weighed a thousand pounds, as if she might never draw a normal breath again. He was standing very close, his expression serious and intent, as if he was looking for an answer in more than words.

She managed a shrug. "At the moment, high school seems far away. I suppose because I have so many other things on my mind... like finding a way to prove you're innocent."

His eyes narrowed. With disappointment? Disbelief? Did he suspect just how vivid her memories of him were and expect her to confess that being close to him like this had a way of making her feel like an awkward, love-struck teenager all over again?

"Your time would be better spent reminiscing about high school," he said dryly as he turned and punched in a five-digit code to open the combination lock on the door of Room 1562. "But as long as you're determined to do this, you might as well do it in comfort."

"Is this your room?" she asked as he pushed the door wide and invited her inside.

"No. It's yours."

She stopped and spun back to face him. "Mine? Do you have the combination to all the room locks committed to memory?"

"You give me too much credit," he murmured, his mouth curving in a self-deprecating smile. "What I have is the code to override the combination to all the room locks."

"Is that how you got into Addison's room that night?"

He hesitated a second, as if caught off guard by the question. "Yes."

"I see."

She moved into the room, barely noticing the luxurious decor of what was actually a two-room suite done in the same soft shades of white, gold and moss as the hallway, but with added accents of peach. She was too busy thinking.

"What do you see that's making you pinch your eyebrows together like that?" Luke asked her. He came around to stand before her, taking her totally by surprise by touching the pad of his thumb to the spot between her brows and kneading lightly. "If you're not careful you'll get wrinkles."

"The way it's going so far," Claire replied, trying not to be distracted by the tiny shivers his touch sent coursing through her, "I fully expect to walk away from this with a few wrinkles and a few gray hairs."

"Not very glamorous souvenirs from your first trip to Atlantic City. We'll have to see if we can't do better."

"How do you know it's my first trip here?"

A spark of amusement flashed in his eyes. "The way you kept trying to peek into the casino over Brad's shoulder. And," he added, "the fact that you're not a gambler by nature."

"Are you?" she asked, forcing herself to move away from him. "A gambler by nature, I mean?"

Luke nodded. "Born and bred. As far back as I can remember my old man bet on anything that moved...not to mention his share of things that were supposed to move and didn't," he added, his voice heavy with cynicism. "And since my mother always said that marrying him was the biggest chance any sane woman ever took, I figure I come by it honestly on both sides."

"What do you gamble on?"

"Now?" He shook his head. "Not a thing. That was one of the conditions I accepted when I took the job here."

"How about before you took this job? What did you gamble on then?"

"Cards, dice, the spin of a wheel, who would score the most points in the third quarter of the Super Bowl—things like that."

"Sounds like a full-time job," she remarked. "When did you find time to work?"

Luke shot her a surprised look, then laughed softly. "I thought you knew."

"Knew what?"

"Until Max hired me five years ago, gambling was my full-time job."

"You were a professional gambler?" she asked in dismay.

"Why, Claire, I do believe you look more shocked by that than by the very real possibility that I may be a murderer." His expression held a note of mockery.

"That's probably because I'm thinking about how your background is going to play for a jury."

"I see. On the disreputability scale it's okay that I might be a cold-blooded killer, but not that I played five-card stud to pay the rent."

"Stop smirking. No one is condoning murder, but the fact is that the murder charge is something we have to deal with, and it would be nice if you had a long history of responsible, respectable employment to offset some of the negatives."

"Sorry. If I'd known I was going to be charged with murder, I would have volunteered to teach Sunday school on the side."

"It wouldn't have hurt," she shot back, searching for a bright spot in the shambles caused by the grenade Luke had just tossed her. A professional gambler, of all things. She supposed she had looked shocked, and she was. Her surprise, however, came more from being confronted with a way of life so far from her own realm of experience than from the thought of Luke having such an unorthodox occupation.

On the contrary, it was easy to imagine him in a black tuxedo, idly watching the spin of a roulette wheel, or in rolled shirtsleeves at a poker game, his eyes hard, his expression inscrutable as he carelessly signaled the dealer for another card. There was, and always had been, something about Luke that was slightly untamed. A hundred years ago he probably would have been found squared off in a gunfight in the main street of some rowdy cowboy town. Today that craving to live life close to the edge might be satisfied by risking everything on a roll of the dice.

She regarded him with a small shake of her head. "A professional gambler, hmm?"

"I guess you could call it that," he said, a slight smile playing at his lips. "Not that it ever felt like much of a profession. More like a hobby, really."

"Or an addiction."

His expression grew somber. "I've seen plenty of people addicted to it, but that's not how it was for me. When I decided to stop gambling to handle security here, instead, I just stopped."

"Why?"

He looked startled by the question. Or maybe trapped was a more accurate description, Claire noted.

"I'm not sure what you mean."

"Why did you decide to stop and do this, instead?"

He shrugged. "I guess I was ready for a change."

"What made you become a gambler in the first place?" she asked, telling herself her interest was strictly related to the case.

"I was good at it," he said simply. "Very good."

"I've been told I'm pretty good at watercolors, too," she replied, her tone slightly exasperated, "but I don't spend my days painting seascapes, instead of working."

"Maybe you should. You sure don't seem real happy doing what you're doing."

Claire folded her arms across her chest. "I'll have you know I love my work."

"Is that why you're here, instead of back in your office doing it?"

"For the last time," she retorted through gritted teeth, "I'm here to try and help you. That's what I do—I help people who need legal advice. This is not a game or a whim. I'm not running away or trying to use you to make a name for myself and, to tell you the truth, I'm getting pretty tired of your comments to the contrary."

Claire was braced for an argument or, at the very least, a sarcastic retort. Instead, he unleashed the same irresistible smile he'd used on the reservations clerk downstairs, and to her disgust, she found herself just as susceptible to its magic as the other woman had been.

"Then I apologize," he said. "You have my word, no more comments."

She felt her irritation dissolve into a warm cuddly feeling that was slowly spreading through her. "So you finally believe me?"

"No," he countered matter-of-factly. "I just promise not to comment on it."

She sighed. "I guess that will have to do."

"So what time would you like to meet for dinner?" he asked.

"Thanks, but I don't expect you to take me to dinner."

"Why not? We have a deal, remember?"

"Yes, but having to entertain me was not part of it."

"Entertaining you wasn't exactly what I had in mind," Luke countered, the sardonic curve of his mouth causing Claire to flush uncomfortably. "Although if you have your heart set on it, I'll give it my best shot."

"I'm sorry, when you suggested dinner, I assumed..."

She trailed off. She'd assumed what? That he was proposing a date rather than simply an addendum to the bargain she'd forced on him? She'd rather starve to death than admit any such thing.

"Claire, our deal was that for the next two weeks, you do what you can to prove I'm innocent and I make sure you don't get yourself hurt or killed in the process. Now, working here has made me pretty good at deflecting trouble," he explained with a self-effacing shrug, "but even I'm not so good that I can do it without being present."

Her eyes narrowed. "What are you saying?"

"I'm saying that you better get used to the idea of us being very... close."

"How close?" she countered warily.

"Except for the time you spend in that bed," he explained with a nod at the king-size bed to his right, "I intend to be right by your side."

"But what about your work?" she protested.

"Brad was all set to handle things while I was gone. We'll leave it that way. If he does need help, at least I'll be around."

"And the personal matters you said you had to handle? Surely you'll need—"

"We'll work it out," he interjected, his tone firm. "I figure that dinner tonight should give us plenty of time to coordinate our schedules for the next two weeks, and for you to tell me, step by step, exactly how you intend to go about proving that I didn't kill Nick Addison."

Luke was half-right, Claire mused as she gathered her things and waited for the bellhop to arrive to help her change rooms. Dinner would give them a chance to discuss their schedules for the next two weeks, but not for her to tell him how she planned to prove his innocence. Mostly because she had nothing to tell.

Love in the First Degree

No plan. No agenda. No schedule, really. The awkward truth that she hadn't admitted to a soul—not Luke or Gerald Rancourt or anyone back home—was that she wasn't exactly sure how she was going to pull this off. She'd barely acknowledged her uncertainty to herself, in fact. Now, with her back to the wall, there was no avoiding the possibility that she might be in over her head.

Except for a few minor cases handled mainly to accommodate important clients, all of her experience since law school had been in the area of financial law and liability. The criminal-law classes that had been her favorites in school seemed a lifetime ago. What she did recall from those classes dealt with standard cases involving eyewitnesses or, at the very least, a defendant who proclaimed his innocence and was willing to fight to prove it. Luke clearly wasn't planning to fight the charges against him. She wasn't even sure he was willing to cooperate with her.

So far, she hadn't wanted to push him too hard or pin him down to specifics. For him to believe so strongly that his case was hopeless, and to so thoroughly distrust anyone who wanted to help, meant that he had some pretty deep emotional scars to overcome. She hoped to win his confidence first and then ease him into opening up to her. That wasn't going to happen, however, if she was forced to confess to him that she hadn't yet decided what her first step should be, never mind having a step-by-step battle plan for the next two weeks.

So, she told herself, zipping shut the garment bag holding her suits, she would just have to devise a battle plan. A plan clever and comprehensive enough to convince Luke she knew what she was doing. A plan to inspire his trust and renew his hope that he really did have a chance. A plan he could believe in and that would give him reason to believe in her. And, she thought, groaning as she glanced at the bedside clock, she had to come up with it in less than three hours.

For the first time since returning to her room, she noticed the blinking red light on the phone and dialed the hotel operator for her messages. There had been one call from Gerald Rancourt and three from her father. Claire grimaced. Was she ready to speak with her father?

Their last several meetings had quickly degenerated into shouting matches. He was outraged by her decision to come here and help defend a man whom he considered guilty by nature. And Claire was more than outraged—she felt used and betrayed and angry as hell—over her father's covert role in the Henderson matter.

When she had first been assigned to defend Stuart Henderson, a prominent bank president and longtime friend of her father, against charges of fraud and unfair banking practices, she had been flattered by the firm's apparent confidence in her and was eager to prove she could handle such a high-profile case. Not until the jury was already out did the private detective she'd hired turn up a final bit of evidence in the very convoluted paper trail of Henderson's undeniably suspect dealings, opening her eyes to the fact that she hadn't been assigned the case because of her ability, but rather her naiveté.

Too late, she realized that she'd been chosen because she was one of the few qualified attorneys in the firm of Mackenzie and Dwyer who wasn't privy to the knowledge that her father had at one time been involved in the same questionable land deal that had caused Henderson's fortunes to come crashing in on him. And, she reflected bitterly, the one most bound by family loyalty to proceed even if she should find out.

Oh, her father swore to her when she confronted him immediately after the trial that his involvement had been minimal and that he'd pulled out of the deal long before the transactions for which Henderson was being tried had taken place. Just as he'd sworn that if his involvement had become known during the trial he would have come forward to reveal the full truth and ensure that she was not subject to a charge of conflict of interest.

For her own sake, Claire had to believe he would have. Just as she had to believe that she would have withdrawn from the case had she discovered the truth in time. But none of those belated good intentions changed the fact that her father had used her, and in doing so he had done more than steal the sweetness from what should have been her greatest victory. He had also thrown a shadow across her very reasons for becoming a lawyer in the first place, reasons that had been inspired in large part by a little girl's fascination with her father's noble words on the importance of truth and justice. It was going to take her awhile to come to terms with that.

With a sigh, Claire reached for the phone to return Gerald's call first.

"I just wanted to let you know that I spoke with the D.A.'s office and a police contact I have," he told her when she reached him.

"How did it go?"

"Just about like this whole case is going... slow and frustrating as hell."

"Did you learn anything new?" she asked, wondering if he'd called simply to whine.

"Not half as much as I need to know, but then, anything is more than I've gotten from my recalcitrant client. You know, usually I have to sift through everything a client tells me, trying to separate the half-truths from the total bull that will never stand the light of day in a courtroom, and I'm always wishing I didn't have to hear half of what they want to tell me. But I never before had a client who didn't want to tell me anything. Nothing. *Nada.* Squat. No confession, no denial and no emotion. What's with this character?"

"I'm still trying to figure that out myself."

"So he hasn't talked to you about what happened that night?"

"Not yet, but he's only been out a couple of hours. Tell me what you found out."

"Like I said, it's not much, but it's interesting. For starters, Cabrio wasn't even a suspect until he fingered himself."

"You mean he admitted it?" Claire asked, feeling every muscle in her body tighten anxiously. "I thought you said—"

"He didn't exactly admit anything," Gerald broke in. "It's like this. Cabrio was already on the scene when the local police arrived, standing over the body, with the gun still in his hand."

"Right, that's all in the police report," she said impatiently.

"But what's not quite so clear in the report is that the responding officers assumed he was there because he handles security for the hotel. They had no intention of questioning him as a suspect."

"What changed their minds?"

"He did. Out of the blue he up and announces he wants a lawyer. I get the feeling he shocked the daylights out of those two cops. They're probably still wondering how it would have looked on their records if they'd let a murder suspect sashay away from the scene with their blessing."

"Why would Luke do that?" she wondered out loud.

"Good question. The D.A. favors the old shock-and-remorse theory. In other words, upon viewing the corpse and being confronted by the cops, Cabrio was so overcome with guilt he spilled his guts."

"Except he didn't. As you said, he hasn't actually confessed to killing Addison."

"He also hasn't actually denied it," he reminded her. "A fact that is sure to make a jury of reasonably normal individuals scratch their heads in wonderment. As for why he did it, personally, I've been doing this long enough to have

Love in the First Degree

learned never to underestimate the human capacity for stupidity."

"Not Luke," Claire said firmly. "If he gave himself up, he knew exactly what he was doing."

"Maybe. Then again, you haven't heard the second half of my news... what the D.A. has latched onto as a motive, at least for the moment."

"What is it?" Claire demanded anxiously.

"Jealousy."

"What?"

"You heard me, jealousy. I had a little trouble imagining Cabrio as the hotheaded, blinded-by-passion type myself, but that's what they plan to go with. Seems the argument that he and Addison had in the lobby earlier in the evening was definitely over a woman, and at least one witness heard Cabrio warn Addison that if he didn't stay away from her, he'd kill him."

"I thought no one was close enough to hear exactly what they were saying," she said, reeling inside from what Rancourt had revealed.

"Apparently someone was. I have a copy of the guy's statement, as well as several others. I'll fax them to you at the hotel. Maybe you can follow up on them."

"All right," Claire agreed, thinking she'd just found out what her first step should be. "But what I really want to know is who's the woman involved?"

"You and me both. I'm working on it, but the police and the D.A.'s office are both playing this close to the vest... which might be a sign that they don't have much and don't want us to know it."

"They'll have to tell us eventually," she said, thinking out loud again. "In the meantime, I'll ask Luke about it."

Rancourt's chuckle was biting. "Good luck. Tell me something, Claire, just between you and me, do you really believe this guy is innocent?"

"Absolutely," she replied without hesitation.

"Then why the hell doesn't he say so?"

"I don't know for sure," she admitted, "but I suspect he believes he's going to take the fall for this, one way or the other, and in his mind he's doing what he needs to in order to set himself up for the best deal possible."

"The only thing he's setting himself up for is an ironclad guilty verdict on murder one. The fact that he's not proclaiming his innocence from the rooftops, like everyone else ever arrested, only encourages the D.A."

"I know that and I know how this whole thing looks, but I still believe that Luke is innocent."

"If you say so."

"You sound dubious."

"If I am, it won't affect my efforts to defend him, you can count on that."

The lawyer in her could accept that. She herself had argued and won cases she didn't believe in on an emotional level. But the woman in her wanted to rant at him for not sharing her faith in Luke.

"So tell me," she said, "just between the two of us, what do you believe?"

"The truth?"

"Of course."

"I believe the guy is guilty as hell."

After hanging up the phone, Claire stood with her arms folded across her chest and stared without seeing through the hotel room window. So now it was out in the open. Luke's own attorney believed he was guilty. She'd gathered from Max Feiffer's remarks that although he was squarely in Luke's corner, he, too, was convinced that Luke had shot Nick Addison. Even Brad, after listening to her demolish his theory about the shooting, had retreated to the position that if Luke had killed Addison, he must have had a good reason.

Love in the First Degree

That left her. Apparently she was the only one who believed Luke couldn't have murdered anyone, simply because she believed so strongly in him. Certainly no one back home had shared her belief, much less the strength of her conviction. Not her parents or the few friends to whom she'd mentioned her intention to try and help him. They had all expressed the same shock, followed by well-intentioned arguments to the effect that although her desire to help him was admirable, there was no way she could know for sure that Luke was innocent, since, after all these years, she didn't even really know him.

Claire couldn't explain, then or now, exactly how she knew, only that she knew Luke wasn't a murderer. And she'd convinced herself that that was all she needed to know to do her job. Now she wasn't so sure. For instance, she hadn't known that Luke was involved with someone: The mystery woman whom he and Nick Addison had apparently argued about that night in the lobby. A woman Luke cared enough about to threaten violence.

Why hadn't Claire even considered the possibility that there was a woman in his life? She should have, she realized with a self-derisive grimace. After all, there had always been some female in Luke's life. Make that *females*, plural, a steady string of them, sometimes several at the same time, like bees swarming around a saucer of honey.

So why hadn't she considered it? The answer was obvious, and embarrassing. She hadn't considered it because it hadn't fit into her fantasy of rushing down here and rescuing Luke, and maybe having a chance to put a different ending on their last meeting. A meeting he didn't even remember, she reminded herself harshly.

Lord, she was an idiot. And she probably shouldn't have come in the first place. But the fact remained that she was here and she had given her word that she would do whatever she could during the next two weeks to prove Luke's innocence. Somehow, some way, she was going to do exactly that. This mystery woman might not be part of her fantasy, but she was a big part of the reality of Luke's case. And, Claire told herself, she was just going to have to find a way to deal with that, professionally and personally.

Chapter 5

Her phone conversation with Gerald Rancourt left Claire preoccupied and on edge. To add to her trouble, the bellhop was delayed, and suddenly every one of the outfits she'd brought with her looked all wrong.

She showered, dried her hair and did her makeup, and then proceeded to dress and undress a half-dozen times, discarding one suit as too stiff, another as too fussy, before she settled on one of raw silk with a knee-length skirt and a softly fitted jacket in a flattering shade of deep sapphire. Beneath the jacket she wore a white lace chemise that was visible only when she leaned forward.

Ordinarily for a business dinner she would have opted to wear a more-conservative blouse. But this wasn't exactly a business dinner, she thought defiantly. Of course, it also wasn't a date. Luke had made that clear. She checked her reflection in the full-length mirror outside the bathroom and fingered the top of the lace chemise indecisively. What it was, she decided, was nerve-racking.

Shrugging, she turned away from the mirror. What the heck? This was Atlantic City, a risk-taker's paradise. If opting to wear a lace chemise, instead of a blouse, was the biggest risk she took while she was here, she would be pretty safe.

All in all, it was an accomplishment to be dressed in time to meet Luke for dinner, much less come up with a brilliant legal strategy guaranteed to inspire his confidence and trust. He showed up exactly on time, wearing a dark charcoal suit and crisp white shirt. He wore the suit as effortlessly as he had the prison-issue jeans and work shirt, but the effect was infinitely more devastating. There was something about knowing a man had gone to the trouble of shaving and donning a tie and splashing on the barest hint of cologne that made a woman feel special. Even if it was just business.

He had made dinner reservations at Lebellecour, an elegant and intimate restaurant tucked away in the west corner of the hotel's tenth floor. They were seated at a table in a windowed alcove with such a spectacular view of the ocean that Claire was sure it was a spot reserved for special guests. For a moment she felt even more flattered that Luke had put himself out for what was essentially, in his mind, babysitting duty.

Then she recalled that charm was the most effective weapon in Luke's arsenal... when he chose to use it. He'd always had an uncanny gift for making a woman feel special, as if at that moment, with his attention focused solely on her, she was the most important woman in the universe. And when the moment was over? As Claire recalled, for Luke there had always been another willing woman waiting to be charmed.

Had he ever reserved this table for dinner with the mystery woman? she couldn't help wondering as the black-tie-clad waiter brought them menus and recited the evening's specials in a slow southern drawl. The maître d' had also

Love in the First Degree

spoken with a drawl. Not for the first time since checking into the Delta Queen, Claire almost believed she was in New Orleans.

"Are the accents phony?" she asked Luke when the waiter had left them alone. "Or does Max really import the staff from down South?"

"A little of both, actually," he replied. "In some of the more informal restaurants and clubs downstairs, there's less emphasis on authenticity, but here the staff, like the French Creole cuisine, is the real thing."

"Do you come here often?"

He shook his head. "Hardly ever. When I'm working dinner is usually a burger grabbed between crises. And when I'm not working, I usually like to get away for a while."

"I can understand that, especially since you live at your workplace."

"It's not so bad." A wry smile lifted the corners of his mouth. "I've lived in worse places, believe me."

Claire, recalling where he'd lived growing up, nodded. "I've stayed in worse places myself," she said lightly. "My new suite is beautiful, Luke. Thank you for arranging it."

"My pleasure."

His dark eyes gleamed with amusement in a way that made Claire lower her gaze to her menu. Damn him for being able to distract her so easily.

"Since you're not a regular here," she said, determined to behave as if sitting across a small, candlelit table from him was no more unsettling to her than brushing her teeth, "I suppose it won't do me any good to ask you to recommend something."

"It's worse than that, actually." He leaned forward, quite purposely adding an air of intimacy to his conspiratorial whisper, she was certain. "I can't even read the menu."

For just a moment, Claire frowned in confusion. "Oh, you mean because it's in French?"

He nodded, his smile beguilingly rueful. "That's why I brought you along."

"To read the menu to you?"

"That's right. You mentioned that you used to tutor me in French verbs and I wanted to..." His eyes darkened to near-black in the candlelight. "To see if you were telling the truth."

"I see," she replied, scanning the menu once again. "I'm sorry to tell you that there aren't many verbs on this menu, unless you count the chicken over rice." She read to him the more exotic-sounding French name for it.

"Again," he said, letting his own menu slide shut as he stared in fascination at her mouth.

She said it again.

Their eyes met and held, his gaze lazily seductive, hers unable to break away. Her knees shook beneath the table and when she drew a breath it made her ache inside.

"Are you ready to order?" asked the waiter who had soundlessly materialized beside their table.

"Yes," Luke replied, handing him his menu without taking his eyes off Claire. "I'll have the chicken over rice."

"Very good, Mr. Cabrio. And for the lady?"

Claire felt the waiter shift his attention to her. A lifetime of good manners dictated that she look at him, instead of at Luke, but it was impossible. How could that one single moment be more powerful than years of good breeding?

"The same," she said quietly, and without turning her head. "I'll have the same."

Still gazing at her, Luke ordered a bottle of white wine and several appetizers for them to share. Alone with him once more, she felt shaken and embarrassed by the undisguised emotion of the moment. Or had she imagined it and made a total fool of herself? She forced herself to drop her gaze. She rearranged her napkin in her lap, cleared her throat and took a sip of water.

Love in the First Degree

Luke smiled. "So, tell me," he said, "exactly how do you plan to go about clearing my name?"

"Well, I have several possible strategies in mind," Claire lied. "But my first priority is to gather more information from all parties involved."

"That might be difficult," he countered, a familiar hint of dryness in his deep tone. "Since I seem to be the only involved party still available for questioning."

"Then I'll start with you," Claire retorted instantly, feeling herself back on solid ground. She'd been referring to the witnesses whose statements Gerald had faxed to her earlier, but since Luke's comment had given her an opening to do precisely what she wanted to do—ask him some questions—she seized it. "How well did you know Nick Addison?"

"Barely."

"What were you doing in his hotel room?"

He shot her a twisted smile. "I'd say the answer to that one is rather obvious."

"Humor me."

"Why was I there?" He paused. "There were some things I needed to talk to Addison about."

"What things?"

"It doesn't matter. We never got around to talking."

"The man is dead, Luke. You were found standing over his body holding the gun that killed him. Everything matters."

"If you say so."

"I do. Did these things you wanted to discuss with Addison have anything to do with your position here at the Delta Queen?" she asked, not sure why she was tiptoeing toward the question she wanted most to ask. She was usually very direct when she wanted to know something. Did she or didn't she want to know about Luke's mystery woman? Claire suddenly wasn't sure.

"No, nothing," he said in reply to her question.

"Then what was the nature of your relationship with Addison?"

"We didn't have a relationship," Luke uttered, his tone contemptuous.

Claire leaned forward in sudden exasperation, unconsciously running her fingers through her hair to sweep from her forehead the silky lock that habitually fell forward.

"Listen to me, Luke Cabrio. The man was found dead in a room in a hotel to which you have full access, killed with a gun registered to you, and you've been arrested for the murder. If you didn't have a relationship with Addison before, like it or not, you definitely have one now. So what was it? Personal? Professional?"

"Neither."

"Then what?"

He hesitated. Claire watched him closely, without seeming to. She was a great believer in body language. She found it odd that Luke appeared neither anxious nor resentful, simply disinterested, as if his fate was sealed and none of this mattered one way or the other. She felt a giant wrenching of sympathy for him.

"Chance," he said finally.

Claire lowered her brows, perplexed. "Chance?"

"Right. It would probably be easier to explain if you were a gambler. You see, even gamblers have a code of honor. When you make a bet, you accept the risk that goes along with it, all the risk, and win or lose, you deal with it. I might have quit gambling per se, but I still have a gambler's heart. For me, Addison represented a gamble. I lost and now I have to deal with it."

"Are you trying to tell me that you owed him money?"

Luke laughed softly. "No. It wasn't that kind of gamble. It wasn't anything that simple."

"Do you want to explain that to me?"

"No."

"Then how can I help you?" she snapped.

"You can't. I tried to tell you that. It's not too late to change your mind and go home, Claire."

"Yes, it is. You may not care about winning this case, but I do."

"Why?"

Because I owe it to you, Claire thought. She owed it to him for rescuing her from a situation that had felt pretty hopeless to her at the time. And because after twelve years she needed to shake the memory of that night at the Phantom Bar, the roughest roadhouse in Rhode Island. She needed to settle the score and this was a chance to do it.

"Let's just say I'd like to win one for myself for a change," she said, shrugging.

"What's that supposed to mean?"

"It means," she returned, reaching for the wineglass the waiter had unobtrusively filled, "that you're not the only one who can talk in circles."

"Does this have something to do with your problem back home?"

Claire frowned slightly. "What problem?"

"The one that sent you hotfooting it down here. You'll notice that's a question," he said dryly. "And not an insinuating comment of the type I've sworn not to make."

"Let's just say my last case was less than…satisfying and I needed a breather professionally."

"I thought you said you just won your last case and it was a big one?"

"It was, and I did. But it's over now and I'm sort of between cases at the moment and it's my turn to ask you a question." She met his eyes directly. "Who was the woman you and Addison argued about the night he was murdered?"

Luke remained absolutely still.

He was very good at hiding his feelings, but now and then something came along that put that talent to the test. All those years of sitting at poker tables, and not revealing even a hint of the cards he was holding in his hand to the others in the game, came to his aid now. There wasn't a glimmer of alarm in his eyes or the slightest tensing of his facial muscles, in spite of the fact that at that moment he couldn't have been more stunned if Claire had reached across the table and landed a punch on his jaw.

Of course, he'd known from the beginning that no matter how little information he volunteered or permitted to be dragged out of him, eventually the all-but-invisible threads that had connected him to Nick Addison would begin to surface and unravel. He just hadn't expected Claire to play this particular card this early in the game. It was one hell of a leap forward, and he had a sudden vision of the next two weeks stretched before him like a dark chasm, just waiting for him to make a wrong move and tumble in.

He remained silent, thinking. It was possible she was bluffing, attempting a blind fishing expedition. Two men had argued. One was dead. He'd already told her that he hadn't owed Addison money. That left only one logical guess as to what they'd argued about.

"Woman?" he echoed, frowning as if totally bewildered.

"That's right. The woman you warned Addison to stay away from or else you would kill him."

So maybe she wasn't bluffing.

Luke leaned back against the tufted velvet seat and wondered how the hell he was going to extradite himself from this one.

"You do recall threatening Addison, I presume?" she pressed.

"Not in those exact words."

"Perhaps it would help refresh your memory to hear the exact words you used, at least according to several witnesses who were in the lobby at the time. I have copies of their statements in my room."

"How—"

Love in the First Degree

"Gerald," she interjected.

His mouth twisted. "It's amazing how he's had a sudden surge of interest in my case."

"You have me to thank for that, I imagine."

"That's what I'm afraid of," he replied sardonically.

"So, would you like me to run upstairs and get the statements?"

"Not especially. I remember all I want to of what was said that night."

"You two argued?"

"That's right."

"Over a woman?"

He hesitated before nodding. "You could say that."

"Did you threaten to kill him?"

"Probably. I was pretty ticked off at the time and, in spite of what Brad told you, I do lose my temper on occasion. The way I was feeling that night, killing Addison wasn't a problem."

He thought he saw her shudder.

"Who's the woman, Luke?"

Luke started to tell her it didn't matter, but stopped himself. Of course it mattered to her. Any fool could see that just by looking into her eyes. Claire Mackenzie was a woman out to prove something—to him, herself, to the world. Luke wasn't sure exactly why, only that she'd chosen his case as the means to do it. And that she had no idea what she was setting herself up for. She was trying to help, and he was going to have to derail her at every turn. She deserved the truth, he thought, wondering how much of it he could risk telling her.

"Could you do me a favor?" he asked.

"What sort of favor?"

She looked wary. She ought to, Luke thought grimly.

"Could you put this whole thing on hold until tomorrow?"

"For heaven's sake, Luke. I only have—"

"Two weeks," he broke in. "You have two weeks. Let me have this one night."

"We're going to have to discuss this sooner or later," she argued. "And you're going to have to answer my questions. All you're doing is postponing the inevitable."

"For tonight, I'll settle for that. Hell, Claire, I've been sitting in a jail cell for nearly a week and I didn't expect to be out walking around, going to dinner, spending time with a beautiful woman for a long, long time. Let me enjoy it just for tonight."

She was wavering, thinking it over. He could tell by the way her bottom lip curled out just a fraction.

"First thing tomorrow we can get back to all the questions and statements and things I'd rather not have to think about," he continued. "Just for tonight, I'd like to pretend that we're simply two old friends, that you're in Atlantic City for only one night and I'm showing you the sights. What do you say?"

"I say it's ridiculous. I—"

"Please," he interjected softly, leaning forward as he watched the play of emotions on her face.

"All right," she agreed finally. "But on one condition. You answer one final question and that's it for the night."

Damn, Luke thought, she was going to ask him again who the woman was. The one question he didn't want to have to answer.

"Did you kill Nick Addison?"

Wrong, Cabrio, he thought disgustedly. This was the one question he didn't want to have to answer.

"Do you know," he said softly, "that except for a homicide detective the night I was arrested, you're the only person to ask me that directly? Not even Rancourt ever asked."

"That doesn't surprise me. I imagine Gerald would rather avoid hearing anything... awkward," she suggested. "For the purpose of providing you with a defense, it doesn't matter."

Love in the First Degree

"I guess that explains my friends' reactions, too. Max and Brad and a couple of others who came to see me in jail avoided that question like the plague. Like you said, they didn't want to hear any awkward details."

"But I do," she said, her fingers laced easily around the stem of her wineglass. At that moment, Luke could picture her in a courtroom, cool, composed and in control, and he worried that he might have broken one of his own rules: Never underestimate your opponent.

"Did you kill him, Luke?"

What could he tell her? Certainly not the truth, he thought a little desperately. He had sidestepped this question each time the detective put it to him, reluctant to confess and unable to deny it. After that first night, Gerald Rancourt had done the sidestepping on his behalf. Even the day Claire had met with him in jail, he had managed to avoid giving her a direct answer.

That wasn't going to be possible tonight, he realized as he looked into her eyes. The candlelight cast soft shadows on her face and made streaks of gold dance in her hair, but it did nothing to soften or disguise what shone in her eyes.

Trust, he thought disgustedly. *Trust, belief, faith.* Call it whatever you like, Claire had this crazy conviction that he was innocent, and it was up to him to shatter it. There was no way around it. With just one word he could wipe that look from her eyes forever.

"Did you?" she asked again, her voice calm and steady.

He was the one trembling inside over what had to be said.

"Did you kill Nick Addison?"

Tell her.

Get it over with.

Luke felt separated from himself as his head shook back and forth a split second. "No."

Claire ran her fingertips along the table edge as if smoothing papers on her desk. Her smile was serene and satisfied. "Good. Now that we have that settled—"

"Whoa, hold on," he said, stunned and cursing himself for a fool at the same time. He was torn up inside over the choice she had just forced him to make, a choice between responsibility and branding himself a murderer in her eyes, and she seemed about as affected by it as if he'd delivered a weather report. "You don't look at all surprised."

"I'm not," she said, lifting her slender shoulders in a shrug. "I've already told you that I know you didn't do it."

"Then why the heck did you ask me?"

"To see if this time you would trust me enough to tell me the truth. And you did. I'd say we've just taken a major step together."

Yeah, right, Luke thought, still seething as the waiter arrived with their appetizers, and Claire reached enthusiastically for a broiled shrimp. A major step, but in which direction?

Since he was the one who'd proposed dropping the subject of his case for the rest of the night, he had no choice but to let her question, and his damned answer to it, be the final word. For now. Later he would have to work on damage control. And figure out why the hell he had been unable to look Claire Mackenzie in the eye and tell her he was a murderer, something he was fully prepared to let the rest of the world accept as truth without a qualm. He wasn't looking forward to his fate, to be sure, but public opinion had nothing to do with it.

With his first bite, he discovered he was hungrier than he realized. Prison food hadn't been that bad, simply bland, and what flavor there was had been more than offset by the bleak surroundings and the constant antagonism of his tablemates. This setting was so different from that of recent nights it struck Luke as almost surreal. The food and wine were excellent, the atmosphere mellow and, for whatever reason, at that moment there was no one he would rather have for company than Claire.

Love in the First Degree

No matter how much he enjoyed being with her, however, he wouldn't have been surprised if, under the circumstances, they had to grope for things to talk about. That didn't happen. On the contrary, their conversation moved smoothly across a variety of topics, his work and hers, movies, music, politics. She asked provocative questions and made thoughtful comments, and at some point it occurred to Luke that his pleasure was rooted in being with an intelligent woman who wasn't afraid to show it.

Eventually the subject turned to home. The small town where he'd grown up was something Luke made it a practice to avoid, both physically and in conversation. If he could have, he would just as soon have wiped it completely from his memory. Tonight, with Claire, even his memories of Oaklawn and the people there didn't seem so bad.

Over the years he'd forgotten that there had been happiness mixed in with the pain, and moments of excitement and accomplishment in spite of coming from a home where there was never enough of anything, not money or food or safety. And in spite of a father whose idea of weekend fun was getting drunk, blowing his paycheck at the dog track and taking it out on his wife and kids.

Somehow, Claire led him on a safe, winding path through a place he never would have ventured alone, the mine field of his own memories. He was amazed by the things she recalled—the petition he'd started in favor of a student smoking lounge; the yearbook picture of him at the senior prom dressed in tails and black jeans; the basketball game in which he'd scored forty-two points, been hit with a technical foul for brawling with a kid who had at least eight inches and fifty pounds on him, and somehow landed in Claire's lap, where she sat courtside with the school band.

That was the very first time he'd ever noticed her, a skinny sophomore with beautiful eyes.

"You played . . . the cymbals, right?" he asked.

"Close. The clarinet."

Luke grinned. "I knew it began with a *C*."

"Sure you did, Cabrio. You know, if not for that little scar on your jaw, I could easily believe that you're an impostor and that you've never even set foot in Oaklawn, Rhode Island."

He looked at her in amazement, his fingertip moving automatically to the white line on the right side of his jaw that was so faint it became invisible if he permitted a five o'clock shadow to develop.

"You remember this scar?" he asked.

"I have an eye for detail," she explained, shifting uncomfortably on her seat. "The night you fell on me I was staring right down into your face and..."

"And?" he prompted softly, finding her discomfit very interesting. It was hard to tell for sure in candlelight, but he'd swear her face was flushed.

"And I noticed the scar," she continued, obviously attempting to sound offhand. "I remember wondering how you got it."

Luke dropped his hands to the table, but his gaze remained melted to hers.

"I'm still wondering," she said softly.

I fell and hit my chin on a rock. The explanation he'd recited every time he'd ever been asked about the scar formed automatically in Luke's mind, but he couldn't seem to say it.

His fingers curled into fists on top of the starched linen tablecloth and he felt himself begin to reach for his shirt pocket and a cigarette, something he hadn't done in the two years since he'd quit smoking. He dropped his gaze to the rim of his coffee cup.

"It happened one night when my old man came home drunk," he said, his voice thick and uneasy. "He evidently lost his wallet somewhere in his travels that night, or else had it lifted from him in some bar. He swore one of us pinched it and I ended up getting shoved down the front steps."

"He thought you stole his wallet?" Claire asked, her eyes as wide as if he'd declared his father was from another planet. But then, he supposed in the home where she'd grown up, the two were equally preposterous.

"No. He thought my mother took it. He only came after me when I tried to stop him from going after her."

"Oh, Luke, I'm so sorry."

"Don't worry about it. It was a long time ago," he added, the knot in his stomach as tight and hard as if it had been yesterday. For her sake he managed a stiff smile, lightly touching the mark on his jaw. "It doesn't even hurt anymore."

"I meant that I'm sorry for asking about it. I should have known better."

"Why?" he countered, his tone turning harsh. "Why should you have known better? Oh, that's right, I almost forgot that everyone in that damn town knew that Tony Cabrio beat up on his wife and kids. And so, whenever one of us missed school or wasn't around for a while, everyone automatically knew that it was because of a black eye or split lip."

"No, that's not it at all. I should have guessed that, however you got the scar, it wouldn't have been a pleasant memory and I shouldn't have gone dredging it up."

Luke looked at her, at the shimmer of regret in her eyes, and the resentment drained from him as quickly as it had flared.

"I'm glad you did. It was worth it to be reminded that not all my memories are bad. You dredged up some good ones, too, Claire. Come on," he said, signing the check and getting to his feet. "Let's get out of here."

"It is getting late."

"Not in this town. I promised to show you the sights, remember?"

"I thought you were kidding."

"Not a chance." He placed his hand lightly on the small of her back as they left the restaurant, enjoying the silky feel of her clothing and the subtle movement beneath. "You're an old friend just here for one night, remember? And since we're playacting, anyway, let's pretend that you're a gambler at heart." He pressed the elevator button for the lobby.

"Where are we going?"

"To the casino, of course."

Excitement sparked in her eyes even as she shook her head cautiously. "I don't know, Luke..."

"I do," he assured her, taking her hand as the elevator doors opened and leading her toward the casino. "I promise I won't let you lose more than your net worth."

She slowed nearly to a halt as they stepped inside the casino. Luke turned to see what was the matter and understood instantly. He broke into a grin at the expression of absolute amazement on her face, a look he'd seen hundreds of times on people entering a gambling casino for the first time.

He couldn't precisely recall his own first time, but he imagined it had felt something like stepping into a chamber of pure oxygen, a heady overload of the senses, with bright lights all around, music, laughter and the nonstop tinkle of coins pouring from the slot machines, the sound of money being won. And lost.

He didn't have to look around to know that, if he did, he would have no trouble finding faces with expressions the polar opposite of Claire's at that moment. Grim, desperate expressions worn by people who came here too often and stayed too long. Some in that category he'd gotten to know personally, and though it certainly wasn't part of his job to see that they left with something still in their pocket, he did what he could. He remembered his own childhood too well not to.

Gambling had always elicited very mixed feelings in him. He hated it and he was excited by the challenge of it at the

Love in the First Degree

same time. Often he wondered if he'd chosen to make his living as a gambler to prove he was a better man than his father, and if he'd given it up at the first opportunity for the same reason. Most times, however, it was simply what he did to earn a living, either by playing himself or seeing to it that those who played at the Delta Queen did so by the rules. Tonight it was even simpler than that; tonight was for Claire.

"What do you want to try first?" he asked.

"The slot machines," she replied instantly.

He'd known she would. He resisted the urge to tell her that slot machines were for suckers and bought her ten rolls of quarters.

"Pick a machine," he instructed. "Any one with a red dome is a quarter machine."

"Aren't they all the same?"

"In execution, yes, in style, no. Some take four coins, some five."

"Five quarters? At one shot?"

"In order for the maximum payoff. It's possible to put in just one coin at a time, but you'll lose out if one of these other combinations comes up." He used a nearby machine to quickly explain the basics to her.

"So three lemons and two gold coins is the best combination, right?"

"On this particular machine. On this one," he said, tapping the one next to it, "you want to get three silver bars and two hearts. Different style, same execution." He gave her a quick, one-armed hug. "Don't look so worried, it's only money...and remember, tonight you're a gambler at heart."

"I'll try," she murmured, glancing down the row of slot machines. "Double Diamonds," she declared, pointing to one near the end of the aisle. "I want to try that one."

Luke settled her at the seat in front of the machine she'd selected, handed her a plastic bucket, emblazoned with the hotel logo, to hold her coins, and said, "You're on."

The first time she pulled the lever, bells sounded, pink and purple lights flashed and quarters poured from the front of the slot machine.

"Oh, my God," Claire exclaimed. "I think I won."

"See, you're a natural," Luke said, laughing as she scooped her winnings into her bucket.

"How much do you think is here?"

"Ten dollars and fifty cents," he replied. At her quick look of astonishment, he showed her how to read the payoff amount on the machine.

"It sounded like so much more," she grumbled. "I thought I was rich."

"This definitely is not the way to get rich. It's just a way to have fun. Want to quit while you're ahead?"

She shook her head, her eyes sparkling with the excitement he understood well. "Not on your life."

At first she insisted on pulling the lever the traditional way on every try, but when her arm tired, she began simply pushing the button on the front like a regular. She also jumped machines like a regular and quickly picked up the trick of moving to a machine someone gave up on under the theory that it was due to hit. At the end of an hour, Luke pronounced her a winner for ending up with a quarter of the amount she'd started with.

They moved to the baccarat table, where she would only watch, but he persuaded her to try her hand at blackjack and roulette. He stayed close to her side to offer advice and because he'd become hooked on the light floral scent that clung to her and drifted his way whenever she moved or tossed her head. Not even on the nights when he was playing and winning big had he ever had as much fun as he was having watching Claire have fun. The conservative, cautious-lawyer side of her had taken the night off. This was a looser, freer Claire whom he'd glimpsed on only one other occasion. That was a long time ago, but he remembered that then, like now, wanting her had made it tough to think straight.

"I won," she cried suddenly, drawing his attention back to the table and the little black ball nestled in the slot she had bet on. "I really did win, right?"

"That's right, miss," said the dealer, chuckling at her amazement. "The house pays."

She'd won over two hundred dollars on a ten-dollar bet, in spite of the fact that he'd been daydreaming about her and had forgotten to tell her to play the odds and leave her markers where she had them for the next spin. There was something to be said for beginner's luck.

Luke might have worried that he'd created a monster by bringing her there if he wasn't so sure there was too much else going on in Claire's life for gambling to become an obsession. First impressions aside, the shiny veneer of the casinos was really very thin. He knew from experience that gambling could only fill a life that was pretty empty to begin with.

"Now I'm ready to quit," she announced, after he'd helped her gather the chips she'd won.

Luke didn't argue. He was tired of sharing her with everyone in the brightly lit casino. And tired of his own resolution to resist Claire at all costs. The feeling of connection he'd experienced earlier, when they talked about home and old times, had persisted. If anything, it had grown steadily stronger throughout the night.

It was perfectly understandable, Luke reasoned as he stood by while she cashed in her chips at the teller window. It had been a long time since he'd connected with anyone from his past, and on some level he'd obviously missed that connection more than he wanted to admit. Then, too, he was facing a long stretch of prison time. As hard as he tried not to dwell on it, it was always at the back of his mind. It was normal that he should want to make the most of every moment he had to spend with a beautiful, intelligent, exciting woman.

The fact that it was easily explained and normal and probably to be expected did not diminish the strong sensation that Claire was somehow the missing part of himself, something he'd been searching for even without knowing it. A mind trick. It had to be. A weird collision of timing and hormones. False positive. But genuine or not, it was, Luke realized, a very dangerous situation. Feeling this happy could make a man do stupid things, and right now he couldn't afford that. He still didn't want it to end. For just a while longer, for this one night, he wanted the feeling to last.

Tomorrow, as he'd promised Claire, it was back to reality. She would ask her questions and he would have to give more in the way of answers, and he had no doubt that would put an end to this thing between them—this magic or chemistry or insanity or whatever it might be. But for now, tonight, he wanted to pretend this was real.

He was going to go on pretending that Claire was simply an old friend with whom he shared a few good memories. He was going to forget about complications and resolutions and the need to watch every word he said and let whatever happened happen.

The prospect filled him with a heated sense of anticipation as they left the casino. When he reached for Claire's hand, she glanced at him, a look that acknowledged the deliberate nature of the gesture and said that she recognized it as something more than the casual touches and brushes he'd indulged in all evening. She didn't pull her hand away. Luke was amazed at the thrill that shot through him. How long had it been since holding a woman's hand had made his heart pound?

"Want to take a walk along the boardwalk?" he asked.

"I don't know, Luke. Now it really is late and—"

"Shh." Still holding her hand, he stopped and swung her around so that they stood facing each other in a quiet stretch of the walkway that surrounded the hotel lobby and casino. He cupped her chin with his other hand so that his thumb rested against her lips, silencing her. "Tonight's not for worrying about getting to bed on time, or what we have to do tomorrow. Tonight is for having fun...and for taking chances."

Her lips were the softest thing he'd ever touched, and the hint of warmth from her breath made him stir inside.

"So what do you say?" he whispered, thrilled by her tremulous nod of acquiescence and the hint of surrender in the way her body swayed gently toward his.

Another signal, like the one she'd sent when he took her hand. If he tried to kiss her, she wouldn't stop him. Luke slid his arm around her and lowered his head slowly. Her eyes fluttered shut as her mouth parted under his lips. He was hungry for her in a hundred different ways, but right this minute he wanted to taste her mouth more than he could recall ever wanting anything.

"Luke, is that you? Thank God...I've been looking everywhere."

Luke jerked his head up and turned angrily toward the woman who'd interrupted. His anger faded as soon as he realized who it was.

"Sherry," he said. "I...ah, didn't know you were working tonight." He gestured feebly at the costume she was wearing, a white bodysuit adorned with sequins and feathers that fit her petite frame like a second skin. There were more feathers arranged in her curly auburn hair and trimming her four-inch heels. White silk gloves that climbed to above her elbows completed the gaudy outfit. He was painfully aware of Claire by his side, smoothing her own hair and clothing.

"I switched with one of the other dancers," Sherry explained distractedly. "I couldn't believe it when someone told me you were here. What's going on? Did you—"

"Sherry, this is Claire Mackenzie," Luke interrupted. "Claire is working on my case along with Rancourt. Claire, this is Sherry. A friend," he added simply.

The two women exchanged the obligatory greetings, followed by a silence that he understood was up to him to break. The problem was he was suddenly too damn tired and frustrated to even attempt it. What a fool he'd been to think he could put reality on hold for even one night. Sherry was his reality and she was standing right there, looking scared out of her mind. And Claire didn't look at all soft and yielding as she had only a minute ago. She looked alert and on guard. She looked like a lawyer, Luke thought.

"Luke," Sherry said, obviously unable to contain herself any longer. "I've been calling your room all night, but there was no answer. I really need to talk with you." Her eyes darted toward Claire. "Privately."

As hints went, it wasn't very subtle. Luke understood that Claire had no polite choice except to excuse herself, but he was disappointed just the same.

"I'll leave you two alone," she said.

"I didn't mean to interrupt anything," Sherry began with a cautious look at Luke.

"You didn't," Claire told her.

"At least let me see you to your room," Luke said hopefully. To Sherry he added, "Then we can talk."

She frowned apologetically. "My break is over in ten minutes and I have to get right home after work. My regular baby-sitter couldn't make it and the woman downstairs will only—"

"All right." Luke cut her off, thinking that the less Sherry said in front of Claire, the better, until he had a chance to talk with her. "Claire, I'm really sorry about this."

"Don't be," she said. "It's late and I really am tired. I'll see you tomorrow."

Tomorrow, Luke thought, watching her walk away and wishing he could have held tomorrow at bay forever.

Chapter 6

Claire told herself that the interruption by Luke's friend, Sherry, had been a gift from the gods. Fate's way of saving her from her own reckless desires and wherever they may have led her tonight.

Of course, she assured herself, even without that reprieve she wouldn't have allowed things to go too far. She would have let Luke kiss her, might even have kissed him back, but only for the sake of curiosity. After all, she'd spent a lot of time back in high school fantasizing about what it would be like to be kissed by Luke Cabrio.

She smiled ruefully as she peeled off her stockings and belted her robe, remembering the nights she'd practiced her technique on her pillow, wanting to be ready when it finally happened. She'd been so sure it *would* happen. Back then she'd even dreamed about Luke's kisses. Her eyes closed and her skin warmed as the memory of those dreams came rushing back to her. At least in her sleep, she'd had quite a vivid imagination for a seventeen-year-old virgin.

Love in the First Degree

She supposed it would have been interesting to find out, once and for all, if Luke measured up to her imagination. Not that she'd been pining for him since high school. She'd just never quite forgotten him completely. Months, maybe even a year or so, would pass without her even thinking of Luke. Then something would happen or someone would say something that would bring it all back and she would remember. And wonder.

That's what kept the fantasy alive, she thought, the wondering, the thrill of speculation. If Luke had ever shown any real interest in her back in high school, or if he had gone ahead and kissed her that night outside the Phantom, as she'd been so certain he was going to, no doubt he would have long ago been relegated to the mundane status of all her other high school memories. Pleasant, but finished.

In which case she might not have felt as if she'd grabbed hold of a live electrical wire when she saw his arrest photo staring up at her from the local paper. She wouldn't have been haunted by thoughts of the trouble he'd gotten himself into. She probably wouldn't have felt compelled to get involved, and she definitely wouldn't be sitting here right this minute, still wondering what it would be like to be kissed by Luke Cabrio.

And wondering just how close a friend Sherry, with her dancer's legs and sleek curves, was to him.

Luke had certainly looked uncomfortable when the woman intruded on them at such an intimate moment. Good old Sherry hadn't looked too thrilled at the sight, either, Claire recalled with a very juvenile stab of satisfaction. But she had to admit, the woman hadn't really reacted like a jealous lover. She'd been too apologetic, for one thing. And if she and Luke were romantically involved, would he have felt free to offer to see Claire—the other woman—to her door while Sherry stood there waiting? Not likely.

Claire paused in the middle of brushing her teeth. Still, she had been visibly upset over something. No doubt the same thing she needed to discuss with Luke so urgently. And privately. Claire stuck her tongue out at the mirror and rinsed.

She wished she'd gotten Sherry's last name.

Not that she should be too hard to track down. How many of the hotel's dance acts included feathers? On the notepad on the desk she wrote the name Sherry followed by a question mark, and underlined it twice.

The fact that Sherry had seemed upset wasn't proof that she knew anything about Luke or the murder. Everyone around here was upset about Luke. Not convinced he was innocent, Claire reminded herself, simply upset that he'd been arrested. Believing in Luke against all odds seemed to be her affliction alone. But there had been an edge to the exchange between Luke and Sherry that she hadn't sensed in his conversations with anyone else.

Also, there was something familiar about the woman, something Claire couldn't quite put her finger on. She tried to imagine what she would look like without the feathers and stage makeup, but still couldn't figure out what it was about her that made Claire think she'd seen Sherry before. She shrugged finally and pushed the matter from her mind. From experience she knew that if she tried too hard, it would never come to her.

Climbing into bed, she rearranged the pillow, reached to turn out the light and paused.

Had Sherry known Nick Addison?

Interesting possibility. There was one sure way to find out, Claire thought. She would ask her. She made a mental note to check with Brad in the morning about the possibility of getting a list of the names and home addresses of all hotel employees. The last thing she saw before the light went out was the note she'd written to remind herself to return her father's call.

Too late now, she thought with only a faint twinge of guilt. Only a week ago it would have been unthinkable for

Love in the First Degree

her not to return his calls as soon as possible, not to do exactly what was expected of her at all times. She wasn't sure if it was time or distance that made the difference, but heeding her own instincts was getting easier with each passing day.

Still, he deserved to know that she was all right. Tomorrow she would call him for sure, she told herself. Early. Before he arrived at the office. That way she could leave a message with Caroline, his secretary, and not have to take any flack in return. She would tell Caroline to let her father know that she was fine and very busy and not sure when she would be back. All true.

She didn't even feel guilty for taking advantage of the fact that her father was president of the firm and embarking on this extended, unplanned leave of absence. She had cleared her desk and delegated like crazy before taking on the Henderson case. That had dragged on for months, with a decision coming only last week. Claire curled herself into a ball, a familiar bitterness knotting inside her at the memory of that decision, the biggest victory of her career. Supposedly. Three cheers for the system.

Afterwards, her father had even urged her to take a few days off. A few days, not several weeks. Or longer. Maybe forever.

It was the first time Claire had even allowed herself to think of the possibility of not returning to the firm. She waited for guilt to come crashing in on her, and when it didn't, she felt as if she'd passed a major milestone. She even grinned in the darkness and stretched her legs full length. Anything was possible.

Maybe she would move here to Atlantic City and spend her time playing the quarter slots. No, that had gotten pretty repetitious after an hour or so. The law was her life and she loved it. Maybe she would start her own practice, here or back home. Now that idea tempted her more than anything in the casino downstairs possibly could. Her own practice.

Choosing clients based on need rather than dollar value. She lay awake for a while, turning the idea over in her mind, marveling at it as if it were a bright penny she'd found in the gutter. Here, away from family expectations and machinations, anything really did seem possible, she thought, surrendering with a yawn to the fatigue that came in a sudden rush....

She was sitting on the bleachers in the high school gym. The game had ended hours ago and everyone was gone. Claire wasn't sure why she was still there. It didn't seem to matter. Suddenly Luke appeared, coming from the direction of the boys' locker room and heading straight toward her with that lazy, lean-hipped stride of his that was like no one else's. He stopped in front of her. His long hair was still damp from the shower and he had a navy canvas gym bag slung over his shoulder.

He dropped the bag at her feet.

"I'm glad you waited," he said.

"I wanted to congratulate you," Claire replied. "You had a great game."

She wasn't tongue-tied or nervous or anything. Her palms weren't even sweating the way they did whenever she sat across from him in tutoring. It was easy to talk with him now. She felt relaxed and sure of herself, the way she always longed to feel around Luke. He noticed the difference, too. She could tell, because for once he wasn't looking at her with that sort of amused, indulgent smile he might use on a six-year-old. He was looking at her the way he would look at a woman.

"The band sounded pretty good, too," he told her.

"Really?"

"Nah, not really," he said, grinning, "but it's worth putting up with all those wrong notes to get to spend the whole game looking at you."

Claire's heart pounded recklessly. "Did you? Look at me during the game, I mean?"

Love in the First Degree 101

His dark eyes flared as he leaned closer, bracing his hands on the bleachers on either side of her so that she felt surrounded by him. "Didn't you notice?"

"Actually, I did." Her laugh was soft, throaty, provocative. "I never before saw anyone make a foul shot without looking at the basket."

"I'll bet there's a lot of things you've never seen," he countered, bringing his face to within inches of hers. His voice was pitched deliciously low. Just the sound of it, so close, sent shivers of excitement racing through her. "Or tried."

"Such as?"

"This."

In a heartbeat, his mouth was on hers, already open, hot, hungry, demanding. Being kissed by Luke wasn't like being kissed by the other boys she'd dated. It wasn't like being kissed by a boy, at all. There was no fumbling, no hesitancy. Luke made it clear he knew exactly what he wanted and he made Claire want it, too.

His tongue was in her mouth. It felt new and wonderful. He moved it slowly, in and out, and with each stroke he claimed a little more of her. Claire felt his hands on her back, moving restlessly over her, tugging up the sweater of her band uniform. His palms felt warm against her skin. He slipped his fingers under the strap of her bra and like magic it was open.

Claire reached out to touch him. She knew just how to run her hands up and down his sides, just how to arch her neck so he could kiss her there, too. She was made for this.

"You were made for me," Luke whispered right on cue. "You're perfect." Slowly he moved his hands around to the front, and for once she had no qualms at all about her breasts being too small. "Perfect," he said as his hands closed over her and she went up in flames.

Claire's eyes flew open. The room was dark and the pillow beneath her head was unfamiliar and slightly damp. The back of her neck was sweating, she realized, and the sheet was twisted around her legs as if she'd been wrestling with it half the night.

She'd been dreaming. That same old dream, she thought, aware of a lingering heat at her core. The feeling was disturbingly real. Damn, she hadn't had that dream in years, but it was every bit as powerful as it had ever been. She didn't need to wonder why it had returned tonight.

Being around Luke had resurrected so many unresolved feelings, it wasn't surprising that it had also brought to life an old dream. Claire wasn't sure how she wanted those feelings resolved, only that she didn't want to be still dreaming that same dream when she was sixty. She punched the pillow into shape and rolled to her side, willing herself to stay out of high school gyms for the rest of the night.

She was awakened by the ringing of the telephone.

Dad, she thought guiltily, then caught herself. So much for last night's milestone. Clearly she still had a way to go before she figured out what she wanted for the future.

She grabbed the phone. "Hello?"

"Claire? Is that you?"

It was Gerald. Relief swept through her.

"Yes. Good morning, Gerald."

"You sound funny."

"I just woke up."

"Oops. Sorry, but I'm going to be tied up in court all morning and this couldn't wait."

"What's up?" Claire asked, coming fully awake as she sat up in bed.

"I found out who the woman is whom Luke and Addison were arguing about that night...at least as far as the D.A. is concerned."

She pressed her fingers to her throat, where her pulse had started to flutter wildly. "Who is she?"

Love in the First Degree

"Addison's ex-wife. She works right there at the hotel, as a matter of fact, and she and Luke are evidently quite chummy. She's a dancer by the name of—"

"Sherry," Claire intoned.

"Hey, you *are* good. How did you find out?"

"I didn't. It was just a lucky guess. Do you know her last name?"

"Wakefield. She dropped the Addison when she divorced him, evidently."

"Sherry Wakefield," she repeated, hoping the name might hold a clue to why she seemed familiar.

"Right," Gerald said. "I think you should try and talk with her."

"I intend to, as soon as possible."

"Maybe we'll get real lucky and it will turn out she and Luke were shacked up at the actual time of the murder, giving him an ironclad alibi, so to speak."

Claire grimaced, but said nothing. She wasn't sure she could stomach that much luck.

"I was only kidding."

"I know," Claire told him, "but you did give me an idea. Did the coroner pinpoint the exact time of Addison's death?"

"I think he put it down as close to the time the police arrived on the scene, or words to that effect."

His nonchalance rankled.

"You're not getting paid to think," she shot back, using one of her father's favorite retorts, "you're getting paid to win."

"And not very well paid, at that." His stiff tone made Claire regret her impatience. "I'll fax you a copy of the coroner's report and you can figure it out."

"Better yet, have a copy of the entire file delivered to me, will you? Please."

"Sure. What are you planning?"

"Luke had to be somewhere, doing something, at the time of the murder. Maybe I can work backwards to his alibi, but first I have to know the exact time of death."

"That's a lot of ifs and maybes."

"Reasonable doubt, Counselor. That's all it takes."

Claire showered and dressed in a hurry. A glance outside suggested it was going to be another hot, sunny day and she longed to throw on something loose and comfortable. Unfortunately, she couldn't. If she had to resort to a power play to get Sherry Wakefield's home address from Brad, she wanted to be dressed for it. It also wouldn't hurt to project an air of competence and authority when she questioned Sherry. She settled on a pale yellow suit over a white silk T-shirt and prayed she wouldn't have to spend too much time away from air-conditioning.

She managed to leave her room before Luke called or came knocking on her door, which was her intention. She wanted to talk with Sherry alone before she confronted Luke.

The concierge directed her to the security offices, located a short distance from the main lobby, and she found Brad seated at the desk in the office with Luke's name on the door. The office was spacious and well-appointed in the same relaxed, but elegant style as the rest of the Delta Queen.

There were a massive desk and bookcase that looked to be antique reproductions, oversize chairs upholstered in burgundy leather and several brass urns holding lush ferns, but not a single photograph or memento. Unless, Claire thought, taking in the entire room with one well-trained glance, you counted the jigsaw puzzle half-completed on the table behind the desk.

"Claire," Brad said as she knocked on the open door and entered. He shot to his feet, looking more than a little

Love in the First Degree

embarrassed. "I hope you don't get the wrong idea from me using Luke's office, instead of my own."

"What wrong idea would that be?"

"That I can't wait to step into his shoes around here. This office is just more convenient and the files are all here and..." He broke off with a sheepish smile so dazzling it would take him far in this world. "And I admit it, I get a kick out of sitting in the boss's chair. That doesn't mean I want him out of here for good."

"I believe you," she replied. "And it's just as well, because Luke's not going anywhere... not if I have anything to do with it, which I do."

"That's great. How can I help?"

"In two ways. First, I'd like to have a look at the room where the murder took place."

"Six-seventeen," Brad supplied, nodding.

"It hasn't been cleaned, yet, I assume?"

"No, the police haven't given us the go-ahead to do more than remove the yellow tape from the door." He shot her a wry look. "Max felt it didn't project quite the desired ambience."

"I'll bet. When can I see it?"

"Whenever you like. I'll give you the current combination for the lock." He swiveled to face the computer on the side table, hit a few keys and jotted a series of numbers on a piece of paper. He handed it to her. "Here you go... unless you'd rather not go in alone. I'd be happy to keep you company."

"Thanks, but that's not necessary."

"Of course," he said, shaking his head at himself. "I'm sure you're an old hand at checking out grisly crime scenes."

"Mmm," she countered, wondering just how grisly a sight it was. "I also need the address of one of the hotel's employees. Her name is Sherry Wakefield. I believe she's a dancer."

Brad nodded as he swung back to the computer. "Right. At the Riverboat Lounge. Let's see... Wakefield, Wakefield." He frowned. "This can't be right."

"What can't?" she asked, peering at the computer screen, but unable to read it.

"Her address. I know for a fact that Sherry lives on the other side of the city, because I've given her a lift home a few times. She probably moved since she started here and Luke never updated this list." He slanted her a sardonic smile. "The man doesn't much like computers. He says he doesn't trust a machine that's smarter than he is."

"I'm not convinced they are smarter," she remarked. "For instance, I'd like to see a computer put together that puzzle." She nodded at the table behind him, strewn with puzzle pieces in an intimidating array of colors, it seemed to her. "Luke's?"

Brad nodded. "Two-faced."

"I beg your pardon?" Claire said, frowning.

"Oh, sorry, I was referring to the puzzle. It's one of those printed with a different scene on each side, just to make things really difficult."

"Now that does sound like Luke."

"I guess it does at that," Brad agreed. "Just give me a minute and I'll get that address for you. I update the list on my computer weekly."

Alone in Luke's office, Claire wandered over and picked up a piece of the puzzle. Sure enough, blue sky on one side and something green and murky on the other. Couldn't he do anything the easy way?

"Here you go," Brad said, returning to hand her a slip with Sherry's address. At her request, he also supplied her with simple directions.

"Eventually I'd like a list of all hotel employees," she told him.

Love in the First Degree

"No problem. Like I said, I update it weekly and I can give it to you alphabetically or broken down by job classification or security clearance."

"I'm impressed. Maybe Luke had better watch out for his job, after all," she joked as she turned to leave.

Brad shook his head firmly. "Not a chance. All the computer expertise in the world can't replace what Luke has—gut instinct. Ninety-five percent of this job is thinking on your feet. Luke can size up a situation in a second. He always knows the right thing to do and just does it."

Like the commercial says, Claire thought, still mulling over Brad's words as she followed his directions to Sherry's house. *Just do it.* She understood exactly what Brad meant about Luke's gut instinct. She had witnessed it in action years ago. She'd seen firsthand how quickly and confidently he reacted to trouble.

She would never forget that night at the Phantom. It was her first and only visit to the tavern on the outskirts of town, a hangout for bikers and other assorted riffraff, a place so unsavory it would never even occur to her parents to warn her to stay away from there. Not that the devil himself could have kept her away that night.

It was the last summer before she left for college, her third summer of watching Luke tear through town on his motorcycle with some other girl clinging to his back. Not even Michelle and Jenny, her best friends in the world at the time, knew how desperately she longed to be that girl on the back of Luke's bike. Her fascination with the town's acknowledged bad boy was something she couldn't even understand, much less share with anyone.

Through the grapevine, she'd learned that Luke, too, would be leaving town in the fall. For good, some said, and good riddance to him. The thought of maybe never seeing Luke again made her crazy and desperate in the way only a seventeen-year-old in love can be. Somehow she persuaded Jenny and Michelle to go with her to the Phantom on the pretense of a final summer adventure. It was the one place she felt certain of running into Luke on a weekend night. It was her last chance.

It hadn't taken her friends long to realize that going there had been a big mistake. Jenny insisted on leaving before someone spotted her father's car in the parking lot and told him she'd been there. Michelle was right behind her going out the door. Only Claire stayed. Sitting alone at a table in what she hoped was an inconspicuous corner, she nursed a tequila sunrise and fended off the attention of guys she'd be afraid to pass on the street. And she waited, stubbornly, for her last chance with Luke. Stubborn as she was, however, the action inside the bar finally turned brawl-like enough to scare her into using the phone in the entry to call for a taxi.

It was while she was dialing that the three guys who'd followed her out grabbed her arms and hustled her outside. Even now Claire's pulse rate zoomed and her grip on the steering wheel tightened as she recalled what followed. It came back to her in a rapid-fire sequence of impressions she had never quite sorted out and wasn't sure she wanted to.

She remembered a huge hand that smelled of garlic and something else disgusting being clamped over her mouth, making it impossible to breathe, much less scream, as she was half carried, half dragged to a dimly lit spot at the far corner of the parking lot. They let her go with a warning not to make a sound, and by then she was too scared not to obey.

She remembered the strong, blended stench of sweat and beer as the three men circled her, like dogs eyeing a bone. The starry summer night gave way to what seemed to be a solid wall of black leather, silver chains and hard, leering faces. She tried not to remember the things they said to her, the lewd comments and terrifying promises, but she would never forget the moment she moved past mere fear to the horrific, paralyzing understanding that she was about to be gang-raped, and maybe worse.

Love in the First Degree

She tried to scream when one of them grabbed the front of her thin cotton blouse and ripped it completely open, shoving her hands and bra aside while they all laughed and cheered. But someone muffled her mouth again, wrenching her head back in the process so that in the moments that followed she didn't know for sure whose hands were touching her where.

Even now, years later, her breath came in short, panicky pants whenever she let herself think about that night. She remembered feeling the snap on her jeans being opened and her legs flailing desperately as she tried to get away. It was hard to stay on her feet, the way they were jostling her. All part of the game, no doubt. Once or twice she caught a glimpse of sky or nearby cars before the circle closed in on her again.

Then one of the men dipped his head to put his mouth on her breast, and for a second she had a clear view all the way to the street. She saw streetlights and Harleys and Luke. He was coming toward her exactly as he always did in her dream, with the same easy stride, the same sense that he knew exactly where he was going and why.

At first she thought perhaps it was only a dream, or a hallucination. Then she realized the others saw him, too, and she knew he was real.

Relief pounded in her ears, blocking out whatever he said as he approached her attackers, and most of the brief conversation that followed. At first the fact that he was smiling along with them startled her, and for one awful instant she feared he had come to join in the fun. Then the other men grudgingly backed away and suddenly she was alone with Luke....

A classic illustration of that old proverb about being careful what you wish for, Claire thought as she turned onto Sherry's street and began checking the house numbers. She had wanted to be alone with Luke that night and she had gotten her wish—just not in the manner she would have chosen. Funny how life has its own way of delivering on the gifts you ask to receive.

When she thought about it afterward, she understood the reason for Luke's smile, and that in a physical confrontation, he would have stood little chance against the three of them. He'd handled it the only way he could, and she could only wonder what he had said to them that made them back off. She still wondered.

Whatever it was that he said, he had saved her from hell that night, and now she had a chance to do the same for him. Another of life's bizarrely presented opportunities. But whether she was successful in helping him or not, she would always be grateful to him for not simply walking past as others had that night.

He had seen what was happening and, just as Brad said, he'd known what to do and had done it. Gut instinct. If anything, Claire imagined that the passing of time had only honed Luke's instincts and his noble impulses. Could that have something to do with the trouble he was in now?

She located Sherry's house without any trouble. It was in the middle of a block of three-story tenements. In spite of the fact that the neighborhood had obviously seen better days, there were plenty of signs that the people who lived there were trying to turn things around. There were freshly painted front doors and window shutters, and small flower gardens planted around the towering maple trees that shaded the narrow street.

Sherry lived on the third floor. Since the front door was unlocked, Claire opted to bypass the doorbell and climb the three flights of stairs to knock on her apartment door. No wonder Sherry had great legs, she thought as she reached the top.

The woman who opened the door looked younger and considerably less glamorous than the Sherry she'd met last night. She also looked exasperated. She was holding a metal spatula in one hand, and wisps of reddish gold hair had escaped her ponytail and were plastered to her damp forehead and neck. In spite of the fan mounted in one window, the apartment was hot enough to make anyone sweat.

Claire's attention was drawn by the little boy with a tear-streaked face who was clinging to the oversize white T-shirt Sherry wore with cutoff denims. He looked to be about five, with reddish hair like his mother's and a dusting of freckles across his nose. Another boy stood a few feet away, regarding Claire with a solemn and wary expression. He had dark silky hair and olive skin, leading her to conclude that he took after his father.

"Yes?" Sherry prompted impatiently.

"I hate to drop in on you unannounced this way," Claire began, then paused at the soft whimpering coming from the younger boy. Her knowledge of children and their reasons for crying was nil. "Is everything all right? Perhaps—"

"He stubbed his toe," the other woman countered. "He wants me to sit and hold him, and I will, as soon as I finish fixing his brother's breakfast and find out what you want."

"Oh, of course. Ms. Wakefield...Sherry, we met last night...at the Delta Queen."

Recognition flashed in her eyes. Evidently the fact that Luke had been about to kiss another woman had not made a lasting impression on her. For some reason that pleased Claire.

"Right," Sherry said. "You're the lawyer Luke was talking to outside the casino."

Claire nodded. She supposed that was one way of describing what they had been doing.

Sherry gave her a quick once-over and shrugged. "You look different in daylight."

"So do you."

Their eyes met and they both smiled slightly.

"Sherry, I'm helping the public defender with Luke's case and I'd like to talk with you about it if I could."

Claire saw her stiffen. Her smile fled.

"I'm sorry," she said quickly, "but I really don't know anything that can help you. I was working all that evening and have no knowledge of what Luke or my ex-husband were doing at any time."

The little speech definitely did not have a spontaneous feel to it.

"I understand. What I'd really like to do, if I might, is to get some background information from you. It will help me to help Luke."

Sherry shook her head. "I'm sorry. I really can't talk now."

"I'd be happy to wait until you finish fixing breakfast," Claire said.

Sherry was already shaking her head in refusal. She looked nervous. No, not nervous exactly. Trapped. Claire decided to try a slightly different tact.

"Please, Sherry. My job is to work on the possibility of a plea bargain on Luke's behalf. In order to secure for him the best possible deal, I need to gather as much background information on the victim as I can."

It wasn't a lie. A plea bargain was always a consideration in a murder case. Even a financial attorney knew that.

"A plea bargain?" Sherry said quizzically. "You mean, like a less-serious charge than—" she dropped her voice, her gaze darting to the children "—than murder?"

"That's right, and a much shorter sentence, as well. Possibly with most of the sentence even suspended."

Sherry's eyes widened, as if Claire had flashed her a vision of heaven. "Could that really happen? Even if Luke admits he did it, they could give him a suspended sentence?"

"It's possible," Claire replied, not mentioning that there was a whole lot of room between possible and likely. "I'll know better what kind of deal we can expect the D.A. to offer after I talk with everyone involved."

Love in the First Degree 113

Sherry absently smoothed her son's hair where his head was pressed to her side. For the moment, Claire's interruption had distracted him from his sore toe.

"So I'm not the only one you're talking with about this?" she asked Claire.

"Definitely not. As a matter of fact, I've requested a list of all hotel employees. I simply thought that since we had already met, and you were acquainted with both Luke and the victim," she added, also glancing cautiously at the two boys, "I would start with you."

Sherry bit her bottom lip before nodding. "Okay, but you'll have to wait a few minutes while I finish feeding them and send them off to play. The less they hear about any of this...you know."

"Of course," Claire agreed, stepping inside and closing the door behind her.

It was even warmer in the small kitchen than it had been by the front door. Claire slipped off her suit jacket and looked around for a safe place to put it. It wasn't that the apartment was dirty. On the contrary, though worn, the floor and countertops were clean and tidy. The blue plaid seat cushions matched the place mats on the table and crisp, white ruffled curtains brightened the windows. However, the open jelly jar, maple-syrup bottle and half-full juice glasses crowded onto the small table made the whole area a danger zone for a woman wearing pale yellow.

"You can put it on my bed if you want," Sherry offered, observing her plight. "It's that way," she added, pointing with one hand while she used the spatula in the other to expertly flip a piece of French toast.

Claire found the bedroom and hung her jacket on one post of a dark four-poster bed, noting that in this room, too, Sherry had created an appealing atmosphere without much to work with. A crocheted white coverlet on the bed made the tiny space look larger, and the same pretty rose-and-white flowered chintz used for the window valances, toss pillows and skirt of the dressing table pulled things together nicely. Lacking any decorating talent at all, Claire was impressed.

The top of the dressing table held a mirrored tray with cosmetics and a group of small framed photographs. Without thinking, she paused to look at them on her way out. Most were of the two boys. There was a vintage photograph of a young couple on their wedding day, which she guessed was of Sherry's parents. Toward the back of the table was a shot of Sherry holding a newborn in her arms, and suddenly Claire knew what was so familiar about the woman.

The picture on the dressing table was the same one she had seen Luke shove into his wallet the day he'd left prison. She'd had such a quick glimpse at the time that she couldn't even have described the picture, but seeing it again, she was certain it was the same photo. There was something about the way Sherry was smiling in the picture and the carefree lift of her chin that had stuck in Claire's mind. That and the fact that Luke chose to carry a photo of a woman and baby.

She hurried back to the kitchen just as Sherry finished cutting up the boys' French toast.

"What are your sons' names?" she asked, taking a seat at the table.

"This is Ben," Sherry told her, placing her hand on the shoulder of the older boy. "And the little guy with the stubbed nose is Nicky."

"Mom," Nicky said, rolling his eyes. "It's not my nose, it's my toe."

"Oh, that's right," his mother said, tapping him on the nose lightly. "I always get those two mixed up."

Nicky laughed at her silliness. Even Ben, clearly the quieter of the two boys, smiled as he ate his toast. Claire sensed genuine warmth and love among the small family.

Love in the First Degree 115

She accepted Sherry's offer of coffee, and by the time it was ready, the boys had finished eating and disappeared into their bedroom to play a video game.

"I like to make sure they get outside on nice days," Sherry said as she placed a blue-and-white flowered mug of coffee in front of her, "so I hope this won't take too long."

"It won't, I promise. I see you named your second son after his father."

It was an observation, not a question, but Sherry launched into a quick explanation.

"Yes. I had a favorite uncle named Benjamin, so when Ben was born I really wanted to use that name. Then when Nicky came along, it was Nick's turn and so..." She trailed off with a shrug.

"They're both fine, strong names."

"I think so." She shrugged again. "Anyway, it's done now. Those are their names for better or worse. I just wish..."

"What do you wish, Sherry?" Claire prodded gently.

"Nothing." Sherry shook her head, obviously banishing whatever thought had brought such sadness to her face. "What did you want to ask me?"

"Mainly I want to know more about your ex-husband," Claire explained, slipping a small notepad from her purse. "Tell me about Nick Addison."

Over the next hour or so she filled several pages of the notepad with facts supplied to her by Sherry. Details about Nick Addison's family background and his childhood in Massachusetts. Sherry revealed that they had met in Atlantic City, when Nick stopped into the lounge where she was working at the time. They'd fallen in love, married and Ben had been born all within a year. Nicky was born two years later. During their marriage they'd lived in a small town that was the home office for the insulation company Nick worked for. His job as a salesman kept him on the road most of the time. As their marriage began to disintegrate, that wasn't such a bad thing, Sherry told her.

As interesting to Claire as everything Sherry told her was what she didn't tell. It was obvious at times that she was holding back. It was equally apparent that some questions brought her face-to-face with some personal demons from her past. At those times she jumped up to refill their still-full coffee mugs or check on the boys.

Claire didn't press her. She simply observed, and made a separate column of notations about which subjects made the other woman most tense and jittery.

Her marriage just died, she told Claire several times. There was no single big blowup, no abuse, no unfaithfulness on either side. Just two everyday people who fell out of love as simply and quickly as they had fallen into it. Claire didn't say so, but she didn't buy it.

When she had finished, Sherry accompanied her to the bedroom to retrieve her jacket.

"Your home is lovely," Claire told her. "You have a real knack for decorating."

"Thanks, I enjoy it," she replied, obviously pleased by the compliment. "And I think it's important to make things as nice and as... normal as possible for the boys."

Claire nodded in agreement. "I couldn't help noticing your photographs," she said, stopping next to the dressing table and picking up the one of Sherry holding a baby. "Is this Ben or Nicky you're holding?"

"Ben," Sherry replied, staring at the picture over Claire's shoulder.

"You look very happy here."

"I was happy. It was a beautiful day, I had a beautiful new baby."

Claire noted the wistfulness in her tone.

"And a new husband. Did Nick take this picture?"

Love in the First Degree

Sherry's expression changed and became anxious. She glanced quickly at Claire and took the picture from her hand. "No. It was taken by... a friend."

"Do you have any pictures of your ex-husband?"

Sherry shook her head.

"Maybe even a snapshot of him with the boys?"

She shook her head again, her jaw noticeably tight. "When I left, I wanted to make a fresh start, without any reminders of the past."

"I understand. Thanks for talking with me, Sherry. If I think of anything else, I'll be in touch."

Sherry looked less than enthusiastic about the prospect of seeing her again, and Claire left the apartment convinced that the woman's version of her marriage and divorce had been as artfully put together as her apartment decor. Luke wasn't the only one with gut instinct. Claire's gut was telling her that Sherry had not only come to hate the man she married, she'd been scared to death of him. And was now scared to say so.

Outside, she hurried toward her car, eager to get the air-conditioning working. She had unlocked the door and opened it before she realized there was someone in the passenger seat. Her heart jolted and raced and she took a reactive step backwards just as a hand shot out and caught hers.

"Going somewhere?"

"Luke," she said, recognition bringing a heavy sigh of relief. She collapsed onto the driver's seat and whacked him on the shoulder. "You jerk, you scared the daylights out of me."

"Then we're even. I lost a little daylight myself when I knocked on your door this morning and found you weren't there. No note, no explanation." He made a *tsking* sound. "What happened to your small-town manners?"

"I don't use them professionally. How did you know where to find me?"

"Same way you knew where to find Sherry, I expect."

Their eyes met and they spoke at the same time.

"Brad."

"You can see," Luke ventured, "how his helpfulness can be a double-edged sword."

"Apparently. What I'd really like to know, though, is how you got into my car when I'm sure I left it locked."

"You'd be amazed at the useful tricks I know."

"I'm sure."

"Why did you take off without me this morning, Claire?"

"I didn't want to wake you."

His dark brows lifted dubiously.

"All right, I confess, I wanted to talk to Sherry."

"Why?"

"I don't know. I just had this crazy idea it might be more useful to talk with her without her speech writer present."

He ignored her implication. "And did she? Talk to you, that is?"

He was slouching with his back against the door, his tone offhand, but Claire had a hunch he wasn't feeling nearly as relaxed as he wanted to appear.

"Yes, although she didn't want to at first. Did you perhaps have something to do with that?"

"*Moi?*"

"Why, Luke, you lied!" she exclaimed, feigning surprise. "You can speak French, after all."

"You got me."

"Not yet. But I will."

"So how did you change Sherry's mind about talking?"

"I told her that I was only interested in arranging a plea bargain and that I needed her help to get the charges against you reduced...making clear, of course, that the charges would remain lodged against you and you alone."

He didn't even blink. "Why would any of that matter to Sherry?"

"Oh, knock it off, Luke. For starters, I already know that Sherry was married to Addison and that according to the police she was the woman you and he were arguing over."

"Not bad," he allowed, his smile grim. "Do my compliments go to you or Rancourt?"

"Both. We're a team. Care to join?"

"Thanks, but I'm not much of a team player."

"Really? Somehow I'm getting the distinct impression you're playing on a different team entirely."

"What are you getting at?"

"The truth, I hope."

"And just what do you think the truth is?"

She noticed he wasn't slouching any longer. "I think the truth is that Sherry Wakefield killed her ex-husband," she informed him in a blunt stab in the dark, "and that for some crazy, noble, misguided reason, you're taking the fall for her."

Chapter 7

"I rescind my compliment."

Luke managed to sound suitably disdainful even as he struggled to get a grip on the havoc Claire's little announcement had caused inside him. Stay cool, he warned himself. Breathe slowly, relax muscles, maintain eye contact lest your opponent think you've got something worth hiding. Much better.

"I'm crushed," Claire retorted.

"You should be embarrassed, instead. The idea that it might have been Sherry who shot Addison isn't even worth discussing," he said dismissively.

She glared at him in indignation. "Why not?"

"Because the police already have their man. Me," he reminded her. "Why go chasing shadows?"

"Because Addison's dead and you didn't do it. Have you forgotten you admitted that to me only last night?"

"I haven't forgotten anything about last night. Last night I wasn't thinking straight."

"And now you are?"

"Now I am."

"The fact remains that you didn't kill Addison and someone else did. So why not Sherry?"

"Because I say so, that's why."

"Oh, please. That line hasn't worked on me since I was five years old."

"No? Then try this one," he snapped, his voice rising. "Back off on Sherry Wakefield, Claire."

"Or else?"

He nodded. "Or else."

He saw her recoil slightly and watched as she sat in silence, studying him with wounded eyes. Luke hated being the one who'd put that look on her face. He had to fight to keep from reaching over and pulling her into his arms and telling her he hadn't meant to yell at her, that he wasn't angry with her. Just at life in general.

This anger was new to him and he hadn't quite figured out how to handle it. That ticked him off even more. After all, he was a master at playing whatever hand he was dealt, accepting his losses and moving on.

Instead, he found himself suddenly boiling over with resentment and with nowhere to direct it. No one had forced him into this situation. Sherry herself was aghast at the sacrifice he insisted on making to keep her out of prison. You have more to lose than I do, he'd told her. And he'd meant it. He'd never expected to be sitting here, hurting inside over a loss he couldn't possibly have envisioned.

He supposed most people wouldn't even call it a loss, since you can't lose something you never had. Strictly speaking, Claire wasn't his to lose. But Luke had always preferred possibilities to reality and, like any man who'd ever risked fifty dollars to win five thousand, he knew you didn't have to hold something in your hand to feel as if it was already yours.

"Sorry," Claire said finally, drawing herself up in her seat, "but we made a deal, and as far as I'm concerned,

Sherry Wakefield and anyone else who might help me prove your innocence is fair game."

"Didn't I tell you? I'm changing the terms of our deal."

"You can't do that."

"The hell I can't. Dealer's prerogative, new deck, new deal. Here it is. If you want to stick around and do exactly what you told Sherry you were trying to do—come up with circumstantial evidence that will put enough dents in the D.A.'s case to convince him to offer me a deal—then I'll be grateful to you. But I don't want you running around trying to save my ass by pinning the murder on someone else."

"Such as Sherry?"

"Such as Sherry."

"And if I don't accept your new terms?" she inquired, her chin coming up defiantly.

"Then the deal is off entirely. I'll turn myself back in today and plead guilty to the first cop who'll listen."

She stared at him, trying to gauge the seriousness of his threat, and Luke watched as anger, frustration and finally acceptance flashed in her eyes.

"So what's it going to be?" he asked.

"You don't leave me much choice, do you? It's a real catch-22. If I try to prove you're innocent the best way I know how in this case, by finding whoever did kill Nick Addison, you'll go ahead and plead guilty, anyway."

"Does that mean you're staying or going home?"

"Staying," she snapped. She shook her head in disgust as she thrust the key into the ignition. "Although for the life of me, I don't know why I'm even bothering."

"Sure you do," Luke drawled, unleashing a mischievous grin as relief spread through him. Relief that Sherry was safe and Claire was staying. It was a feeling as close to contentment as he could expect to enjoy for a long time, and it made him reckless. "You're sticking around for the same reason you came to see me in the first place—because you're

Love in the First Degree

an honorable woman, a woman who always pays her debts in full, and because you think you owe me."

"I owe you?" she echoed, slanting him a wary glance, the barest hint of nervousness in her laugh.

"That's right."

"What on earth for?"

His grin broadened. "Services rendered."

"I have no idea what you're talking about," she declared, hiding behind the hair that fell like a silk curtain whenever she tilted her head.

"Then let's see if I can jog your memory."

Luke reached out and threaded his fingers into her hair, pushing it back from her face. Laying his palm against her cheek, he slowly drew her toward him as he leaned closer.

The urge to kiss her had been building in him ever since last night, when Sherry had interrupted them. It was so strong by now that just touching her made him tremble inside. It took all the willpower he possessed to keep from dragging her into the kind of hard, fast kiss he needed to take the edge off his craving.

Instead, he did something he'd been thinking about almost from the minute she'd showed up at the jail and turned his life upside down. He held her face in his hands and slowly traced her mouth with the tip of his tongue, lingering on the soft, damp spot just inside her lower lip. It was, he knew, a gesture much more intimate than a kiss.

Drawing back slightly, he met her gaze. "How come you taste so good?" he asked softly.

Her lips parted slightly, the look she gave him a blend of caution and surprise. "I—I've been drinking coffee."

"Trust me, Angel, it's not coffee I'm tasting."

"Oh, God," Claire whispered. "You *do* remember.... That night at the Phantom, everything."

"Everything," he confirmed, nodding. "The way you looked, and felt and what we said to each other. And the way you tasted. But it was not coffee I licked off you that night."

She withdrew from him, bewildered. "You told me you didn't remember anything about me, not the tutoring or the—"

"I lied," he interjected.

"But why?"

He shrugged. "Old habits die hard, I guess. It just came naturally for me to play things close to the vest until I figured out what cards you were holding."

"So you remembered me all along?"

He nodded. "I just might surprise you with all that I remember about you...Angel," he added, smiling at her. "For instance, I remember how I started calling you that after you slipped me the questions that were going to be on old Madame LeClerc's final exam in French."

A smile softened her lips. "Because you said I was your angel of mercy."

"And you said I didn't deserve any mercy. You were right, you know. I didn't deserve to have you stick your neck out for me. Not then and not now, Claire."

"Why not? You stuck out more than your neck for me when I was in trouble that night outside the Phantom."

"That was different."

"Why? Because you were the one doing the rescuing?"

"Maybe," he said, not sure how to explain to her that stopping those guys from hurting her hadn't been an act of bravery or heroism on his part. It was just an impulse, something he'd had to do, like breathing or sleeping. You didn't take credit for things like that. He couldn't have ignored what was happening to her any more than he used to be able to cower beside his brother and sisters while his old man was hitting his mother in the next room. Even if it meant taking a beating himself, he'd always had to try and stop him from hurting her.

"Maybe I don't deserve to be rescued because I walk into trouble with my eyes open. For instance, I knew all that last semester that I had to pass French in order to graduate. LeClerc warned me, you warned me, hell, I even warned myself from time to time. But there was always something else I'd rather do than study French."

"In the end you still had to study," she reminded him. "I simply used those questions to give you a nudge in the right direction."

"A nudge?" he groaned. "By the end of that last tutoring session with you I felt as if I'd been run over by a French-speaking bulldozer."

"You passed."

"Barely."

"You graduated."

"True. Thanks to you."

"Then why won't you trust me to help you now?" she implored.

"It's not a matter of trust," he countered, shifting restlessly in his seat. "Believe me, this situation is a lot more complicated than a high school French exam...or being pawed by some drunks in a parking lot."

"Evidently your memory isn't as good as you think it is," she snapped, rolling down her window with jerky motions, as if she desperately needed a shot of fresh air. She curled her fingertips over the edge of the steering wheel and stared grimly through the front windshield. "I wasn't simply being pawed by those men. They had ripped my clothes half off, touched me—"

She broke off, squeezing her eyes shut as she struggled to hold back the tears that quivered in her voice. Luke's heart wrenched inside him.

"Hey, Angel, come on. I didn't mean..."

She lifted a hand to stop him from trying to stop her. After a few seconds she continued, still not looking in his direction as she forced the words out.

"The things they said to me made it very clear that they intended to rape me. All three of them." Her shoulders shook. "I was never so scared in my life. I remember being scared to death that they might end up killing me. I've learned and seen enough since then to know that wasn't an idle fear by any means." She turned to look at him, tears still shimmering in her eyes, but her voice becoming strong and full of conviction.

"I might be alive today because of you. So don't try and tell me I don't owe you something or that I was wrong to come here and try to help."

"I never said you were wrong," Luke told her. "I admit that I may have resisted the whole idea at first, mostly because I couldn't believe you had come in the first place, at least not for the reasons you claimed. Even when I figured out what was really going on in that stubborn head of yours, I couldn't believe that after all this time you would go to so much trouble to return a twelve-year-old favor."

"It was a little more than a favor. Besides," she continued, shrugging, "it's not all that much trouble. As I told you, I'm more or less between cases at home—"

"It's not just the legal stuff," he said, cutting in. "I guess what really blew me away was that right from the start you actually believed I was innocent."

The tinkling melody of an ice-cream truck broke the late-morning quiet. It stopped a few car lengths in front of them and kids came running from yards up and down the street. Luke used the distraction to corral his thoughts. The way Claire made him feel, it would be easy to open up too much, to say things he couldn't risk saying. For a minute he watched to see if Sherry and the boys might appear, and he experienced a twinge of disappointment when they didn't.

What would it feel like, he wondered, if they did come out and get on line and he joined them there? He would buy Ben and Nicky the biggest cones the driver sold, watching their eyes go wide when he handed them over. He would find a shady spot for them to sit and eat, wiping the drips that dribbled onto their chin and never telling them to hurry up because he had better things to do.

Snap out of it, Cabrio. How it would feel to do that was something he was never going to know. Even with a plea bargain and time off for good behavior, by the time he was out of prison they wouldn't be little boys anymore.

He turned back to Claire. "You're the only one who does believe I'm innocent, you know. Rancourt told me outright he didn't want to know, and the others who came to see me in jail just sort of tiptoed around my reason for being there. Not that their reaction came as a big surprise."

"What do you mean?"

He gave a careless shrug. "Most of my life people expected the worst of me and I delivered on it. I was a fool to think things had changed that much. That I had changed enough so that maybe Max and Brad and the others—" He broke off, giving in to a rueful smile. "What the hell, I can't blame them for accepting the obvious. I was caught with the body and the murder weapon.... How did you put it? Motive, means and opportunity?"

"From what I've seen, both Max and Brad support you wholeheartedly."

"Oh, they've made it clear they're in my corner, all right. But there's a difference between supporting someone and believing in him. You're the only one who was able to look me in the eye and tell me she knew in her heart that I couldn't have done it. Why is that, Claire?"

"I guess you'll have to ask the others."

He shook his head, stretching his arm along the back of her seat, permitting himself the luxury of brushing her shoulder with his fingertips. "That won't help, because I'm really less interested in why they don't believe in me that way than I am in why you do."

"I don't have a nice, neat answer for that," she replied. "I only know that when I read the news of your arrest in the paper, and saw the photo of you that ran along with it, about a thousand memories came crashing in on me, memories of high school and some of the silly things we laughed at when I was supposed to be helping you study and... and the way you held me that night in the parking lot. Mostly that, I guess.

"I just kept staring at that picture of you," she went on, "and telling myself that people change, that I had no idea what kind of man you'd become, that I was hardly an expert on Luke Cabrio—or criminal law, for that matter. Nothing helped. You say you've spent a lifetime playing things close to the vest? Well, I've spent my time constructing logical, legal arguments to support whatever position I'm being paid to defend. I'm very good at being logical. But all the logical arguments in the world didn't change the fact that every time I looked at your picture, I knew I was looking into the eyes of a hero, not a murderer."

"Hell, Claire," he muttered, wincing, "I'm no hero."

"Yes, you are," she insisted softly. She reached out and touched his jaw. "That's why you have this scar. It's also why I wasn't gang-raped when I was only seventeen. And it's why you're going to prison, instead of Sherry."

He focused his gaze on the ice-cream truck as it drove out of sight. "I told you I don't want to talk about Sherry."

"You must care about her very much."

"We're friends."

"She said that you dated for a while, but it was over a long time ago."

"A very long time ago," he confirmed.

"It's obvious you still have strong feelings for her, though. Tell me, did she leave you for Addison?"

The question caught him unprepared, stirring a bitterness in him that Luke thought he'd left behind. "She left me, but not for Addison."

"Were you trying to win her back?"

"I told you, we're friends. Period."

"'Friends' covers a lot of territory. Think you could be a little more specific?"

He jerked his head around and met her gaze. "I'm not sleeping with her, if that's what you want to know. Is that specific enough for you, Counselor?"

That was only part of what she wanted to know. "Are you in love with her?" she asked.

"No."

"But there is something between you. Don't bother to deny it because—"

"Because it would only prolong this discussion I swore I wasn't going to have with you. So I won't deny it. Yes, there is something between Sherry and me, and what it is is none of your business."

"Look, if you don't want to tell me, just say so."

He smiled sardonically. "I just did, Angel."

"Fine," she snapped. "If you don't want to talk, I'll go question the witnesses who overheard you and Addison arguing over her. All in the interest of developing circumstantial evidence, of course," she added, tossing her hair back and twisting the keys to start the engine. "Luckily, two of them live here in the city. I can drop you off at the hotel on my way to see them."

"Thanks, but all things considered, I'd rather tag along."

"You can't be present when I question them," she warned. "It might be construed as intimidation."

"Then I'll wait in the car."

"It could take awhile. Hours even. That's a long time to be cooped up."

"No problem," he countered dryly. "I can use the practice."

She was right. It did turn out to be a long afternoon, and a frustrating one. Worse, the next few days were more of the same. Claire wasn't sure whether to blame it on the heat or bad karma, but everything she attempted seemed to take longer and cause more aggravation than it ought to.

One week down and one to go, she told herself on Monday afternoon. She was alone in her suite, reassessing Luke's situation and not particularly pleased with her progress on his behalf. After several wasted trips to his home, she'd finally managed to speak with one of the men who had witnessed the argument between Luke and Addison, and she was almost sorry she'd bothered. He remained adamant that he had heard Luke threaten loudly and clearly to kill Addison unless he stayed away from "some broad," as the witness put it. No matter how she approached it, she couldn't shake him from his recollection of the word *kill*.

The second witness seemed to be less damaging. According to the police report, he'd maintained it had been difficult to hear exactly what was said during the argument. Unfortunately, the address he'd given the police proved to be phony. Not a good sign. She had Brad at work trying to trace the man through the credit card he'd used, but so far he hadn't had any luck.

At least she had made some headway toward establishing a possible alibi for Luke by extending the range for the time of death. According to her calculations, there had been at least a twenty-minute delay between the time the couple in the next room heard what they thought was a gunshot and the time they finally reported it to the front desk. First they had debated between themselves about getting involved and then they'd had trouble with the phone in their room.

That was explained by the fact that there had been a problem with the hotel's computerized phone system that night, which, coupled with unusually high usage, had resulted in fewer than half the usual number of lines being available at any time. The reference to unusually high usage immediately made Claire wonder whether Luke might have spent any time on the telephone that night.

A telephone call made a questionable alibi, but it would at least help make the case against Luke less clear-cut, which is what she was supposed to be doing. If she could show evidence that Addison might have been killed even earlier than first thought and that Luke might have been on the phone at that time, it would add weight to the theory that he could have arrived on the scene after the shooting had already taken place.

The D.A. wouldn't buy it, of course, but it should serve to make him less confident of his chances of getting a conviction for murder one and hence more willing to deal. Gerald agreed that it was an angle worth pursuing and had arranged for a forensic scientist to analyze the bloodstains on the carpet in relation to the temperature in the room at the time...a handy little detail she'd gleaned from a blowup of one of the crime-scene photographs that showed the thermostat in the room.

She'd discovered that good investigative skills were as crucial to a criminal case as to a financial one. Her initial uncertainty had disappeared once she began actually exploring the facts and finding herself in the familiar pattern of one small revelation leading to another. Unbeknownst to Luke, who claimed he hadn't been on the phone at all that evening, she had also thought to ask Brad for a list of Luke's phone calls for the past month. Who knew what she might glean from them?

In spite of all that, however, she couldn't shake the feeling that she was simply spinning her wheels. Which, of course, she was. That's exactly what Luke intended for her to do. His threat to confess on the spot if she tried to prove that it was really Sherry who'd murdered her ex-husband prevented her from digging for evidence the way she longed to. It was like running a race that she'd already been told she couldn't win.

And it was frustrating as hell, she thought as she curled up on the sofa in the sitting room, going over the police and medical examiner's reports for what seemed like the hundredth time. She wasn't sure what she was looking for, only that she had to keep looking. It sometimes took a very small key to unlock a very big mystery. Her father had taught her that when she complained about the hours she spent poring over a client's tax returns or financial statements. She was certain that same principle applied to criminal cases, also. It was just a matter of looking for the needle in a different sort of haystack.

She paused to rub her temples. Eyestrain and frustration were combining to produce a whopper of a headache. She was accustomed to winning and she didn't like the prospect of losing one bit. Sure, even with the case they'd already built, they would probably secure a decent plea bargain, but that wasn't the same as winning, and Claire wanted to win this case more than she could remember ever wanting to win any other. The reason was obvious and becoming more so every day. She was falling in love with Luke.

Shoving aside the paperwork strewn across her lap, she jumped up from the sofa and went to the small refrigerator for a can of soda. Unfortunately, it didn't help wash away what she was feeling, or distract her from what she was so afraid to feel. To her dismay, she'd already discovered that there was no way she could run away or distract herself from thoughts of Luke.

Of course, the fact that she was with him practically every waking moment didn't help. But even when they were apart, like right now, he was always on her mind. She'd racked her brain to think of a way to convince Luke not to throw his life away for something he hadn't done, and after a string of preoccupied days and sleepless nights, she'd been forced to accept that it was hopeless.

Spending hour after hour alone with a man gave you a chance to get to know him pretty well. In fact, they'd joked that their situation strongly resembled being stranded together on a deserted island, even teasing each other with the

Love in the First Degree 133

nicknames Professor and Mary Ann from the old "Gilligan's Island" television series.

It was a closeness so sudden and intense that it had a way of lulling you into saying things you might not otherwise. During the past week they had both done a lot of talking, and listening, and everything new she had learned about Luke only reinforced what she'd known before she came here.

He was a strong and honorable man, perhaps the strongest and most honorable man she'd ever known, and he wasn't afraid to put himself at risk to help someone who needed his help. What he was doing for Sherry was an act of sheer kindness and self-sacrifice. A sacrifice she couldn't imagine anyone else making, and she loved him and hated him for it at the same time.

At a knock on the door, she glanced at the clock and frowned. She'd made plans to have dinner with Luke, the same as she did every night, but that wasn't for several hours. It was all part of his round-the-clock surveillance. She wasn't sure if he was as concerned with her safety as he professed or simply didn't trust her out of his sight. It didn't matter. She cooperated without protest because deep down she wanted to spend every minute with him that she possibly could. If this week was all they had, she intended to make the most of it.

"Who is it?" she called out, eschewing the peephole, which in her opinion made even a friendly face look distorted.

"It's Brad, Claire."

She hurriedly unlatched the dead bolt and opened the door with a smile.

"Hi, Brad."

"I come bearing gifts," he said, waving what looked like a computer printout. "I've had it since yesterday, but you asked me to keep this quiet and I haven't had a chance to see you alone."

"Thanks, Brad, I appreciate your cooperation on this."

"It wasn't easy... getting you alone, I mean. I was beginning to think you and Luke were attached at the hip or something."

Claire just smiled and shrugged.

"So are you? Or something, that is?" He flashed her a smile she would have found irresistible if not for the fact that she found Luke's a hundred times more irresistible and she was a one-smile woman. "I've never seen Luke so... captivated by a woman."

"Really?" she returned, pleased to think that if Luke had been captivated by Sherry any time recently, Brad would surely know it. So why on earth was he throwing his life away for her? "I guess that just shows how serious he is about his case."

"He's serious, all right, but I'm not sure it's only about his case. The man hardly lets you out of his sight."

"I know. Speaking of which..." she murmured with a wary glance at the door of Luke's room, wondering if she should ask Brad to step inside.

"Don't worry," he assured her. "He's down in his office clearing up a few things. That's why I'm here."

"Now I see why you left modeling for security," she teased. "You're a natural. So what do you have there?"

"Not everything you wanted, I'm afraid. I'm still doing battle with the credit-card company over that guy's address, but I'll get it out of them eventually. In the meantime, here's a copy of the record of all activity on Luke's telephone for the past month."

"Terrific!" she exclaimed, taking it from him.

"It's pretty self-explanatory as far as date and time," he explained, "and there are separate columns for incoming and outgoing calls."

Claire wrinkled her forehead as she quickly scanned the list. "Why aren't there any numbers in this column?"

"Because we don't have numbers for incoming calls," he said, glancing over her shoulder, "just the calls Luke made."

"I see," she said. "Well, that's better than nothing. Thanks, Brad."

"I'm glad I could help. I took a look at the calls for the day of the murder and circled in red the ones made from any of the security phones here in the hotel... which is most of them, since Luke was working that night. Those calls are all routinely recorded. I have the tapes downstairs, if you're interested."

"I'm not sure, yet. I'll let you know."

"Fine. I also checked out the number that Luke called that night."

"Wow, you're good. That was my next step. What did you find out?"

"It's the number of a private school just outside the city. I asked around and found out this place, Brighton Academy, is pretty exclusive... and expensive."

Claire's eyes narrowed thoughtfully. "What would Luke be doing calling a school? Did you happen to find out whom he spoke with there?"

Brad nodded, his carefully shuttered expression in itself revealing.

"Who was it?"

"The headmaster. The guy's a real egghead. He not only remembers speaking at length with Luke, he took notes of their conversation and recorded the exact time it began and ended."

"If the times are right, that could really help us," she exclaimed.

"It could, except..."

"Except?"

"Except for the reason Luke called. It seems he was looking into enrolling Sherry's son, Ben, in the school. With Addison being her ex and that argument in the lobby and all, well, it doesn't look good for him to be so involved, does it?"

"It doesn't look as good as I'd like it to," Claire replied, concealing the sinking sensation going on inside her, "but it doesn't look hopeless." She glanced at the printout once more. "I just wish there was some way of finding out who placed these two incoming calls."

"Sorry I can't be more help with that," Brad said. "I have no way of knowing where a call is coming from."

"Unless," Claire countered, excitement flashing in her eyes, "it's coming from another room here in the hotel."

"Of course. In that case I could—"

"Brad," she interrupted, unable to wait. "I want you to get me a list of calls placed from Nick Addison's room the night of the murder."

Brad stared at her, startled. "You think maybe he called Luke? That maybe he lured Luke down there in the first place?"

"I think someone might have placed a call to Luke from that room," she said, "and I think you're wonderful for helping me figure it out."

Claire was so thrilled, she threw her arms around Brad's neck in a quick, spontaneous hug, without giving a thought to the fact that they were still standing in the open doorway of her room, with her dressed only in the oversize T-shirt she'd been lounging in, and that someone walking by might easily misinterpret the gesture. Or that the someone in question might be Luke.

She first saw him over Brad's shoulder and immediately drew away. Luke folded his arms across his chest and leaned one shoulder against the door frame as if stopping for a friendly chat.

"You kids having fun?" he asked, his mouth twisted into a cynical grin.

"Luke," Brad said, freezing.

Love in the First Degree

Claire couldn't help noticing that he looked about as guilty as she suddenly felt, and for absolutely no reason. They were both simply reacting to the air of cool speculation that Luke wasn't bothering to hide.

"I was just..." Again Brad fell silent, glancing quickly at her for a cue. She understood. He'd been about to try to explain the hug by telling Luke what he was doing there and had ended up feeling twice as guilty.

"Thanks for dropping off this information, Brad," she said brightly, taking the precaution of rolling the papers in her hand into a cylinder. "I'll look it over later."

"Anytime." He smiled reflexively and glanced at his watch. "I just remembered something I have to check on. If you'll excuse me..."

"Of course. Don't let me keep you," Luke said, his tone quietly mocking.

Brad turned his head and shot her an apologetic look. "See you later, Claire."

With Brad gone, she turned and walked back inside. Luke followed.

"So, what was Brad doing here?" he asked, a bit too offhandedly for Claire's peace of mind.

"He was dropping off some information I asked him to get for me," she replied, slipping the printout into her briefcase and snapping it shut.

"Mind if I have a look at it?"

"Not at all," she said, turning to find him standing right at her shoulder. She smiled sweetly. "As soon as I've had a chance to."

His return smile was pure, unadulterated ice. The look in his eyes was a little tougher to decipher completely, but the black gleam of suspicion was unmistakable. Claire just wished she knew if he was more upset over finding her in Brad's arms or the fact that she was doing business behind his back.

"What sort of information is it?" he inquired, still wearing that damn smile.

"Do you remember me telling you I asked Brad to try to track down the second witness's real address? He was just getting back to me."

Claire told herself that it wasn't a lie. Exactly.

"You mean he came up with this guy's address?"

"Not yet."

"Then what were those papers he gave you?"

"A list of possibilities. He wants me to look them over."

Now *that* was a lie. A dumb one, too. What on earth could she hope to learn from looking at a list of possible addresses for a missing witness? Luke's expression told her he was asking himself the same thing.

It didn't matter. Even if he pressed her, she would have to bluff her way through this. She couldn't reveal to him her suspicion that Sherry might have called him from Addison's room that night or that she had asked Brad for the records to confirm it. If it proved true, she wasn't sure, yet, how she would use the information. She did know that she couldn't risk having Luke jump to the conclusion that she was still trying to pin the murder on Sherry and use it as a reason to call off their deal.

"I see." He crossed his arms. Claire had felt less jittery waiting for a judge to hand down his verdict. "So that was his only reason for being in your room?"

"He wasn't in my room," she corrected, instantly regretting that she'd felt it necessary to do so.

"No, I guess technically he wasn't. But then, he didn't need to be invited in."

"What's that supposed to mean?"

"Only that you two seemed to have gotten pretty chummy standing right there in the open doorway."

"I was simply thanking him for his help."

Luke grinned maliciously. "Imagine if he had actually found the guy."

"For heaven's sake, I gave Brad a friendly hug. Big deal."

"It's more than you've given me."

She shot him a look of exasperation. "Do you want a hug, Luke? Is that what this is all about?"

"No," he retorted, jamming his hands into the front pockets of his jeans. "I just want to be kept informed about what's going on with my case."

Back to the case. She still didn't have a handle on what he was really annoyed about. She wondered if he did.

"I am keeping you informed." Sort of, she amended silently. "I'm still waiting for the forensic report on the bloodstains on the carpet and I'm doing everything I can to locate this witness."

"With Brad's help."

"That's right, with Brad's help. Is that a problem?"

"Not for me. I do recall telling you, however, that Brad has a reputation for being lethal on women, and you saying that you could understand that. Something about how he gives new meaning to the term gorgeous."

"I believe my exact words were 'drop-dead gorgeous,'" she retorted, her temper flaring. "What's your point, Luke?"

"The point is that you should be careful. And maybe not waste so much time trying to find a witness who probably isn't going to provide much help anyway."

"I'll disregard most of that, since it's your pigheaded restrictions that have me wasting my time as it is." She tossed the hair from her eyes and braced both hands on her hips. "As for what this witness can provide, he just might be able to cast doubt on the D.A.'s prime motive by testifying that he never heard you tell Addison you would kill him if he didn't stay away from Sherry, thereby making you look a little less like a flaming jealous lover."

"I'm not her lover."

"Well, you're not mine, either. So don't you dare—"

"I could be."

Chapter 8

Claire fell still and studied Luke warily. She was having trouble relating what she thought she'd heard him say with the angry scowl on his face. "What did you say?"

"I said I could be your lover," he shot back in the same tone. "It's what I want, damn it. I have a feeling it's what you want, too."

Admittedly, she didn't have much experience with men bluntly announcing they wanted to become her lover, but in her opinion, even such a direct approach ought to be made in a less-caustic manner.

She regarded him with disdain. "When you put it so romantically, I don't know how I could possibly resist."

Luke caught her arm as she tried to move past him and whirled her around to face him. Ebony flecks glittered in the usually placid gray of his eyes. "Sorry, I'm not feeling very romantic at the moment."

His grip on her arm tightened. "You asked me if I wanted a hug from you—"

"And you said no," she broke in to remind him.

"That's right. I don't want a hug, or a kiss on the cheek when I walk you to your door at night, or to talk for hours about old times with you sitting so damn close to me I swear I can taste you every time I draw a breath. I've had all of that I can take."

"So what do you want?" she demanded, anger pushing her onto ice so thin she would ordinarily avoid it at all costs.

"This."

She might have protested if not for the fact that he had claimed her mouth and occupied it before she could react. Twice now, first outside the casino and again the morning they had sat talking in her car outside Sherry's, she'd been prepared for Luke to kiss her and it hadn't quite happened. Now she was caught totally off guard, and yet she had such a strong sense of familiarity that it seemed the most natural thing in the world to melt into his arms and kiss him back.

Her dream, she thought hazily, *this was like her dream.*

Except he wasn't gentle as he always was in her dream. His mouth took hers roughly, his hands raked over her back and clenched the soft curve of her bottom, and nothing could have made her happier. The urgency in his passion and the underlying knots of tension she sensed in him bore testimony to the intensity of his feelings. Good. She wanted him to feel some of what she'd been feeling for days now.

She felt the imprint of his body all along hers, sending enough sensations to her brain to threaten total meltdown. She felt the heat and power in his muscles as he urged her closer and closer; she felt his desperation and his hunger, and then she felt nothing but his mouth, his hands and her own explosive response.

He finally let her catch her breath, but his lips still hovered close above hers. When he spoke, the anger was gone from his voice, but not the heat. His husky whisper sent a thrill straight to the core of her.

"This is what I want," he said, and he tilted her hips to let her feel his arousal, using it to caress the ache building deep inside her. "I want you, Angel. All of you. I want to make love to you, over and over again."

Her dream never progressed this far, but if it ever had, she was certain that the Claire in the dream wouldn't have hesitated, but would have known exactly what to say. She knew now, too.

"Hurry," she said. It was the briefest summation she'd ever made, and the sweetest.

Surprise flickered in Luke's eyes, but he didn't waste time questioning her response. There was no need to. Claire was already reaching for him, signaling her own desire. She swayed against him, eager to feel once again the sensation of his body pressed to hers from shoulder to thigh.

She tugged at his shirt. She wanted his skin beneath her fingertips. Luke beat her to it. He pushed his hands beneath her loose T-shirt and worked it up above her waist. Claire's knees went weak as she felt his hands on her at last.

She wasn't wearing a bra. Luke cupped her breast with one hand and fumbled with her panties with the other. Claire reached to unfasten his belt, then opened the snap on his jeans and slipped her hand inside to caress him. He was hard and hot and silky.

Her touch made Luke tremble and he shoved his hand deeper inside her panties, his fingers thrusting between her thighs. The sound of the lace panties ripping seemed amplified in the silent room.

To Claire, it was proof of how badly he wanted her, exciting her even more.

Luke froze.

She immediately sensed the change in the tension she felt rippling through his muscles, resistance replacing fervor. He tried to pull away gently, but her arms were still locked around his waist.

"Luke?" she said softly. "What are you doing?"

"Good question," he muttered. "What the hell am I doing?"

He lifted his head, and something in his expression suggested to Claire a man who's just wandered in on a scene he doesn't quite understand. That made two of them. A strange coldness began to seep through her.

"I was under the impression you were making love to me," she said uneasily.

"Take a closer look," he advised, his tone harsh. "This isn't about love."

Claire flinched.

It probably took less than sixty seconds for him to remove his hand from her panties, tug down her shirt and fasten his jeans and belt, but they were, without question, the most humiliating seconds of her life.

"I'm sorry," he said without looking at her.

"You should be." Claire stared at him, hurt and confused. "Talk about giving an all-new meaning to things."

He looked away. "You don't have to tell me anything. I already know I'm a jerk, all right?"

She twisted away when he reached for her. "Don't you touch me."

His chin came up as if she'd slapped him. A heavy sigh lifted his chest and she saw the cords in his throat flex, once again, as if he was fighting for control.

"You're right," he said finally. "I shouldn't touch you."

Claire shrugged. His agreement was a hollow victory when she was standing there with her heart still pounding from his kisses. What the hell had gone wrong?

"After all," he continued, "touching you is what got us into this in the first place. Just like I knew it would. Why do you think I've been avoiding putting my hands on you for the past week?"

"I wasn't aware that you had been."

His expression turned sardonic. "Think about it, Claire. Think about that flimsy lace thing you were wearing when I stopped by the other morning—"

"My robe?" she interjected, frowning in disbelief.

He shook his head vehemently. "No. Robes are big and bulky and plaid. That was..." his eyes darkened with the memory "...something else. Think about a man spending day and night with a woman who can turn him on just by brushing back her hair. Think about him knowing every minute of that time that in just a few days he won't ever see her again. Yeah, I was afraid to touch you. Hell, sometimes I was even afraid to look at you for too long, because looking makes me want to touch you and touching you makes me crazy."

He stalked away from her, moving all the way to the other side of the room and hooking his fingers in the back pockets of his jeans before turning back to her. "What just happened here is proof of that. Damn it, Claire, you've got me thinking and acting like a fifteen-year-old, my hormones surging into overdrive just because I catch you hugging another guy. Ripping your clothes off...and forget about a bed. I didn't even need the back seat of a car. I was more than ready and willing to make love to you standing right where you are."

"This wasn't about love," she reminded him.

"Because it can't be. Don't you think I want it to be different?"

"As usual, I don't have the slightest idea what you want."

He tilted his head back to stare at the ceiling and Claire could actually see weariness claim his body.

"For the first time in a long, long time, you've got me wanting what I can't have," he said when he finally looked at her once more. "Claire, a week from now I'll be back behind bars, and even if things go better than we expect, I won't be getting out for a lot of years."

"It doesn't have to be that way," she told him, unconsciously knotting her slender hands.

"Yes, it does. For me, it does. Not for you, though. Look at you," he said, a tender smile lifting the corners of his mouth in spite of the grim resolve still in his eyes. "You're young and smart and beautiful. You deserve the very best from life."

"What if I say you're the best thing for me?"

"You'd be as wrong as you've ever been. I know I hurt you a minute ago, but believe me, if I hadn't stopped I would have hurt you more in the end. Us making lo—sorry, us screwing, would have been a big mistake."

His crudeness pierced like a knife, making her want to retreat and lick her wounds, but she had crossed a line when she surrendered to his arms and she wasn't going back without a fight.

"Shouldn't I be the one to decide that for myself?" she demanded.

"Sure, but not in the heat of passion. When you have a chance to think about it rationally, I know you'll see I'm right."

"I have been thinking about it," she replied. "For years now."

"What are you talking about?"

"I'm talking about you and me, and the fact that you were the real reason I was at the Phantom that night twelve years ago. I went there hoping I would run into you. I was leaving for college in a week and I'd told myself that if anything was ever going to happen with you, that was my last chance."

He slowly dropped his hands to his sides, his expression baffled. "What did you want to happen?"

"I'm not sure I really knew, exactly," she confessed. "But I'd had a wicked crush on you for a long, long time and I was desperate. Just once I wanted you to look at me the way you looked at me a few minutes ago, to finally notice that I was alive."

When she finished, Claire felt exposed and vulnerable. She'd never revealed that to another soul and never dreamed she would end up telling Luke himself. She prayed he wouldn't laugh or make fun of her. There was no way she could handle that added rejection right now. But no matter how he reacted, she wasn't sorry it was finally out in the open after all this time.

He wasn't laughing. He looked astonished. And miserable. "Oh, I noticed you, Angel, believe me. I just never realized..." He shook his head regretfully. "Did you know that the only reason I even stuck it out in French class was so that I'd have a reason to be tutored by you?"

"No," Claire countered, frowning as her mind struggled to make sense of that. "No, that can't be true. You never paid any attention to me. Even when you were forced to talk to me, it was always very offhand, like I was a pesky kid sister or something."

The bold look that flared in his eyes stunned her. "Trust me, I never thought of you as my sister. Not even close. I don't know if you'd define what I felt as a crush, but I was definitely aware of you... in every way."

"Then why didn't you ever do anything about it?"

"Like what? Ask you out?"

"Yes," she declared, struggling with a whirlwind of new emotions. "That would have been a start."

"I guess because asking you out would have raised that age-old question—do I pull my motorcycle right up to your door and watch your old man's jaw drop when he sees who's there to pick up his little girl, or simply ask you to sneak out and meet me at a dive like the Phantom?"

"I would have." She shook her head. "What am I saying? I did."

"And look what almost happened to you."

"But it didn't happen, because of you. You saved me."

"Twice in the same night," he countered, his smile heavy, deepening the lines at the sides of his mouth. "Bet you never knew that."

"I don't understand."

"It's simple. You were in more danger that night than you realized. Do you remember what happened after I got rid of those guys?"

"Remember?" She tugged at the hem of her shirt as she moved closer to him. "I don't think I thought about anything else for months afterwards." She didn't add that she'd also thought about it often in the years since. "You held me until I stopped crying and asked me if I wanted you to call the police...."

"And you said absolutely not because then your folks would find out where you'd been. You see, even you knew there was something wrong with that place and with the people who hung out there."

"It was pretty rough, I grant you, but you were never like those other guys."

"I never had a taste for rape or hassling women, it's true. But don't kid yourself, Angel, I was at home at the Phantom... much more at home than I would have been sitting in your living room."

"How do you know? You never even—"

He raised a hand to cut off her protest and at the same time stopped her from moving any closer. "We were in different leagues, Claire. Just think about it. Your old man was a lawyer and now you're one, too. I spent my formative years staying a half step ahead of the law and then graduated to gambling full-time. As you pointed out, it's not the most illustrious career choice.

"I may not have been able to conjugate verbs," he went on, "but I knew the score where you and I were concerned. I knew if we hooked up it would only be trouble—for both of us. That didn't stop me from wanting you, though, when I was supposed to be comforting you. The buttons were all off your shirt and it kept sliding open so that your breasts were right up against me, and I never wanted anyone the way I wanted you right then."

Claire felt dazed, as if she'd stepped into one of her own dreams.

"You kissed me. Well, almost anyway," she amended, recalling the way he had used his tongue to make her feel things no one else ever had. "And then all of a sudden you stopped and I thought it had to be because of the way I'd kissed you back, because I wasn't good enough or experienced enough for you to want to bother anymore."

"Not quite," Luke replied, a ragged edge to his laugh. "It's true that I could tell from the way you reacted to my kiss that you weren't very experienced, but it didn't make me want you any less. It just reminded me of why I couldn't do what I wanted to do with you. And believe me, back then I wasn't very good at self-denial."

"Obviously, you've gotten better," she observed, tears stinging like acid as she tried to hold them back. With every word he said, the knot of dread in her stomach got bigger. She felt as if she'd been handed the most beautifully wrapped present she'd ever seen and then had it ripped away before she could even open the ribbon.

"Not a whole lot better," he responded, "so don't push me, okay? And don't cry, please, Claire."

She wiped at her eyes with the back of her hand. "I'm not crying. I just think you're wrong.... I think when two people feel what we've felt, what we still feel, they shouldn't shut the door on it."

"We're not shutting the door, the state penitentiary is."

Claire tried to turn away from that cold slap of reality.

"Face it, Claire," he said, stopping her. "I have even less to offer you now than I did back then."

"It didn't feel like nothing to me," she retorted, staring at the hand he dragged through his hair, remembering how it had felt moving roughly over her body.

"Well, that's about all it amounts to. A few days of sex and a whole bunch of regrets."

"I'm not still seventeen years old," she insisted. "Even if that is how it turns out, I can handle it."

"Maybe so. But I can't."

Ordinarily, Claire felt a twinge of regret whenever Luke left. Not this time. It was a physical relief when he returned to his own room. She barely heard his promise to call later about dinner. Alone, she threw herself on the sofa and faced the torrent of emotions that were rioting inside her.

They were in layers, like the fancy parfaits served at the hotel's dessert bar, but not all her layers were sweet. Some were so bitter the bad taste lingered, running through her like poison. She hadn't thought her feelings for Luke could get any more complicated and confusing than they already were, but that's exactly what had happened.

Even now, excitement and dismay chased each other around inside her, like puppies vying to be on top. The realization that Luke had actually been attracted to her twelve years ago and still wanted her now brought the sweet, sharp thrill of a dream coming true, followed immediately by the crushing blow that he had no intention of doing anything about it.

She wanted to argue with him about the senselessness of what he was doing by allowing himself to be sent to prison for a crime he didn't commit. She wanted to plead with him to give them the chance they should have had years ago and beg him to just this once find a way to temper his heroic side with a little selfishness.

In her heart, however, she'd already accepted that Luke wasn't the kind of man to be argued or pleaded with or manipulated out of doing what he had made up his mind was the right thing to do. Sure she could go ahead and try to make a case against Sherry and her instincts told her she would be proved right. But where would that get any of them? She knew in her heart that even if she could somehow trick or seduce Luke into telling the truth about Addison's murder, there was no way the two of them could ever find happiness by shifting their misery onto Sherry and her two young children.

The boys had already lost a father. While no expert on child psychology, even she understood that it would be devastating for them if the mother whom they clearly adored was sent away to prison for murdering him. The more she thought about it, the more she was convinced that it was concern for them that was motivating Luke. It made perfect sense, especially knowing what she did about him and about his own less than idyllic childhood.

Knowing also that he wasn't in love with their mother helped her accept it. At first, it had seemed to her that he must still be in love with Sherry, no matter what he claimed to the contrary. No longer. She believed Luke when he told her that whatever he and Sherry had once felt for each other was over, because he had proven that he wasn't able to look her in the eye and lie. And because when he'd held her in his arms, his body had told her without a doubt, that he was not a man in love with another woman.

She understood his desire to protect those two little boys. She even admired him for it. But it still wasn't fair, she thought, getting up and checking the temperature on the air conditioner. It was so cold in her room, she couldn't believe it was set where it always was. It wasn't the room that had suddenly gone cold, she thought, it was her.

Too late, too late, too late... The words ran singsong through her head. She couldn't shut them out. The truth was like that, persistent even when it was unwanted. It certainly seemed to be true that it was too late for her and Luke.

Every thought she had seemed to start with "if only." If only she had been a little more aggressive at seventeen, or else Luke a little less honorable now. If only she had picked up the phone one of those many times she had thought of him and called and said... what? If only she had come to Atlantic City on vacation and run into him unexpectedly.

Love in the First Degree

They could have gotten together and talked. Everything would be exactly like it had been this week, but without the horrible specter of a murder charge hanging over their heads.

She was a firm believer that even a small-chance occurrence could dramatically alter the whole course of a life. If even one of those things had happened, Luke might not be in the position he was in now—facing a prison sentence he didn't deserve.

A sentence of how long? She tortured herself with the possibilities. Ten years? Fifteen? Twenty? If things didn't go as well as they expected, if they, in fact, went all wrong, he could be locked up for the rest of his life.

Fear and anger closed in on her. What then? What if, in spite of Luke's wishes and her own common sense, she couldn't just walk away from him at the end of this week? What did he expect her to do? Smile and say, "It's been fun. Call sometime when you're not facing ten to twenty"?

The sensation of a hand closing on her throat sent her looking for her soda can. She found it on the coffee table, lifted it to her lips and put it back without taking a sip. She knew if she tried to swallow she would choke.

What was she going to do? How was she supposed to just return home and pick up the pieces of her life as if being here and seeing Luke again hadn't shaken them up so thoroughly that she wasn't sure how to put them back together? Or if she even wanted to?

Would she ever be able to meet a man again without measuring him against Luke and losing interest? Would she wait for him?

For how long? The rest of her life, if it came to that? Claire wrapped her arms around herself tightly, tears turning the room into a kaleidoscope of shapes and colors. She saw bits and pieces of her dreams of marriage and a family swirling and breaking apart. No, she couldn't give up the rest of her life because he chose to.

Then how long? What difference did it make, she thought, trying to stop herself from this exercise in heartache. She couldn't. She couldn't stop. How long? Ten years? Yes. Hadn't she already waited twelve? So she could handle twelve years. Fifteen? Eighteen? Twenty?

With one sweep of her hand she sent the soda can flying off the table and across the room. She couldn't take this. She rushed into the bedroom, yanked her suitcase from the closet and opened it on the bed. She had to get out of here. Without thinking of what she was doing she began grabbing things from drawers and the dressing table and tossing them into the suitcase.

Bras, panties, slips.

Gerald would be able to continue with the case alone from this point. If he had a question on something she had handled, he could call her at the office.

Toothbrush, blow dryer, makeup.

No one would blame her. Hell, Luke hadn't wanted her here in the first place. Half the time she felt as if she were facing two adversaries, the prosecutor and the client. It might be a relief to get back to reading financial statements.

She glanced at the half-empty suitcase. What was she forgetting?

Just her clothes, she realized disgustedly, turning toward the closet.

She pulled suits off hangers, folding them haphazardly, with none of her usual care. Each suit stirred memories. The gray one she had worn to see Luke in prison for the first time. The blue one with the very short skirt that she had intentionally chosen for the day he was released. The yellow one... she hugged the jacket to her chest, remembering the day they'd sat talking in her car. She closed her eyes and could see Luke grinning at her a split second before he leaned over and...

Love in the First Degree 153

She forced her eyes open. Where had this masochistic streak come from all of a sudden? As she gave the yellow jacket a shake to line up the sleeves for folding, something flew from the pocket.

She dropped the jacket in the suitcase and reached for what had fallen. A puzzle piece. She turned it over in her hand. Green on one side, blue on the other. It had to have come from the puzzle in Luke's office, but how had it ended up here? She remembered picking up a piece the day she'd met with Brad there. She must have walked out with it and stuck it in her pocket without thinking.

She'd have to return it before leaving. The puzzle appeared challenging enough without pieces missing. Whoever heard of a two-sided puzzle? she thought, a small, grudging smile breaking out as she turned the piece over once again. Trust Luke to find a way to make the difficult close to impossible. He was doing the very same thing with the case against him.

It would all be so simple if she didn't have to deal with his noble instincts. If Luke were like any normal client, willing to do or say anything to be let off, she could simply pursue the case against Sherry and voilà...he would be a free man.

Voilà. She turned the piece over again, watching the contrast of the color against her palm. Blue. Green. Blue. Same shape; different color. Same piece, but a very different effect when the color changed.

Claire curled her fingers tightly over the small puzzle piece, feeling the uneven edge bite into her palm.

She kept rereading those reports, looking for some small key to opening up Luke's case, but just maybe she didn't need a new key. Perhaps she simply needed to take another look at the ones she already had. Perhaps all she had to do was turn over the pieces she'd found and look at the other side.

If she tried to prove that it was Sherry who'd killed Nick Addison, she would only force Luke into a full confession.

He was adamant about going to prison so Sherry wouldn't have to. So what if, instead of proving Sherry did it, she proved that she'd had no choice?

Her body trembled with excitement.

She had no idea why or how Sherry Wakefield had come to shoot her ex-husband. Luke hadn't let her get close enough to the facts to find out. But even knowing as little as she did, Claire's instincts told her that it wasn't murder one and it might well have been self-defense.

She began pulling things out of the suitcase even more frantically than she had tossed them in. She needed to get dressed. And she needed to find the notes from her interview with Sherry.

She could never convince Luke not to do everything in his power to protect Sherry and the boys, but she just might be able to fix things so Sherry didn't need his protection. If she was right about this, and she could prove it, then neither Luke nor Sherry would be going to prison.

Chapter 9

Claire's first impulse was to find out if Sherry was scheduled to dance at the Riverboat that night, charge downstairs and confront her with the truth. A tactic that just might work. She would certainly have the surprise factor going for her. On the other hand, it might also prove to be a lethal mistake.

The last thing she wanted to do was come across as trying to bully the other woman, putting her further on the defensive. It had been obvious when they spoke that the entire subject of her ex-husband and his violent death made her very uneasy. With good reason, Claire thought dryly. Luke might be able to spare her the prison sentence murder carried with it, but not the guilt.

In addition to her understandable nervousness and reluctance to talk about the death, Sherry had obviously been coached on the subject by an expert, Luke. She would have to be approached very carefully, and Claire knew from experience that the more information she gathered beforehand to bolster the arguments on her side, the better chance she had of convincing Sherry that she had her best interests, as well as Luke's, in mind.

Claire cautioned herself that she also had to bear in mind that no matter how much she wanted to help Luke, until she turned up some concrete evidence, her suspicions about Sherry were still only that... suspicions.

The arguments for delaying her talk with Sherry were all very prudent and reasonable. Unfortunately, she wasn't feeling particularly prudent or reasonable... or patient. Especially not patient. She was racing inside, eager to get started doing whatever it took to prove her theory right.

The real reason she resisted the urge to confront Sherry immediately was Luke. He had an uncanny, and infuriating, sixth sense for knowing whenever she slipped out of her room without telling him. She had yet to venture out to the gift shop or to stop by the front desk for something without him showing up a few minutes later. She'd even begun to wonder if he had the entire Delta Queen staff spying on her. It might be funny if it wasn't such a real possibility, making the idea of visiting Sherry at work much too risky for now.

Besides, to find out what she needed to know about Sherry and Nick, she would have to start back at the beginning, with their marriage and divorce. It wasn't enough to prove that Sherry had killed him, she needed to prove why.

Her years as an attorney had taught her a new respect for the old adage about appearances being deceiving, but after meeting Sherry and seeing the home she'd made for her little boys, Claire couldn't conceive of her being a cold-blooded killer. Knowing that the woman had Luke so firmly on her side, only further convinced her that there had to have been extenuating circumstances surrounding the shooting. If she was right and Sherry was the one who had picked up that gun and pointed it at the father of her children, then something had driven her to it. All Claire had to do was figure out what it was and gather the evidence to convince Luke, Sherry, Gerald Rancourt and a jury—in that order—that she was right.

There were at least a half-dozen major points she needed to explain before anyone would be willing to even listen. For starters, how Sherry had gotten possession of Luke's gun and why she had gone to Addison's room in the first place.

Claire realized she had a lot of ground to cover in less than a week, especially since she couldn't let Luke know what she was doing. But for the first time since arriving in Atlantic City, she was free of the subtle, underlying sense of indirection and frustration that had been haunting her. Even on this new playing field, she had her old confidence back.

Somehow she was going to pull this off so that everyone emerged a winner. She was going to see to it that Sherry was cleared of criminal charges and, hopefully, some of her own guilt, as well. Ben and Nicky were going to keep their mother with them. And Claire herself was going to see to it that she and Luke finally got the chance they had let pass them by twelve years ago.

Leaving the open suitcase and half of her belongings strewn across the bed, she was ready to go only a half hour after finding the puzzle piece in her pocket. She'd dressed in a no-nonsense gray-and-white-striped suit and hurriedly applied a little makeup. She wasn't sure, yet, precisely where she was going or whom she would be seeing—she wouldn't know until she'd spoken with Brad—but she did understand the advantage of power dressing when you were seeking information, especially from those who might not be all that eager to talk.

She kept her phone call to Luke as brief as possible, explaining that she had a headache and was going to call room service for dinner and then go to bed early. He didn't try to change her mind or prolong the conversation. His unusually downcast tone lent credence to his comment that he could use a good night's sleep, as well.

If only she could count on that. Since she couldn't, she weighed her options and decided to let it drop that she just happened to have obtained a list of the phone calls he'd made the night of the murder and that, since he couldn't recall speaking with anyone, she was planning to check them out herself first thing in the morning.

They hung up, and a few minutes later she heard the door to his room open and softly close. Standing with her ear to the wall nearby, she grinned triumphantly. She wasn't sure if the headmaster of that school was about to get a visit or merely a precautionary phone call from a telephone Luke felt was safe to use. She only knew that she was about to make a clean getaway and that for the next few hours, she was blissfully on her own.

Brad was in his office and more than willing to provide her with Sherry's former address, the one still listed on Luke's computer file. At least, it had been there a few days ago. She had her fingers crossed that he hadn't updated it since then. He hadn't. What's more, Brad was even able to cross-reference the date when the file was last updated with the date on which Sherry began working at the Delta Queen and assured Claire that Sherry had been living at that address at the time she was hired.

She recalled Sherry saying that she had returned to Atlantic City right after separating from her husband because she needed a job, and Luke had offered to help her find one. That meant that her neighbors at this address might be able to tell Claire something about the divorce, perhaps about Sherry's state of mind at the time or whether she'd received any unwanted visits from her soon-to-be ex.

She was prepared to dig deeper, if necessary, to interview people who knew Sherry and Nick at the time they were still married, as well as current co-workers and neighbors of Sherry's who might have information relevant to the days leading up to the murder. But this was a start. She finally felt

Love in the First Degree

as if she was doing something that mattered, and contrary to what she'd told Luke, she wasn't a bit tired.

She caught a taxi outside the hotel, leaving her car in the hotel garage in case Luke checked and also as a safety measure. She'd discovered for herself that he hadn't been exaggerating when he told her the city had its rough side, and she wasn't sure what sort of neighborhood she would be driving into. A taxi satisfied her need to play it safe.

Brad had frowned when he first saw the address and said he wished there was some way he could get off work and accompany her. Claire thanked him for his concern and his warning to be careful, and refrained from telling him that she actually preferred to go alone. Sometimes an extra pair of ears was all it took to discourage a person from talking.

She handed the slip of paper with the address on it to the taxi driver. He glanced at it, scratched his head and shrugged as he switched on the meter. Leaving the circular drive, they headed west, away from the boardwalk and the hotels that were strung like a glittering ribbon against the setting sun.

Just a few blocks from Atlantic Avenue, the streets narrowed, and tenement houses were lined up like books on a shelf. Instead of color-coordinated gardens, the only signs of vegetation were the scruffy clumps of crabgrass growing through the cracks in the sidewalks. The absence of air-conditioning was apparent from the windows, with ripped screens or none at all, left open to catch whatever meager breeze there was.

This was the side of the city few hotel guests ever saw. Another two-sided puzzle, Claire thought—reality as the flip side of fantasy. Here, gangs of kids roamed the streets and hung out on the corners. Police cars, cruising by slowly, were a common sight. Gazing out the dingy rear window of the taxi at a glass-littered playground, she was thankful she hadn't attempted to find this place on her own. But not nearly as thankful, she suspected, as Sherry must have been the day she moved away from here. The whole area had a grimmer and less friendly feel than her new neighborhood.

They drove for about ten minutes before the driver pulled to a stop. It was plenty of time for Claire to speculate about what kind of a reception she might receive from Sherry's former neighbors.

"Here you go, miss," the driver said, half turning in his seat.

She checked the meter and leaned forward to hand him the fare plus a tip. "Thanks."

"You want I should wait?"

"That isn't necessary," she replied, straining to see which of the three-story houses nearby matched the address. "I might be awhile."

"I don't think so," he countered, what looked like a smile forming beneath his scraggly gray beard. "Not unless you're planning to do your praying sitting on the steps there. Church closes at five, lady. You want to light yourself a candle, you'll just have to come back again tomorrow."

"Church?" she said, ignoring his remarks as she glanced around. Sure enough, across the street, set back from the sidewalk, was an old, redbrick church. The steeple was so tall she couldn't see the top of it from inside the car. Above the arched front doors was carved the name St. Michael's.

"Are you sure this is the right address?" she asked.

"Sixteen hundred Fairfax. That's the address you gave me and this here is it. St. Michael's. Don't worry, you ain't the first gambler who felt a sudden urge to pray," he added with a sly chuckle.

Claire rolled her eyes and got out without attempting to correct him.

"So you want me to wait or what?"

She glanced up and down the street, spying a market on the next corner. There would have to be a telephone there she could use to call for a ride back to the hotel when she was through.

Love in the First Degree

"No, thanks, I'm all set," she told the driver, stepping back quickly as he took off with a squeal of rubber on asphalt.

Alone, she glanced around, hoping to see someone she could ask to verify the address. It was just her luck to end up on what seemed to be the only street for blocks without people gathered on their front steps. Where were all those patrol cars now?

"Can I help you, miss?"

She turned in the direction of the voice and noticed a man sitting in a rocking chair in a corner of a porch. He looked to be in his seventies. Belatedly she caught the fragrant drift of his pipe smoke.

"I hope so," she said. She quickly told him that she was looking for an address a friend had given her and that it had turned out to be a church.

"This is Fairfax Street, right?" she asked him.

"Sure is. You say you're looking for sixteen hundred?"

"That's right. At least I thought it was right. Maybe my friend copied the address down wrong. I know it can't be a church I'm looking for."

The old man slowly got to his feet and crossed the porch to lean on the front railing, squinting at her over the pipe clamped between his teeth as she stood in the light from a nearby streetlight.

"You one of those women?"

Claire stared back at him, perplexed. "Which women are you referring to?"

"Never mind. Whoever you are, you look safe enough to me. Sixteen hundred is the convent. Go down that there alley and around the back," he directed, pointing across the street. "You can't miss it."

"Thank you," she said, hurrying in the direction he indicated.

A convent? She supposed it was possible. Perhaps the nuns had taken Sherry in as an act of charity. Or maybe they rented out spare rooms to women in need. She just wondered if the good sisters would be more or less likely to answer the questions she needed to ask.

Behind the church she found a rambling old house that in the darkness looked to be vaguely Victorian and in need of repair. There was only one light on in the back of the first floor, while the windows of the second and third stories were ablaze. Except for the small fleet of tricycles gathered by the steps, the place could easily pass for a convent.

Nuns on trikes? Claire mused as she concentrated on navigating the overgrown, unlit pathway to the steps. Nah.

Only then did she see the young woman sitting on the top step. Rather, she saw the red nub of the lit cigarette in her hand. It wasn't until the woman stood up and flicked the cigarette into some bushes that Claire realized she was holding a baby and had a toddler beside her. Their silhouettes were huddled together in the darkness.

"Come on," the young woman said, reaching for the child's hand.

Claire was puzzled by the urgency in her tone. She'd seemed content enough to enjoy her smoke a minute ago.

"But, Mommy, I'm still—"

"I said move, Samantha," the woman snapped.

"Excuse me," Claire said, "can you..."

That was as much as she was able to get out before the three of them disappeared inside the house and the heavy door slammed behind them. Claire heard the bolt being jammed into place. How very hospitable.

She marched up the fronts steps. The place was so damn dark she couldn't even find the doorbell and had to settle for banging on the front door. She kept banging until someone finally opened it.

"Yes?" said a different woman than the one whom she'd scared off the steps.

She only opened the door a few inches, and her two-handed grip on the old wood remained unabashedly firm, as if she was expecting someone to storm the gate. Claire would like to see the person foolish enough to try. There was nothing vulnerable or timid about this woman, or nunlike, either, for that matter. She was tall and slim, with intense dark eyes that were themselves a warning not to try and slip anything past her. Her salt-and-pepper hair was cut stylishly short and set off by large, gold hoop earrings.

Even through the narrow opening she permitted, Claire was able to glimpse in the background the young woman who'd fled from her a minute ago. She was still holding the baby in her arms, and the little girl's face was buried against her legs. It was dark inside the convent, as well, but no place would have been dark enough to hide the expression of sheer terror on the woman's face, and in a flash Claire understood everything. The old man asking if she was one of "those women," the presence of tricycles outside a convent, the house's unwelcoming air. Visitors weren't welcome here. Especially visitors of the surprise variety.

"Yes, I'm sure you can help me," she said to the woman at the door. "I hope you will. My name is Claire Mackenzie. I'm an attorney and I'd like to talk with you about a woman who stayed here for a while about two years ago. Her name is Sherry Wakefield and—"

"I'm sorry, I don't know anyone by that name."

"Please," Claire countered, placing a cautionary hand on the door before it could be shut in her face. "I know full well what I'm up against here. I just figured out that this place is a shelter for battered women and that you can't afford to trust strangers who show up at the door unannounced. But if you'll just hear me out, I'm sure you'll see that I'm not—"

"I'm sorry," the woman said again. This time her grip prevailed and Claire found herself staring at a solid expanse of wooden door.

"Drat," she muttered, giving it a small kick. She'd wager it wasn't the first or by any means the fiercest kick the old door had endured. Which is why she couldn't fault anyone for not welcoming her, or any stranger, through it with open arms.

She still had to find a way to get inside and talk with someone who might have been here two years ago. The fact that Sherry had spent time at a battered women's shelter proved she was on the right track. Her frustration at being turned away was more than tempered by a fresh surge of hope.

She knew enough about the running of shelters and the people who dedicated themselves to them to know that neither the police nor the courts could force them to tell her anything they didn't want to tell. She had to do this on their terms, by their rules, and that meant winning their trust through the intervention of someone they already trusted.

Luke came to mind. He must have had some contact with the shelter if he was the one who urged Sherry to return to Atlantic City. Claire would prefer not to involve him in any of this, however, until she was prepared to present her case in full, with all the puzzle pieces in place. If Sherry had taken refuge in a shelter for battered women, it meant her marriage and divorce had not been as harmonious as she claimed and it might well lead to a motive for her to shoot Addison.

Claire tried to slow the racing of her heart by reminding herself that she still only had suspicion on her side. Right now she had to find someone else to act as a go-between for her. It wasn't until she'd trudged to the corner market and dropped her quarter into the telephone slot that it occurred to her that the person she needed might already be on her team. If not, he might be able to put her in touch with someone who could help.

She reached Gerald by beeper and waited impatiently until he returned her call, purchasing a can of soda, a candy bar and small bag of chocolate chip cookies to appease the scowling clerk. Some dinner, she thought wryly.

"What's up?" Gerald asked by way of greeting.

"I need your help," she replied. "I think I've put this whole thing together, who killed Addison and why Luke is so determined to take the fall for it."

"You still think this guy is innocent, huh?"

"More than ever. Just listen, Gerald."

She quickly ran through her version of things, bringing him right up to the slammed door of the convent.

"You're right about it being a shelter," he confirmed. "The convent had been empty for a few years when the priests at St. Michael's decided to convert it into a place for battered women."

"Can you help me get inside?" she asked.

"Maybe." That was enough to make Claire's spirits soar. "The woman you described is Mona Kurtz. She's the director. She's been there forever, it seems, and she's a real tough mother hen."

"Do you know her? Are you friends?" she asked excitedly.

"We worked together fairly closely on an assault case a few years back. But friends? I doubt Mona has any. She's too single-minded. I'll give her a call and see what I can do about getting her to see you, but I have to warn you, Claire, Mona's first loyalty is to those women."

They made arrangements for her to wait there until he tried contacting Mona and got back to her. Claire hung up, very aware that he had used the same words the old man had, *those women*. It sounded so isolating, as if a woman became part of some subspecies of humanity simply by virtue of the fact that the man in her life proved to be abusive.

Her own life had been blessedly free of violence. She'd never even been spanked as a child. The closest she'd ever come to experiencing violence firsthand was that night in the parking lot of the Phantom, and then no one had actually struck her. Even so, the feeling of utter helplessness, of being at the mercy of someone bigger and stronger who could hurt you or rape you or kill you if he chose to, was something she could still taste. It was her connection to the women at St. Michael's.

And to Sherry Wakefield, she realized. Perhaps to women everywhere who'd been reduced to hiding behind locked doors... in their homes or their hearts.

As different as her experience was, in some small way, she thought, being the victim of a man's aggression made her one of "those women," too. Until that moment, her desire to prove Sherry had been justified in killing Addison had been fueled almost entirely by her concern for Luke. Suddenly that changed. She still wanted desperately to keep Luke from going to prison, but she also wanted to help Sherry for her own sake.

It was another candy bar, a pack of gum and a *People Magazine* before Gerald called back. By the time the phone rang she'd read about all the latest Hollywood parties, learned what celebrities were in rehab clinics and which child star was suing his parents for mismanagement.

"What did she say?" she asked Gerald anxiously.

"She said she'll see you. It wasn't easy," he added, "especially when she got the impression you were looking to get a man off the hook...."

"Gerald!" she wailed.

"Calm down. I explained everything and it turns out she remembers Luke from the time he brought Sherry there and came around to check on her. Mona's a little one dimensional, but deep down she's good people. She doesn't want to see *anyone*—not even a man—" he added with wry emphasis, "have to pay for something he didn't do."

Claire thanked Gerald and hurried back to St. Michael's Convent. She took the fact that a light had been turned on over the front door to be a good sign. This time Mona appeared almost as soon as she knocked. She still didn't smile, however.

Love in the First Degree

"Come in, Ms. Mackenzie," she said in invitation. A light had been turned on inside, as well, dispelling the aura of gloom that had been Claire's first impression. The walls in the front hall were painted pale pink and a worn oriental runner in shades of faded cherry and blue covered an equally worn hardwood floor. "I'm Mona Kurtz."

Claire extended her hand. "Thank you for seeing me, Ms. Kurtz." The director's formality demanded the same, although the name Mona fit her so well, it was hard for Claire to think of her as anything else.

"If you'll follow me, we can talk privately in my office," she said, leading Claire to a small room at the back of the house.

Claire did not see anyone else along the way, although the sounds of footsteps, children laughing and a baby crying filtered down from the floor above.

Her first thought upon entering the small office was that it reflected Mona well, Spartan and no-nonsense with its metal desk and file cabinet and highly polished black-and-white tile floor. Then, as she slipped into the seat across from the desk, she happened to turn her head and noticed the wall behind her, the wall Mona must see every time she looked up. It was covered with children's drawings—crayon-colored pictures of houses and families and rainbows. Lots of rainbows, Claire noted. It was a mosaic of hopes and dreams, and it told her all she needed to know about the woman regarding her so sternly from across the desk.

"Mr. Rancourt explained your reason for wanting to see me," she said. "Ordinarily I would reject out of hand your request for information about one of the women we've helped in the past. But as I see it, this situation with Sherry has very troubling implications."

"I agree," Claire replied. "And I do appreciate you agreeing to meet with me to discuss it."

"I should warn you that I tried contacting Sherry after your first visit here this evening and wasn't able to get through to her at work. My policy is to inform all women of any inquiries about them and ask them how they would like the matter to be handled. The only reason I'm making an exception in this case and agreeing to speak with you before I hear from Sherry is because Mr. Rancourt impressed upon me how very much time is of the essence here."

Good old Gerald, Claire thought. "That's true," she agreed, not mentioning that it was Luke and not the courts who made it so.

"I remember Mr. Cabrio very well," Mona continued, "so I was greatly disturbed when I read the news of his arrest in the paper. He appeared to be something I see all too rarely in my work—a decent man."

"When you read of his arrest, were you aware that Nick Addison, the man he's accused of killing, was Sherry Wakefield's ex-husband?"

A look of distaste puckered her lips. "Oh, yes, very aware. Mr. Addison was not the sort you forget."

"Why is that?"

"The man was a snake, pure and simple," she retorted.

"Can you tell me why you had that impression?"

Mona's lips thinned. "I'll do better. I'll tell you about the one-and-only time I had the displeasure of meeting the man, and you draw your own conclusions about him."

Claire nodded.

"Somehow he had gotten the phone number here, and he'd been calling and making threats for days," Mona began. "I remember how terrified Sherry was, convinced that it was only a matter of time until he found her and the boys. She was right. I was out at a meeting when he showed up and somehow smooth-talked his way past the young woman who answered the door." Her eyes narrowed. "Did you know Mr. Addison?"

"No, I didn't."

She flipped open a manila folder on the desk in front of her and riffled through the contents until she found the

Love in the First Degree

photograph she was looking for and pushed it across the desk toward Claire.

"That was Nick Addison at his finest," she drawled, "all white teeth and phony smiles."

"This must have been taken early in their marriage," Claire remarked, closely studying the picture of what appeared to be a very happy couple. "Sherry looks so young here."

"She is young," Mona retorted. "But her last few years have been hard ones."

Claire recalled a similar comment that Luke had made about the differences between himself and Brad. She continued to stare at the picture. The single newspaper photograph of Addison that she'd seen prior to this hadn't done him justice, she realized. He had been an extremely handsome man, blond and broad-shouldered, with a dazzling smile that did indeed dominate his face. Maybe it was simply because she wanted to believe the worst about him, but even in a photograph she could detect something calculating about that smile, a smugness that made it easy to accept Mona's characterization of him as a snake.

"He was a salesman, you know," Mona told her, "so smooth-talking was his forte."

"Did Sherry speak with him the day he came here?"

"Yes, she agreed to see him. As I said, I was out when he arrived, but by all accounts he was extremely charming, right up until the moment when Sherry made it clear she and her sons would not be leaving with him." Mona's jaw tightened. "I arrived in time to see him dragging her down the front steps by her hair, poor little Ben screaming and doing his best to hold onto her."

Claire shuddered as she pictured the scene. "How awful."

"I managed to take hold of Ben. When Addison saw me, he let go of Sherry in order to try to grab him from me. In the process, Sherry tripped and hit her head on the concrete step at the bottom, hurting herself so badly it took over twenty stitches to close the gash in her scalp."

"So she was seen by a doctor?" Claire inquired, instinctively thinking of documenting the incident for the court.

"Oh yes," Mona replied with a small smile. She tapped the folder. "It's all here—photos, statements, a copy of the arrest report."

"Addison was arrested?"

"Yes, indeed. I think the sight of all that blood made him too scared to run away." There was a glassy brightness to her eyes as her smile tightened. "He had tears in his eyes when the police arrived and he told them that he hadn't meant any harm to anyone, that he simply loved his Sherry too much to let her go." Her small laugh was brittle. "I can tell you that it was enough to make this old maid glad to be one."

"You said that you only met Nick Addison once. Does that mean he never attempted to see Sherry after that day?"

"Not here, he didn't. I think he knew better," she said with grim satisfaction. "As part of the deal to drop the assault charges he agreed to go ahead with the divorce, and Sherry was able to leave here and find a little place for her and the boys. That wasn't the end of it, though. I spoke with her as recently as a few months ago and could tell he was still in the picture... and not in a good way, if you know what I mean."

"I'm not sure I do. Do you mean he was still being abusive to her?"

"I'm sure of it... although Sherry never really opened up to me or anyone here about what she had gone through... what she was *still* going through, evidently. After she and the boys left, I kept in touch as best I could. I kept trying to convince her that she should see someone professionally. We have a list of top-notch therapists who devote their time to the women who need them. I told her she should get everything out in the open and come to terms with it before she could truly make a fresh start."

"But you're not sure whether she ever followed up on your advice by seeing one of these therapists?"

Mona shook her head. "Not as far as I know. And she'll need to see someone now more than ever, no matter how things got to this point."

"Ms. Kurtz, you said you remember Luke Cabrio?"

"Very well." She again shuffled through the papers in the file, this time producing a photocopy of Luke's driver's license. "We used this for identification purposes whenever he came to visit Sherry... which was frequently. He always brought a little surprise for the boys, a small toy or a book."

Claire glanced at the photocopy with Luke's full name typed beneath the small photograph. Lucas Benjamin Cabrio. Funny, she'd never known his full name. It was only one of hundreds of little things she didn't know about him. Was it possible to fall in love with a man and then wait twelve years to get to know all the reasons you loved him? Yes, she thought rebelliously. It was possible. She'd done it.

"...simply a decent man," Mona was saying, drawing her back to the subject at hand. "And a good friend to Sherry."

"Did you know the exact nature of their relationship?" Claire asked, leaning slightly forward in her seat.

"Friends," Mona said, shrugging. "As far as I knew they were friends. But as I said, Sherry wasn't one to advertise her business."

"Do you think Luke was close enough to Sherry, that he cared enough for her, to kill her ex-husband if he believed she was in some kind of danger?"

"I really couldn't comment on that. I knew him so superficially, you understand."

"Of course. How about Sherry herself, do you think she was capable of killing him?"

"I think that under the right circumstances, any one of us is capable of killing. From what I saw, Addison's treatment of her more than provided the right circumstances. If Sherry did kill him, it was because he drove her to it. That I believe with all my heart and that I will gladly swear to in any court you name."

"You may get the chance," Claire told her. "I don't have all the facts, yet, by any means, but I believe it's possible that Sherry killed Nick in self-defense after years of abuse, and that Luke was caught at the scene when he went there to protect her, and that he's protecting her now, too, by taking the fall for it so that she won't have to."

"If Sherry is sent to prison, her children will be without a father or mother."

"I've thought of that," she said sadly.

"But if she doesn't stand trial, an innocent man will surely go in her place."

Claire could only manage a nod.

"And so the suffering caused by one man's obsession goes on and on," Mona murmured, her expression weary as she closed her eyes briefly and shook her head.

"I hope not," Claire said. "I hope that I can work this out so that no one has to suffer any more than they already have."

"I'll help in any way I can," Mona said. "Provided..."

"Provided?"

"That Sherry approves. I make no secret of it, Ms. Mackenzie, and no apologies. Sherry is my first concern and will remain so."

"That's fair enough. She deserves to have someone like you on her side."

Surprise flickered in the other woman's eyes, followed by a subtle softening of her expression. "I'm thankful you're able to understand. So many people don't. I will promise you this, however—that I'll do everything in my power to convince Sherry to own up to anything she may have done."

"I'm glad to hear that."

"Violence is never to be condoned, but if she shot that man, I assure you it was an act of courage, not malice, and she will need to have that courage validated, by her friends and family and by the powers that be, if it comes to it. If she doesn't, if she allows the shame and guilt and secrecy that have surrounded her for so long to continue festering inside her own heart, then I'm afraid the anguish that lies ahead for her will be far worse than anything she endured at the hands of her ex-husband."

Claire agreed wholeheartedly. She only hoped that when the time came, she could express it half as eloquently and convincingly to Luke.

"I'm sure you're right," she said.

"It won't be easy for her, I know that. But every time a woman stands up and fights back, it makes it that much easier for the next woman, and the next. It's the only way we'll ever turn this nightmare around."

"At least Sherry's not alone," Claire responded. "I have a feeling that with your help, Ms. Kurtz, we can see to it that this is one fight she wins."

The other woman smiled. "Please," she said, "call me Mona."

Chapter 10

Claire continued to talk with Mona Kurtz for over an hour before she finally asked to use the phone to call for a taxi. Throughout their conversation it was clear that Mona was eager to help with the case, not only because of her concern for Sherry, and for Luke, as well, but because of a deeper conviction that through understanding what had happened to Sherry, people would have a better understanding of the plight of other women who were still trapped in similar situations.

She was a dedicated and impassioned spokesperson for her cause, and Claire couldn't help but be impressed by her loyalty to the women she served. At no time during their meeting did Mona betray Sherry's confidence or reveal anything that she had not heard or witnessed firsthand. Although she didn't offer to let Claire examine the contents of Sherry's file without her permission, she did confide that it contained photos of Sherry taken when she'd arrived at the shelter, showing her bruised and swollen and with a broken arm that had not been set. There was, she assured Claire, her lips thinning with anger, ample evidence of the years of abuse.

She also made it clear that the release of the folder and any further cooperation on her part depended on what Sherry herself ultimately decided to do. Claire suspected that no matter how much evidence she produced, Luke would feel much the same way. Since she couldn't pull this off without their help, she really had no choice but to respect their wishes. The evening had convinced her that her suspicions about Sherry were right and filled her with optimism, but as much as she longed to share that with Luke, she understood that the next person she spoke with had to be Sherry. Like it or not, this was her call to make.

It was after eleven when she returned to the hotel, unconsciously stepping lightly as she passed Luke's door. She let herself into her own suite with a sigh of relief and headed straight for the bedroom. Suddenly she was feeling every bit as exhausted as she had claimed to be when she called Luke earlier.

She flipped the first of the three wall switches located just inside the bedroom and light from above softly illuminated the wide hallway area outside the triple width closet, leaving the rest of the room in shadows. Sliding open the mirrored closet doors, she hurriedly hung up her jacket and slipped off her blouse and skirt. Her slip and panty hose she relegated to the laundry bag and dressed only in her bra and panties she reached for her nightgown on the hook where she'd left it.

"Don't bother," came the gravelly order from somewhere behind her.

Claire froze. A giant lump erupted in her throat, making it impossible to breathe as her heart began to pump furiously. Clasping the nightgown to her chest, she whirled instinctively toward the voice, recognition coming almost before she identified the dark shadow sprawled in the chair in the corner.

"Luke," she breathed, relief and anger surging through her in equal amounts. "What the hell are you doing here?"

"Waiting for you," he replied, making no attempt to rouse himself. He was slouched deep in the easy chair, his long legs fully extended so that his feet rested on the desk chair he'd obviously moved closer for that purpose. He wasn't wearing shoes or socks.

"In the dark?" she demanded.

"It suits my mood tonight."

"I see. Well, make yourself right at home, why don't you?" she invited, heavy on the sarcasm as she waved her hand in the direction of his bare feet.

"Thanks, I did."

She noticed a tendril of smoke curling upward from a cigarette in the hand he held draped over the arm of the chair and chided herself for being so preoccupied she hadn't sniffed it sooner.

"I didn't know you smoked," she remarked. She was trying to remain composed, or at least appear to be so. It wasn't easy when she was standing there in only her underwear, with what now felt like a thousand-watt spotlight aimed at her from above. And skimpy underwear at that, she thought, suddenly regretting her secret passion for hiding the sexiest lingerie she could find beneath the conservative suits her job required her to wear. Judging by the fact that Luke's gaze was burning as hotly as the cigarette in his hand, her secret was out.

"There's a lot of things you don't know about me," he drawled.

"I won't argue with that."

"You don't argue at all, do you, Claire?" he countered, getting to his feet and grinding the cigarette out in the ashtray beside him. "You just smile and speak softly and then go ahead and do exactly as you damn well please, right?"

She stared at him in silence, weighing her options.

Love in the First Degree

"Right?" he repeated, his tone turning harsh and impatient.

Her gaze strayed to the bedside table, to the empty glass and half-full bottle of Scotch that didn't belong to her. "Have you been drinking?"

"Not so you'll notice, I promise you," he retorted.

She had to admit that he didn't sound drunk, and the path he followed as he crossed the room was as straight as any highway line she'd ever seen. In fact, there was something menacing in his stride. She was debating taking a step backward, into the closet, when he stopped just inches away from her.

"Right?" he asked again, more softly.

"I'm not sure what you're talking about."

"I'm talking about the fast one you pulled on me tonight. You knew that dropping that bait about the phone calls would have me chasing my tail, trying to head you off before you had a chance to follow up on it yourself tomorrow."

She gave a one-shouldered shrug. "Practicing a little advance damage control, Luke?"

"You bet your sweet—" He broke off. "But I was too late. It seems Brad had already checked out the number for you."

"Really? I don't recall."

"Cut the crap. The kid's gotten pretty damned fond of you, Angel. Not to mention loyal. I couldn't pry a word out of him about where you'd taken off to tonight. But I know him well enough to read his mind on some things and I know that he'd already told you all about my conversation with the headmaster at Brighton Academy. So the question is, why was it so important for you to give me the slip tonight that you were willing to let me in on the alibi angle you've been playing so close to the vest?"

Her eyes betrayed her surprise.

"I figured it out yesterday," he informed her. "Your mind isn't quite as easy to read as Brad's, but where you're concerned, I pay a whole lot more attention."

"If you knew I was trying to put together an alibi for you, why didn't you cooperate? Why didn't you tell me yourself that you had been on the phone with this man around the time of the murder?"

"Because coming up with an alibi is your fantasy, not mine."

"Then why—"

"It doesn't matter." He cut in without waiting to hear what she had to say. "Where were you tonight, Claire?"

"I can't tell you. Not yet, Luke. I'm working on something, but I'm just not ready to talk about it, yet."

"All right."

"All right?" she echoed, startled by his utterly unexpected acquiescence.

"Where you were doesn't really matter, either. All that matters is that you're here now, safe...and real," he added, his voice soft and deep as he reached out and lightly brushed his hands along her arms, as if to prove to himself that he was right—she was real. He was in a strange mood, Claire thought.

"Do you have any idea how worried I was about you?" he asked her.

"I'm sorry you worried. There was really no need to."

His laugh had a cynical edge. "Yes, there was. There was definitely a need to worry. I needed to worry. Did you really expect me to order room service and go to sleep when you were out there somewhere, alone, hurt maybe, or in trouble—"

"I wasn't—"

"You could have been. That was enough. It's all I could think about. I couldn't eat or sleep..."

"Just drink?" she interjected, glancing at the bottle of Scotch.

Love in the First Degree

"Believe me, Angel, I couldn't even do that the way I wanted to. I checked with Sherry at the Riverboat, thinking you might have gone back to talk with her."

Claire silently thanked God she hadn't. What a wasted night that would have been.

"She said she'd hadn't seen you all night, and after that, I didn't know where the hell to look. You might as well have been in a different universe, and I kept telling myself, 'Get used to it, pal, because this is just a preview of what it's going to be like when you're locked up in some hole and she's out here.' A whole lot of nights of wondering where you are and who you're with, if you're happy or upset, if you've forgotten all about me."

"I won't forget you," she said quietly. "Not ever."

His dark eyes flashed a warning. "You should."

"Luke, this is crazy. We still have time. Maybe it will work out and none of this will even happen. Maybe..."

"Yeah, maybe. But maybe it will happen just this way. I only know one thing for sure." There was a quiet, but desperate firmness in the sound of his voice. His gaze heated as it touched on her bare shoulders and the hollow between her breasts, which was only emphasized by the way she was hugging her nightgown in front of her. Undercurrents of sensuality stirred between them, and inside Claire there was the first small flutter of understanding of what was to come.

"I know I was wrong this afternoon," Luke continued bluntly. "Wrong to walk out on you because of some crazy idea that us making love would only make it harder to be without you later. I know now that nothing could be harder than not being able to see you ... touch you...."

"I was furious with you for leaving me like that."

"It wasn't all selfish. I was trying to protect you, too."

"Oh, Luke, the whole world doesn't always need your protection. I don't always need it. Sometimes I need..." her voice dropped self-consciously " ... other things."

Comprehension gleamed in his eyes. "I know. I did a lot of thinking about those other things tonight. Hell, I did a lot of thinking about you, period. I sat here and I kept picturing the way you push your hair back when you're annoyed and how you curl your bottom lip out when you're upset and—"

"I do not curl my lip. Ever."

His smile was lazy and intimate. In spite of her protest, Claire couldn't help being thrilled by the thought that he was learning little things about her, too. There were so many little things to learn, for both of them. Did he know her middle name? she wondered. Her favorite color? That she sprinkled salt on her watermelon and collected old 45 records? It wasn't fair, damn it. They needed more time.

"Yeah, you do," he told her. He touched her lip with the pad of his thumb, sending shivers through her. "But don't worry, I like the way you curl it."

"What a relief."

He grinned. "Would you like to know what else I thought about sitting here in the dark?"

"Yes."

"I thought about driving you home from the Phantom that night and how good it felt to have you on the back of my bike, your arms wrapped around me tight, and how I wanted to ride by your house and keep right on riding. I wonder what would have happened if I had."

"My father probably would have had you charged with kidnapping and statutory rape."

He shrugged. "Couldn't be any worse than how I ended up."

The bleak wistfulness in his tone made Claire wish she could give him a reason to hope. But his notion of a reason to hope and hers were still different, and she was afraid to show her hand prematurely.

"And I thought about the way you feel and the way you smell—sweet, like walking through a garden in the sum-

Love in the First Degree

mer," he went on, drawing her from her thoughts with his words and the movement of his hands on her shoulders. "And I thought about kissing you. I thought a lot about that, and about how soft you felt against my fingers... the softest thing I've ever felt, and then that was it. I was out of memories. So I just sat there and kept replaying what I had, and after about a hundred times I knew one thing for sure... if I have to live my life without you, I want more to remember."

His grip on her shoulders tightened and Claire trembled all the way to her toes.

"I want all of you, Angel," he continued softly. "I don't want to let them lock me up with a bellyful of regrets, and then have to spend the rest of my life the way I've spent the last twelve years—wishing I had done things differently with you when I had the chance."

The yearning in his voice amazed her as much as his words. "I had no idea. I never expected you would even remember me, never mind have regrets."

"Now you know. I wanted to make love to you then, and I want to make love to you now, Claire. Tonight. All night."

"Oh, Luke..."

"Tell me you want it, too."

It wasn't something she had to think about. This was preordained, the decision made years ago. She believed that with all her heart.

"I do want it," she whispered, lifting her hands to his face. "I want you. I always have. You have to know that, Luke."

He kissed her palms, tasting her with his tongue and closing his eyes briefly as if she was a pleasure to be savored. "Tell me one thing first."

"Anything."

"This work you're doing..."

Claire froze. No. Don't let him be pretending, lying, using her feelings for him to get her to reveal what she'd been doing tonight.

"This business of you being my lawyer," he opened. "Does that matter to you?"

"Matter?" When his thumbs stroked her jaw the way they were doing now, nothing else mattered.

"Mmm. Is it going to bother your conscience later if we make love?"

Claire laughed with relief. "Not at all. Technically, I'm not your lawyer."

"Technically. Is that good enough?"

It was. For tonight, it was. As seriously as she took her career, Claire doubted anything could have stopped her from making love with Luke now that she knew he wanted her as badly as she wanted him.

She nodded. "It's enough."

"Good. Then come here." He wound her nightgown around his hand to draw her closer, then pulled it from her grasp and tossed it aside. "You won't be needing that tonight."

Before Claire could react, he spun her around and backed her up against the wall opposite the closet. When he leaned into her she could sense the night's accumulation of fear and frustration simmering just beneath the surface of his desire, and how hard he was fighting for control.

The mirrored closet doors reflected the image of her slender frame pressed tightly to his broader, rangier body. She was stunned by the sight of them together, Luke looming over her, wearing a black T-shirt and faded jeans, while she was barely covered by the brightly flowered demi-bra and panties. The contrast was wildly erotic. She probably ought to be shocked, she thought, or at least uncomfortable. But she wasn't. Far from it. She was excited, aroused, every muscle in her body primed with anticipation.

Even more exciting was the sensation of his clothed body rubbing against her bare flesh, and for endless moments as he moved slowly against her, that was all she could feel...the heat coming off him and the tremors under her skin as every part of her was awakened by his touch. She wasn't tired any longer, either.

She tipped her head back against the wall and stared into the mirror from beneath half-lowered lids. Beneath Luke's T-shirt, she could see the rippling movement of the muscles across his strong back. His biceps flexed and released and flexed again as his hands roamed over her, his touch light and fleeting as he discovered just some of the places where she longed to be touched by him. She saw the gentle rocking motion of his hips and felt the melting it started between her thighs, and she could only guess what it was costing him to be so gentle.

It was the first time she had ever watched a man making love to her, and she couldn't look away. Watching made her feel sexy, decadently so, and gloriously alive. Her gaze followed the movement of his hands as they sought hers. He interlaced their fingers and then pinned her hands to the wall on either side of her head. The weight of his body held her still as he released the front catch of her bra and let it fall to the floor.

His eyes went smoky and her throat went dry as he leaned back and stared at her breasts. When her hands began to fall to her sides, he caught them, pressing them back against the wall. Claire felt no urge to resist. Slowly, his head dipped and then his mouth was on her, hot, wet, drawing her out of herself and into a world that began and ended with Luke, with the fierce strength hovering just beneath his tenderness, the blended scent of fine soap and good Scotch that clung to him tonight, the ragged cadence of his breathing.

Her hands cradled his head where it was bent to her breast, his hair slipping like silk between her fingers, the dampness at the back of his neck signaling the frantic rise of his own desire. She moaned softly as his teeth closed on her and she let her eyes drift shut. Darkness intensified the sensations that were streaming in a fiery path to her core and then radiating out again, making all of her vibrate with growing pleasure.

Luke straightened suddenly. Claire's eyes flew open and their gazes locked and stayed that way as he hooked the back of her neck and drew her to him, kissing her at last, a wild, hungry kiss, opening her mouth wide, his tongue stroking deeply, making her senses dance out of control.

She felt as if she'd been riding a roller coaster as it slowly, slowly climbed to the top of the track. With each careful caress, each hot tug at her breast, Luke had wound a little tighter the heated coil of desire crouched inside her. Now the ruthless passion of his kiss pushed her all the way to the summit.

She hovered there, a little breathless, a little frightened by the unfamiliar intensity of her own response. It had never been this way for her. With other men, as with everything in her life, she had always been restrained and in control of her own desire. The problem was that, with Luke, restraint had never been a viable option. Now she was quickly moving past desire to need, clinging to him as he pushed her closer and closer to the storm that waited.

He kissed her cheeks and jaw and the soft place behind her ear.

"Ah, hell," he murmured, his lips brushing against hers between words. "I planned to go so slowly with you. I promised myself I would hold back...make the first time the best, make it last, but damn it, I can't."

His mouth devoured hers. Claire could taste the searing need in him and feel his frustration at the way it was driving him, and she understood. Understanding brought her a measure of control over the desire that had been so close to flaring out of bounds.

Love in the First Degree 185

Luke had said he wanted a memory. Well, she was going to give him one. And more. She would give him a reason to fight. When this night was over, Luke would know exactly what he was sacrificing when he chose prison over justice.

"Slow down," she whispered as his hands raced over her, bruising in their hurry to possess.

"I can't," he told her again, his tone a raw reflection of the urgency that was riding him hard. "God help me, I can't."

"I can," she countered softly, taking hold of his wrists and pulling him across the room. "Come with me."

She stopped beside the bed, quickly sweeping it clear of the suitcase and clothes she'd left there earlier, and then turning to face him. When he reached for her, she gently brushed his hands aside.

Wordlessly she slipped her hands inside his shirt and began working it up. His chest was hard, muscle over bone, muscle that tensed beneath her palms. The hair that grew there was black and curly, the feel of it so deliciously masculine that she spent much longer than necessary removing his shirt.

"Please lift your arms," she said at last.

He did as she asked, his eyes watchful, curious, a little amused.

That would change, Claire thought confidently as she tossed his shirt aside and reached for his belt. She opened it, then undid the button at the waist of his jeans and lowered the zipper. When the jeans were off, she looked at him with blatant appreciation. He was lean and hard and fully aroused. She couldn't resist the urge to caress him, drizzling her fingers the length of his shaft, letting the heaviness below rest in her cupped palm.

"Touching you makes it hard for me to breathe," she whispered, swaying against him.

Luke rested his hands on her shoulders. "It doesn't exactly put me at ease myself. Claire, if this is your idea of slowing me down, I don't think—"

"Good," she interrupted, lifting her fingertips to his lips and pressing lightly to silence him. "Don't think.... At least don't think of anything but me and how good I'm going to make you feel tonight."

Sweet heaven, Luke thought as she pushed him down onto the king-size bed. This wasn't quite what he had expected from nice, proper Claire Mackenzie.

For days now he'd suspected that the strong sexual currents he felt pulling at him whenever he was around her worked both ways. This afternoon had confirmed that suspicion with a vengeance. He'd known then that if he let nature take its course, they would sooner or later end up in the same bed. He'd also known it would be good. He just hadn't expected that he would be the one who landed flat on his back there, with her taking the lead and obviously enjoying it to the hilt. Not that he was complaining.

There was nothing to complain about in the way she straddled his hips, the satin skin of her inner thighs making his flesh sizzle where they were pressed together. She leaned forward slightly, just enough to make her breasts sway and his senses spin. He remembered her breasts very well. They were only a little bigger now than when she was seventeen and still as firm, perfect for a woman of her willow slimness. They were crested with pale pink and at that moment they were too damn tantalizing for him to resist.

He lifted his hands to cup their delicate weight, half expecting her to brush him away again or pull back, playing a teasing game intended to either prolong his desire or prove how little the male of the species had actually progressed along the evolutionary chain. He hated playing games in bed, but for Claire's sake he was prepared to try to tolerate this one for as long as he could. Which, considering the pulsing in his loins at the slightest shifting of her weight, wouldn't be too long.

But she didn't push him away. She wasn't playing a game, he realized with surprise, as a smile of genuine pleasure trembled across her lips in response to his touch. She was making honest love to him. It probably said something about the company he kept, but he couldn't recall the last time a woman had been interested in doing that. Or when he'd ever wanted one to.

He wanted it now. He wanted her even more fiercely than he had only seconds ago, something he wouldn't have believed possible. There was a new edge to his wanting, he discovered. It still clawed at him, to be sure, but there was a sweetness there, too, and a kind of power he'd never before felt. The power to receive, instead of simply to take.

His thumbs strummed her nipples as he watched their color deepen and the peaks grow taut. Her heart was pounding furiously enough to keep pace with his own.

"That feels so good," she whispered, taking a soft breath. "Let me show you how good."

Luke went still as she placed her palms on his chest and sought the flat nipples buried in his chest hair. He caught his breath when she found them, flicking lightly, then quickly bending to replace her fingertips with her tongue. With every little move, she made the flames in his belly flare hotter. She shifted her legs so that one rested between his, pressing against him, riding high, higher. His head arched back against the pillow. Sweet heaven.

Claire felt the trembling response that raced through him, then gradually she felt his muscles relax. She sensed him easing into the pleasure she bestowed, giving himself up to it... and to her. Something told her that was a new experience for Luke and that made her even more determined to make it one he wouldn't easily forget.

As tautly muscled as he was, he became like melting wax beneath her mouth and hands—soft, pliant. For long moments, Claire caressed his stomach and played her fingers along his ribs, dazzled by the sensation that they were flowing together, that the pleasure she gave and the pleasure she derived from the giving were both part of the same endless loop. She tasted, she explored, she aroused. Her senses were tantalized by the faint musk of his arousal as she moved lower, and lower still.

Oh yeah, oh yeah, Luke thought. Please. His hand in her hair went taut as he felt the damp heat of her breath on the inside of his thighs. He struggled to keep from moving a muscle, not wanting to pressure her into anything she wasn't ready for by indicating what he wanted. And how badly he wanted it.

There were degrees to intimacy. He knew that and he'd thought he'd experienced them all. He was wrong. He hadn't even come close, he realized as Claire hesitated, glancing up at him, their eyes meeting as her mouth found him. She was a silken vise closing around him, drawing him in. Hot, wet, the pressure exquisite. Fire and ice at once. Pleasure so close to pain. Lightning striking raw nerve, chain lightning that lingered and burned and ran together.

His head was jammed into the pillow. It was a struggle just to fill his lungs with air. The pressure built, getting under and behind him, pushing him deeper, faster, harder. He felt her tongue, her teeth...so much sweetness and heat. He wanted to tell her...say her name...something. But all he could do was shudder and reach for her just in time.

Claire had never been so turned on. She'd never dreamed she could become so aroused herself simply by focusing all her attention on the man she was with. Luke had yet to touch her intimately, but when he dragged her up, rolling with her so that she was on her back with him poised above her, she was more than ready to receive the passion that blazed in his eyes.

He stripped her panties from her in one efficient motion.

"Now?" he asked, letting her feel his swollen need at the tender portal between her thighs.

"Yes. Now. Hurry."

He rocked into her and Claire arched up to meet him. She felt him filling her, plunging deep. Deeper. They moved together, slowly at first, silk against silk. Then harder, hotter, faster.

Claire gripped his shoulders. Luke grasped her long legs and pulled them around his waist, levering up in a way that increased the friction of his thrusts until she felt as if the pleasure would rip her apart. With every instinct warning her to slow down, to get control of herself, she held on to Luke even more tightly, closed her eyes and went with the tremors that were racking her from the inside out.

She was running. Racing. Surrounded by white light that filled her head with heat. She could hear the blood rushing through her, sense the pressure building and feel the unbearably sweet contraction of muscles that she couldn't control if she wanted to.

She was close. So close. Luke could see it in the tension on her face, hear it in each ragged breath that shuddered from her chest, feel it in the delicate ripples of flesh that were coming faster and faster, making her body contract around him like a moist fist.

He could do this, he told himself over and over. He could hold off until he felt her climax first. He had to. It was either that or leave her hanging in the worst way possible, and he wasn't about to do that. Not to Claire. Not tonight.

He gritted his teeth and pumped harder. She rose to meet each thrust. He saw her arch, reaching for it, and he pulled her closer until they were torso to torso. The urgency that burned in her eyes echoed his own. She moaned, eager, yearning, then cried out.

"I can't."

Luke slipped his hand between their straining bodies and found the wet heat where they were joined. He pressed his fingers against her and saw her eyes fly open wide.

"I can," he said, his fingers keeping up the pressure, grinding into her, until he felt her go rigid in his arms, then collapse into convulsive shudders.

He held her tightly until she quieted, then rocked his hips into her, slowly, deeply. That was all it took to send the heat he felt coming off her damp body rushing through him, as well. Now he was holding onto her for anchor as the whole world spun around him, an avalanche of light and sparks and raw pleasure that he wished could go on forever. He wanted to go on holding her forever. Not until the rush of sensation eased did he remember that in all likelihood he was going to be spending the better part of forever in a very different way.

He pushed the thought away, not wanting to think about it right then.

Claire stirred beneath him and he gently disentangled his body from hers. She looked very happy and slightly dazed as she pushed her fingers into her hair and held the top of her head. As if, Luke thought, it was threatening to come off. Great sex after-shock. He knew the feeling and grinned at her.

"You okay?" he asked, stroking her cheek as he rolled to rest on one hip.

"Mmm. Very okay." She turned her head to kiss his palm.

Smiling, Luke brought her hand to his lips and returned the gesture, kissing her palm lazily, flicking lightly with his tongue, then swung off the bed. "Be right back."

He went into the bathroom and returned with a warm washcloth to tend to the stickiness on her stomach and between her thighs.

"Mmm, you're spoiling me," she murmured, rolling her shoulders like a satisfied feline.

Love in the First Degree

Luke managed to smile at her words in spite of the sadness suddenly squeezing his heart. He wanted to spoil her in every way he knew how. He wanted to spend his nights making love to her and his days paying her back for believing in him when no one else did. Unfortunately, it would take a lifetime to spoil her properly and he only had a handful of days and nights left to give.

"I guess I'll have to add this to the list," she said as he stroked her thighs with the cloth.

"What list?"

She lifted her head off the pillow a few inches so that his gaze met hers. "The list of reasons why I love you."

The room might as well have been transformed into a meat locker. Luke felt that cold. And that trapped.

He got out of bed and stalked to the bathroom, hurling the washcloth into the sink. He stood there for a minute, his knuckles turning white as he gripped the edge of the counter. When he lifted his head, he saw Claire's reflection in the mirror. He turned to face her.

She had pulled on his T-shirt. Her lips were puffy and her hair tousled. She would have looked sexy as sin if not for the concern that clouded her eyes. If he could have, without resorting to outright lies, he would have tossed her back into bed and loved away the pain he'd inflicted. Then at least her memory of tonight would be a happy one. One lousy night. He owed her that much. There was only one person in the whole world he owed more.

"I'm sorry if I scared you or something by using the *L* word," she said, clearly striving to appear relaxed as she leaned her back against the doorjamb and crossed her arms in front of her.

"You think you scared me by saying you love me?" he countered, guilt making his voice sound harsher than he intended.

"Yes."

"You didn't."

"Then why did you run away?"

"I didn't run away," he denied hotly, knowing damn well he had done exactly that and was doing it again right now as he squeezed past without touching her.

He needed air.

He needed time to think.

He needed a kick in the ass for getting himself into this in the first place.

She'd said she loved him. There was nothing she could have said that could have made him feel more like a heel than he did at that moment.

He grabbed his jeans off the floor and yanked them on, not bothering with underwear. Shoving his shorts into his pocket, he glanced around.

"All right, then," Claire said, still slouched in the doorway, but looking his way. "I'm sorry I upset you."

"I'm not upset."

"You could have fooled me."

I did fool you, he thought, looking around the room, looking anywhere but into her eyes. He'd fooled her into thinking he was worth her effort. He pulled back the bed covers, which had somehow been wrenched from the bed. Where the hell was it?

"Looking for this?" she inquired.

He glanced over his shoulder to find her watching him with a wry smile. Half a smile, actually. She was plucking at one shoulder of the T-shirt she was wearing. His T-shirt.

"Yes, I am, as a matter of fact. You want to toss it to me?"

"No."

His eyebrows shot up. "No?"

"That's right. No. If you want it that badly, come and take it off me."

Luke didn't want the shirt half as badly as he wanted to meet the challenge he saw gleaming in her eyes. He knew

Love in the First Degree

exactly where it would lead if he did—back to bed. She knew it, too.

"Keep the shirt," he said.

"So you are scared," she declared, following him into the other room. "You're also running away again."

He stopped short and turned back to her. "Claire, for the last time, you didn't scare me or upset me by saying that you loved me. But you did confirm that I was right the first time... this was a mistake."

"Don't say that. Don't you dare say that," she ordered, her voice quiet and controlled. He might not have known how angry she was if not for the way her hands had curled into fists at her sides and the fact that her bottom lip was curled. "Not after you were the one who came here uninvited, lying in wait for me. You were the one who wanted something to remember, something to..."

Luke fought the impulse to go to her and stop the tears he heard threatening before they had a chance to pool and fall. He wanted to take her in his arms and kiss her forehead and tell her... what? That everything was going to be all right? Try again, Cabrio.

So he waited. "I didn't mean that it was a mistake for me," he told her when he judged that her emotions were back under control. "It's the opposite, in fact. I got exactly what I wanted, what I asked for. I got what I came here looking for tonight. For a man on his way to prison, there isn't any better way to spend the night than with a woman who's been driving him crazy since the moment she walked back into his life. I meant that this was a mistake for you."

"Shouldn't I be the judge of that?"

"Maybe, if you had a clear view of what was at stake. Admit it, Angel, you still have this crazy hope that this is all going to magically work itself out and—"

"Not magically," she interjected. "But I do happen to believe in the miracles of hard work and logic, and the fact that when push comes to shove, our justice system delivers."

Luke shook his head. "Like I said, magic. If you saw me the way the D.A. does, as a guilty man, I don't think you'd have climbed into my bed so willingly."

"My bed," she corrected. "And I didn't climb into it with a guilty man, simply a misguided one. But I'm going to change that."

Something in the arrogant lift of her jaw warned him not to brush off her claim too lightly. "Now that would be a miracle. Care to tell me how you plan to pull it off?"

"I plan to use the direct approach. A little while ago you accused me of not arguing, but you were wrong. I do argue when there's something worth arguing over. Think about it, Luke—I get paid to argue in front of a judge...and I'm very good at it," she added, with a verbal swagger that wasn't lost on him. "When there's something really important to me at stake, I don't simply argue, I fight like hell."

There wasn't a shred of doubt in his mind about that. "Is that what you plan to do—spend the rest of the night arguing with me over something that's already been decided?"

"Tonight, tomorrow, as long as it takes. But I have the utmost confidence in your intelligence and your powers of reason," she said, with such an abrupt shift in tone from angry to sweet that he didn't know if she was being nice or sarcastic. "And I know that when you hear what I have to say, you'll agree that I'm right, that there is a way out of this mess for everyone concerned."

Not attempting to hide his skepticism, he dropped into a corner of the sofa. "Shoot," he said.

"All right. First off, I believe we've already established that you didn't kill Nick Addison and that the only reason you're not denying the accusation that you did is to protect Sherry Wakefield."

"Go on," Luke urged, doing his best not to snicker at the sight of her acting so lawyerly while rumpled and half-naked.

"As your attorney—"

"Not technically," he interjected, running his eyes over her suggestively.

"No, not technically," she agreed, her long legs shifting restlessly as she stood before him. "But as someone acting in the capacity of legal adviser, I must vehemently discourage you from that course of action." Her expression softened as she moved to perch on the sofa near him. "But as a woman who knows you and loves you and who was once very grateful to be on the receiving end of your heroic instinct—"

"Claire..."

"Hold your objections, please. I knew there was no way I could force you to save yourself if it meant sacrificing Sherry. I confess that around that time, I began wishing there was some magic spell that I could use to change your attitude and make you put yourself first for once." She reached for his hand, curling both of hers around it where it rested on his bent knee. "But the more I thought about it, the more I realized that I didn't want to change you, that I love you just the way you are. I love you because of the way you are. I always have," she added softly.

Luke shook his head. "Damn it, Claire—"

"No. Please let me finish. I didn't plan on telling you any of this tonight. I wanted to talk with Sherry first, because I know that this all hinges on her and what she decides to do. I hoped that the two of us could work out the details and then talk with you together."

"Just tell me."

"I'm trying to. It took me awhile, but I finally realized that I was wasting time trying to prove that Sherry was guilty or trying to get you to admit it. I realized that the only way

I could save you was to save Sherry first. And so that's what I'm going to do."

"I don't understand. Sherry doesn't need you to save her. The police don't even suspect her."

"Of course not, because you've given them such a nice big easy target to take aim at."

"And I plan to keep it that way."

"To save Sherry from going to prison, right?"

He shrugged.

"But what if there was no chance of her being sent to prison, because there was no chance of her being found guilty?"

"There's always a chance."

"All right," she conceded, "but a very minute chance. I'm not the gambler here, so I can't quote odds. But I am a lawyer and I've followed the trend in cases where battered women have resorted to using violence against the men who were abusing them, whether the charges be murder or maiming or simple assault, and after looking into it, I can assure you that Sherry has an excellent case for acquittal."

He hated the look of unadulterated hope that shone in her eyes, mostly because he knew he was going to be the one to destroy it.

"Did she tell you that Addison abused her?"

Claire shook her head.

"Then what gave you that idea?"

"It was just the impression I got when I listened to her talk about him, about their marriage...."

"An impression?" he interjected. "Oh, that should stand up in a courtroom."

"You asked what first gave me the idea," she retorted. "I know more now. Luke," she said, tightening her hands around his, "I've been to St. Michael's, the shelter you brought Sherry to after she left Addison. I've spoken with Mona Kurtz. That's where I was tonight."

Love in the First Degree

Luke listened as she described her visit to the shelter. He listened to as much as he could. He had to admit, she knew the facts. She knew things about Sherry and the hell she'd gone through with Addison that Sherry hadn't even told him. Just as well, he thought bitterly. If she had told him the whole story, Addison probably would have ended up dead a lot sooner.

He couldn't deny that what Claire said made sense. Even Sherry had tried to convince him that what she'd done might be considered self-defense. He couldn't argue with that, either. He wasn't even going to try. From his viewpoint, it was immaterial. He knew what he had to do and he was going to do it. Nothing Claire said could change that.

"I don't believe you," she exclaimed when he told her that's how it was. How it had to be. She jumped to her feet and planted her hands on her hips, tossing her hair back as violently as he'd ever seen her do it. "I don't believe that you could sit there and listen to everything I just told you and still say you're going to go ahead with a plea bargain."

"Believe it," he countered, getting to his feet.

"No," she shot back, defiance and indignation in every rigid muscle. "No one could be that stupid . . . and cruel."

"Cruel?"

"Yes, cruel. How can you just walk away after what we shared tonight?"

"I'm not just walking away. I'm being sent to prison."

"For something you didn't do."

He grabbed her and jerked her toward him. "Don't you think this is tearing me up inside, too?"

"I don't know. I don't know what to think. I can't understand how you could make love to me the way you did, knowing how I feel about you and knowing how you feel about me—don't even try to deny it, Luke, a woman can tell. . . . I don't understand why you would throw it all away for another woman. I know she's an old friend, but this is ridiculous, service above and beyond the call of friendship. Is she blackmailing you? Is that it?"

"Another woman?" he echoed, the words striking a discordant note. His brow gathered into a frown of disbelief. "You don't think I'm still involved with Sherry? Romantically, I mean?"

"What should I think? You climb out of bed with me and tell me we can't be together because you're going to jail so she won't have to. You're willing to sacrifice what we have, and everything we could have, to save another woman...a woman who doesn't even need saving, I might add. A woman who should—"

"Will you stop?" he demanded, shaking her a little too roughly. He had to make her understand. "I'm not sacrificing a damn thing for another woman. This isn't about Sherry."

Claire went still, the resistance draining from her, leaving confusion in its place. Luke gentled his hold.

"It's not?"

"No. I'm not doing this for Sherry. I never was." He took a deep breath. "I'm doing it for my son," he told her. "I'm doing it for Ben."

Chapter 11

Claire pulled away from him, taking a few steps backward.

"Ben is your son?" she whispered, stunned.

She quickly realized that she shouldn't be. Even before Luke confirmed the fact with a solemn nod, she had absorbed the utter rightness of it. There had been so many signs. If only she had been alert to them. Ben's fiery, dark good looks that were much more reminiscent of Luke than of either Sherry or the fair-complexioned Addison. Luke's interest in sending the boy to a private school and the fact that he carried a baby picture of him in his wallet. Even his name, Ben. She shook her head as she recalled the full name on Luke's driver's license. Lucas Benjamin Cabrio. How could she have missed it?

"Who else knows about this?" she asked. Her gaze narrowed sharply. "Did Addison know?"

"Of course," he replied, a little indignantly, Claire noted. "Sherry's not the type to play games with a guy about a thing like that."

Claire did some quick calculations based on what she had learned about Sherry. "But she must have been pregnant with Ben when she married Addison."

"That's right."

"Did she know then that you were the father?"

"We both knew."

"Then why did she marry someone else?"

He shrugged. "Why not? Addison was everything she was looking for in a man—dependable, respectable, a steady worker... and crazy about her in the bargain."

"You make it sound as if he was something she ordered from a catalog," she exclaimed, puzzled by his offhand tone. "You don't marry a man because he's a steady worker when you're carrying another man's baby."

"Want to bet?" A note of bitterness had penetrated his nonchalance. "Addison was perfect husband—and father—material."

"What about you?"

"Me?" His harsh gulp of laughter tore at Claire's heart. "I wasn't even close. Oh, I was financially solvent—for the moment, at least, but respectable? Dependable? Let's just say that a professional gambler wasn't exactly Sherry's idea of the ideal husband and father." His eyes fixed on her. "I doubt you'd argue with that."

"That's not the point. Your job wasn't the point. We're talking about a child here, a human being. Did you try to take responsibility for the baby? Did you ask her to marry you, or at least offer some sort of support?"

"I offered. I asked," he said, the words falling like ice chips. "Hell, I begged. I promised to find a real job, do whatever she wanted me to do."

"And she turned you down?"

He grimaced. "Yeah, she turned me down. Not that there was much to turn down...materially or romantically. Sherry and I had been involved in an on-and-off way for a year or so, but we were never in love."

Claire wasn't exactly proud of the pleasure she took in hearing that. Not that it made any difference. Sherry and Luke shared a bond even deeper than love. "I take it the baby was a complete accident?"

"God, I hate that word," he snapped, stiffening. "Ben may not have been planned, but he was no accident. That little kid is... a blessing. As insignificant as my role was, I can still say he's about the only thing I've done right in my whole life."

"I'm sorry. I didn't mean to imply..."

"I know you didn't," he cut in. "If I'm touchy on the subject, you can chalk it up to my guilty conscience."

"Why should you be guilty when it was Sherry who chose to marry someone else instead of you?"

"I made choices of my own. Choices I'm not proud of. I chose to step aside when she asked me to, to let another man claim my kid as his own, raise him." His eyes were haunted.

"Addison was willing to take on that responsibility even knowing he wasn't Ben's father?"

"So he said," Luke retorted. "He really fed Sherry a line about how he wanted to take care of her and the baby, how it didn't matter to him who the real father was, how from their wedding day on he was going to be the baby's real father." He broke off with a cynical chuckle.

"And Sherry believed him."

He nodded. "Yeah, she believed him. She was that desperate." He turned empty eyes her way. "I'll let you in on my dirty little secret, part of me wanted to believe it, too. I even felt a little relieved at being off the hook. I told myself that Ben was going to have a good home and family and no one was going to be counting on me to provide it... something I wasn't at all sure I could do for the long haul. If I didn't have to try, I couldn't fail, right? It took me years to understand that you don't have to try in order to fail in the only way that really matters."

"Don't be so hard on yourself. I can understand how what you did might have seemed like the right thing to do at the time. If Sherry was in love with Nick Addison and that was the way she wanted it."

"I'm not even sure she ever was in love with him. I tend to think it was more a case of her wanting to be in love with him, or being in love with what he represented."

"And what was that?"

"Success. A nice house in a good neighborhood, a new car and enough steady income for her to stay home with the kids. The American Dream... one version of it, anyway."

"What went wrong?"

"Evidently Prince Charming wasn't always so charming when they were alone behind closed doors, or after he'd spent the afternoon knocking down a few rounds with clients on the golf course."

"Did you know he was abusing her?"

"Not back then. I wasn't even in the picture for the first couple of years. Sherry wanted a clean break. They moved across state and she asked me to stay away, for her sake and for Ben's, to give them a chance to be a real family without any shadows hanging over them. And I agreed," he said.

He ground his fist against his open palm, his anger and self-recrimination so raw it was painful for Claire to watch.

"I agreed," he said again, "that it would be best for the kid not to have to know that his real flesh and blood lived in hotel rooms and played cards for a living and hung loose from one big score to the next. I was a hotshot with a deck of cards, a big success at the same game my old man had failed at. I figured I was showing the whole world what I was made of, sticking it to all those people who'd said I wouldn't amount to squat."

He stared past her, bringing his fists up, then dropping them again, as if there wasn't anything to strike out at, or else he just didn't have the energy.

"Then, Sherry told me she was pregnant," he continued, striking an even tone that didn't fool Claire a bit, "and I had to take a good, hard look at myself and face the fact that, win or lose, what I was doing with my life wasn't much to be proud of. I had to agree with her that I didn't have much to offer in the way of substance. I figured by going along with what she wanted, at least I would be giving my kid something I never had growing up, a father he could be proud of.... Nick Addison," he concluded with a harsh laugh. "What a joke."

"Oh, Luke," she said, tasting at the back of her own throat the bitterness that simmered so strongly in him. "We're talking about something that happened over seven years ago... you were young..."

"Not so young I didn't know a mistake when I made one. I knew, all right. Not right away maybe, but I knew. The first, hell, the only time I ever held my son in my arms, I looked into his eyes and I knew that what I had done was wrong."

He reached for his wallet and stared in silence at the picture of Sherry and Ben before handing it to her.

"I'd heard from friends when she had the baby and that it was a boy, a son, and I couldn't stop thinking about him, wondering what he looked like. It drove me crazy to the point where I was losing my focus, my edge. That's death for a gambler, so I called Sherry and talked her into meeting me at a park near her house so I could see him and hold him, just once. To get it out of my system, I told myself." His shoulders were rigid. "That's the day I took that picture."

After a minute, he continued. "That was also the day I figured out why I couldn't stop thinking about him, why I couldn't shake whatever it was gnawing at my gut day and night. You don't just shake off your own kid as easily as you do losing a game of blackjack. I knew then I'd made the biggest damn mistake of my life and that I was going to have to live with it forever."

"Did you tell Sherry how you felt?"

"What was the point? It was too late to do anything about it... or so I thought. I had given Sherry my word, I had let her marry Addison. What right did I have to go turning three other lives upside down because I'd made a mistake?"

"A father's right," she said softly.

"Yeah, well, I'm a pretty poor excuse for a father. Then and now. But at least this time I'm not shirking my responsibility to him."

"By going to prison for something you didn't do? Is that your idea of a father's responsibility?"

"In this case, you're damn right it is," he retorted. "The way I figure it, Ben's never had much of a father, but he's got a great mother. Sherry loves those kids and she'd do anything for them. Ben needs that... he needs her. He saw how Addison treated her. He saw more than any little kid should have to see."

Claire could only nod, remembering the incident at the shelter that Mona had described. How many more "incidents" like that had Ben and his little brother been subjected to? she wondered.

"Now the only father he ever knew is dead. Shot by his own mother."

He closed his eyes, pain etched in every line of his face, and Claire felt herself reeling inside from a shock she hadn't expected to feel. After all, she had suspected Sherry had killed Addison almost from the start. No matter how she cautioned herself to keep an open mind, in her heart she had already known the truth. Still to hear Luke finally confirm it out loud made a wrenching impression on her.

She understood that he was thinking of the effect all this was going to have on Ben and Nicky. She couldn't help

Love in the First Degree

thinking about the same thing, and for once she was at a total loss for words.

"I guess all kids need love and stability," he said at last, "but right now Ben needs it more than ever, and he needs all of it he can get. The last time he needed me, I wasn't around for him. That's not going to happen again."

Claire released the deep breath she'd been holding. "I understand how much you want to protect Ben..."

"Good," he cut in. "Then you understand why I'm asking you to back off and let me do what I have to do."

"But don't you see?" she countered, the lawyer in her surfacing once again. "You don't have to do this. I know we can build a case for Sherry—"

"And then what?" he demanded before she could finish. "You expect the D.A. to say, wow, what a strong case, I give up?"

"No, it's seldom quite that cut and dried, I'm afraid. I imagine Sherry will be charged with the murder, although I venture to say it will be a lesser count than murder one, and then—"

"And then the whole ugly mess gets played out in court... and in the newspapers. Right?"

She couldn't deny it.

"And for the rest of his life, Ben gets to live with the gossip and the rumors. And the truth... that his mother killed his father—for whatever reason—only it wasn't really his father, it was just some man everyone told him was his father. His real father was such a loser he was better off not even knowing about him."

Claire went to him, but he moved out of reach, as if whatever was inside him might contaminate her, too.

"No seven-year-old kid should have to deal with that," he declared, his voice thick and wavering.

"Luke, there are ways to control the publicity surrounding a trial. The judge can—"

"The judge can try," he barked. "That's all he can do. My way is a sure bet."

"I wish you'd just listen to me for a minute."

"We all have wishes," Luke retorted. Knowing how much he was hurting inside, and that his sarcasm was a defensive measure, didn't make it any easier for Claire to take. "I wish I'd been a father to Ben from the start. I wish I'd taken care of Addison the first time I found out he'd put his hands on Sherry, the way I wanted to. I wish I hadn't listened to her reasoning that it would only make things worse for her and the kids if I got involved. I wish I'd done something when he first showed his face here at the hotel, instead of playing the professional and waiting for him to make a move. I wish to hell I'd never given Sherry that gun."

"Why did you give it to her?"

"Because she was afraid and she asked me for it. Addison had shown up at her place a couple of times in the middle of the night, making a scene and getting the kids all worked up, making threats. She was so nervous that he'd come back that she couldn't sleep."

"Why didn't she call the police?"

"She was worried that he would retaliate if she did, and she was worried about what the neighbors would think, and because she kept hoping he would just get tired of hounding her and go away."

"That seldom happens in cases like this."

"Right. I guess that guys who get their rocks off hitting women don't usually outgrow it." He plunged his hands into his pockets. His eyes cut away from her to stare at the framed magnolias over the sofa, but Claire knew he didn't even see them. He was focused on something that had happened a long time ago. "I knew all about that. I should have made her listen. I should have..." He broke off with a weary shake of his head. "She said that having the gun handy and knowing how to use it would help her to sleep. She was looking like hell. I knew she needed to get some sleep, for the kids' sake if not her own."

His voice had regained its cool detachment, a newscaster's voice, only this wasn't a newscast, Claire thought, it was his life.

"Do you know why she had the gun with her the night Addison was killed?"

"She always carried it with her," he answered. "She took it to work, the store, anytime she left the kids home alone with a baby-sitter. I told you, she's a good mother. She doesn't take chances."

"I don't know Sherry very well, but I agree with you that she's a good mother. I saw them together and it's hard to fake a good relationship with kids."

"You saw Ben?" he asked, some of the darkness leaving his face.

"Yes, the day I went to see Sherry."

"That's right. Is he a great kid or what?"

Claire smiled, moved by his honest pride in a boy he was never even allowed to acknowledge as his own. "He's terrific. I should have guessed he was your son. He looks just like you."

"I guess that was always part of the problem." Luke drew his lips together tightly. "Addison might have started out with good intentions, but having a kid who looked so much like his wife's former lover really got to him. According to Sherry, once Nicky was born and he finally had a son of his own, he turned on both Ben and her.

"Things between them started to go downhill fast. By the time she decided she had to get out and called me for help, I knew right away the situation was bad. I saw some of the marks he left on her," he said tightly, "but even I didn't know how bad it had gotten. Sherry lets it out in little bits and pieces, but she's the only one who really knows what she had to put up with from that son of a bitch. She keeps it all locked up inside her... even about what happened that last night."

"Why did she go to his room that night?"

He puffed out an exasperated breath. "I wish to hell I knew. We haven't exactly had an opportunity to get together and discuss it at length. First I was locked up and now, well, I'm just not taking any chances on raising suspicion in her direction by having her seen with me... or leaving a trail of phone calls," he added pointedly.

"Speaking of which, did she call you from his room that night and ask you to come down?"

"She called. I went down all on my own."

"Was she still there when you got to the room?" Claire felt as if she was cross-examining him. It came naturally, and she couldn't seem to stop.

"No. When she called I told her to go back to work and make like she'd never even taken her break. That place is such a zoo most of the time, I knew she could pull it off."

"And you had already decided at that point that you were going to take the rap for her?"

"No, I didn't even know he was dead, only that she said she'd shot him and that whatever shape he was in I was a better choice to deal with it than she was."

"You mean because you're in charge of security here?"

He nodded. "That's right. I knew he was dead the minute I walked in the room... and that they'd struggled beforehand. I did some picking up, wiped the gun for prints and made sure she hadn't left anything around that would tie her to the scene. I figured I'd just call it in as a routine B&E that went sour... that's..."

"Breaking and entering, I know."

"Right."

"What made you change your mind?"

"The second the cops got there and asked me for a statement, it hit me that no matter what I said or didn't say, they would zero in on Sherry like she had cross hairs on her back.

Love in the First Degree

All I could think of was how Ben—and Nicky, too—were going to lose their father and their mother in one night. I had to stop that from happening and the only way I knew to do that was to distract them just like you said, by giving them a bigger target to aim at. Me."

"And Sherry just went along with that?"

"Max put a lid on things here so that she didn't even know about it until the news of my arrest spread the next day. Then she came tearing down to the jail to tell me I was crazy."

"She was right."

"She told me she'd had to do what she did and she wasn't sorry. She said that she didn't want me taking the blame for her."

"How did you change her mind?"

"I'm not sure I did," he said, the curve of his mouth sardonic. "I told her that we had done things her way the first time, that she owed it to me to go along with what I wanted now."

"Sherry is lucky to have you for a friend."

He shrugged. "I told you, I'm not doing this for her."

"Ben is lucky, too. You're making an unbelievable sacrifice for them, and I know your heart is in the right place."

Her tone purposely signaled that she was leaving something unsaid.

"But?" he prodded, eyes narrowing suspiciously.

"But I'm not sure you're actually doing them such a big favor. You've seen for yourself how the passage of time can put things in a different light, make what seemed the right thing to do seem suddenly all wrong."

"What are you driving at, Claire?"

"I think that there are other reasons besides the obvious why Sherry should come forward and get everything out in the open. Mona Kurtz said the very same thing to me earlier tonight. Sherry needs to face up to what's happened to her, to everything that's happened, and have what she did validated for what it was, an act of self-defense. She needs to know without a doubt that she's the victim here, not a criminal. Having her day in court just might be the best thing that could happen to her."

"And the worst for Ben. I'm sorry, but Sherry and I got to choose what was best once before and look how it turned out. This time Ben is going to come first."

"Coming to terms with what happened will only make Sherry a better mother to Ben," Claire insisted.

Luke's expression became shuttered. "I really don't want to talk about this anymore tonight... or ever, for that matter."

"Your mind is made up, is that it?" Panic twisted inside her at the look of utter determination in his eyes.

"My mind has been made up from the start. I never made any secret of that."

"No," she agreed. "You had other, more important secrets to keep."

"For what it's worth, I'm sorry you got mixed up in this."

"You didn't ask me to come."

"I also didn't force you to go."

"You couldn't have."

He arched one dark brow. "Trust me. I could have."

She shrugged. What difference did it make? What difference did anything make when Luke was determined to throw his life away and she was absolutely unable to stop him?

"So," she said inanely, banking down the ache in her chest, the leading edge of a pain so big she had no idea where it ended. Or if it did. Don't think about it now, she told herself. Later; she would deal with it later. After all, she was a logical woman. She would approach this logically, sort it all out and figure out a way to pull herself back together and go on. Later. All she wanted now was to get through the next few minutes. "What happens now?" she asked him.

"I'm going to give Rancourt a call first thing in the morning and ask him to put some pressure on the D.A. to come up with a deal as soon as possible."

"Oh no, you can't do that," she cried, professional instincts overriding all else for an instant. "You never go begging. It makes you look desperate."

His lips twisted. "Angel, I *am* desperate. I want this settled before I . . . I just want it settled, that's all."

He reached out and laid his hand against her cheek, then let it drop to his side. The expression in his eyes was so heart-wrenchingly bleak, Claire would have looked away if she could have.

"You know, I taught myself a long time ago," he told her, "not to want what I couldn't have. A dog, a new bike, a house where you could bring home friends without having to run ahead and check to see if there was a raging argument going on or if somebody was passed out, drunk, in the hallway." His mouth twisted into a bitter smile. "I had a lot of practice, so I got real good at not wanting things. I turned it into an art form, and even when I left home and could afford the things I wanted, I still practiced not wanting them just . . . just to stay sharp.

"And now," he went on, "in only a few days, you've managed to undo the work of a lifetime." His attempt to sound amused instead of dejected failed miserably. "You've got me wanting what I can't have."

Claire watched him turn and leave without asking exactly what it was that he wanted and couldn't have. Freedom? A fresh start? Her? Maybe all three. Maybe for Luke, the three were so closely entwined that to want one was to want them all.

He had asked her to back off and that's what she was going to do. She had to.

At the door of the bedroom she stopped, staring at the rumpled bed and the suitcase and clothes she had left lying there earlier and that were now strewn across the floor. She could have tolerated the mess, but not the fresh memories that hung in the air along with the sweet, earthy scent of their lovemaking.

"Oh, Luke," she whimpered, wrapping her arms around herself tightly, twisting his T-shirt in her fingers.

She turned her head and nestled her nose against the wash-softened fabric, smelling Luke...seeing him reaching for her...feeling his hands and his mouth streaking over her body. She jerked her head up. *She had to get out of here.*

Dragging a blanket from the bed, she returned to the other room and threw herself on the sofa.

An odd feeling settled over her. She knew how it felt to win and how it felt to lose, but this was neither. It was something in between. It was giving up, she realized, and that was something she never, never did.

She was doing it now, though. She had no other choice.

She could have fought this if it was only Sherry whom Luke was trying to protect, and she would have fought, tooth and nail, to the bitter end. She would have argued and cajoled and used every lawyer's trick and feminine wile at her disposal to get him to change his mind and think of himself first and to consider what he was losing...what they would both be losing if he went to prison.

She would have fought because she loved him. And it was for the same reason that she knew she had to give up now. It was because she loved him that she understood why he could never put his own happiness before his son's, and it was because she loved him that she would never ask him to do it for her. She would never ask him to make a choice between the woman he loved and his own son.

Luke let himself into his room, grabbed the first shirt he saw, jammed his feet into his running shoes and left. He didn't need to climb into bed and spend an hour wrestling with the bedclothes and his own thoughts to know he was too wired to sleep.

Love in the First Degree

He pulled on his shirt during the elevator ride to the ground floor and took a seldom-used exit to the boardwalk. Usually he did his running early in the morning, racing the sun along the horizon, and usually he spent the recommended length of time stretching beforehand. Tonight he just hit the boards and started running, flat out, legs pumping as if they were part of some super engine that would never break down, instead of part of a man who could be broken all too easily.

Tonight he was racing with himself, trying to outdistance the part of him that was saying that maybe he ought to compromise. That maybe, just this once, he could have what he wanted and no one else would have to get hurt in the process. At least no one would get hurt too badly. Define "too badly," he taunted himself. What the hell does "too badly" mean to a seven-year-old?

No.

No compromises.

No surrender.

No. No. No.

His feet pounded out that refrain as they hammered the wooden decking of the boardwalk. Past resorts and the plaza. Past the dozens of fast-food stands and amusement rides, all quiet now. Past TropWorld. Farther. Running harder. Out of breath and almost out of boardwalk and still running. Running until it hurt so much to run that maybe, for just a little while, he wouldn't feel any other pain, like the pain of knowing that Claire was lost to him forever.

Sorry, pal, he thought as the end of the boardwalk came into sight, you just can't run that far. Beyond the end rail, the sand fell away, leaving a stretch of black sky peppered with stars, a little glimpse of what forever looked like. How apropos. It looked cold, Luke decided as he dropped, gasping for air, onto the rough wooden deck. It looked cold and lonely. He closed his eyes.

Welcome to forever, pal.

Chapter 12

Claire was stalling and she knew it. She was showered and dressed and her bags were packed. There was nothing to stop her from leaving Atlantic City the same way she'd arrived, with her life in disarray behind her.

She'd thought she'd had problems at home, boredom with handling one look-alike project after another, irritation with her father for passing her over for the really big cases and then finally assigning her one that had forced her to walk a personal line between ethics and loyalty. That's what had pushed her over the edge and sent her off chasing windmills. When she left, she'd been fed up with the world of Mackenzie and Dwyer and fed up with the way she was spending her time at work. Up until two weeks ago, her work had been her whole life.

This little excursion to gambler's paradise had certainly changed that in a hurry. More accurately, falling in love with Luke had changed it. It had also put her work-related problems in perspective. She'd choose boredom or a bruised ego over a broken heart any day.

Love in the First Degree 215

Unfortunately, Claire thought, sighing as she checked the room one last time to see if she was forgetting anything, she hadn't known that that was the choice she was making until it was too late.

Too late. That seemed to sum it all up nicely. It was too late for Luke. Too late for her. Too late for second chances. She shook her head, recalling how she had fantasized about quitting the family firm and moving to Atlantic City to start her own practice, specializing in the kinds of cases and clients that were important to her. And to be near Luke, of course. There was no denying the tempting part he had played in this most recent fantasy.

Let it go, she told herself, because it just plain wasn't going to happen. She wasn't feeling together enough at the moment to contemplate any major career changes. And she wouldn't be moving anywhere close to Luke anytime soon. Like the rest of this century, she thought bleakly. Not unless she planned to give new meaning to the expression "jailhouse lawyer."

Not funny. She couldn't even make herself smile this morning. Which was probably a good thing. Smiling would probably hurt as much as breathing did. All of a sudden it seemed as if every muscle in her body was connected directly to the giant ache in her chest, and every time she moved it just got a little bigger and harder to bear.

She checked the clock. Nearly ten and still no sound of life in Luke's room next door. She didn't want to wake him up to say goodbye. Who was she kidding? She didn't want to say goodbye at all. If breathing hurt this much, she didn't want to think about what it was going to feel like to stand close enough to Luke to touch him and have to tell him goodbye.

Coming to an abrupt decision, she moved to the corner desk and found a piece of hotel stationery. She didn't even bother to sit. After last night, there wasn't a whole lot to say.

She hurriedly wrote his name at the top of the sheet, and then below it, "Good luck. Take care of yourself." She hesitated before scrawling "Love, Claire."

She would stick it under his door on her way out.

She wiped at the corner of one eye and phoned the front desk to ask them to send someone for her bags. Then on impulse she punched out the number of her office in Providence. Her father would doubtlessly be overjoyed to hear that she would be home this afternoon. After dodging his phone calls the entire time she'd been away, she supposed she owed him a little joy. Besides, it would make reentry that much smoother.

He was in court, his secretary told her.

"No, no message," Claire said in reply to her request. She would just have to surprise him. Maybe she would even drive straight to the office and throw herself back into her work right away. Nose to the grindstone, an idle mind and all that. Just the thought of it made her grimace as she pulled the door shut behind her.

She slid her note under the door of Luke's room, wishing in spite of herself that he might see it right away and come running out to stop her and tell her that he couldn't let her go after all and that somehow, some way, they were going to find a solution to this no-win situation.

She wished so hard that she could almost hear his footsteps on the thick carpeting behind her and his voice calling to her to wait. It was so real that for a second after the elevator doors slid open and she saw Luke standing on the other side, she half expected him to launch into the lines she'd written for him.

Instead, he just stared at her in silence, looking as startled as she felt. Then he frowned.

"My God, Luke, is everything all right?" she asked at last, noting that he was still wearing the same jeans as last night, with a white cotton dress shirt that had seen better days, or rather, better nights. It was wrinkled and smudged

Love in the First Degree

with dirt and had a jagged tear up near the collar. His hair was ruffled. Whiskers darkened his cheeks and jaw and his eyes were bloodshot. He looked as if he'd been in a brawl.

"Fine," he replied. "Why do you ask?"

She shrugged uneasily. "You just look sort of... awful."

"Awful." He nodded with mock thoughtfulness. "Yep, I'd say awful just about covers it. I never made it to bed last night."

"Any special reason?"

"None you don't already know all about."

"I see. Where did you go?"

"Running. Then I ended up in my office."

"Working?"

"On a puzzle." There was a gruff sheepishness in his voice.

"How's it coming?" she asked, thinking she probably ought to mention the missing piece and wondering what she had done with it.

"It's finished, except for one stinking piece. I just spent an hour crawling around on my hands and knees looking for it. Really ticks me off," he said, scowling.

Claire forced a flicker of a smile. This was definitely not the time to mention that she might—just might, mind you—still have the missing piece. "That's a shame. Well, maybe it will turn up."

Maybe. If she could find it and send it to him. In time.

"Yeah, maybe." He moved to hold the doors open with his back. "Where are you off to so early?"

"Home."

"Home?" He looked shocked, as if he hadn't spent most of the past two weeks advising her to go home.

"That's right. There's really no reason for me to hang around."

"No. No, I suppose there isn't."

"I wrote you a note," she said, shifting the strap of her handbag to her other shoulder. "I stuck it under your door."

"What does it say?"

"Not much. I just wanted to tell you good luck and to take care of yourself."

"That's it?"

She swallowed and her throat burned. It was a lot easier to write the word *love* than to say it when he was standing so close, staring at her, his eyes ablaze with a dark, unmistakable heat.

"That's it," she said.

"Well. Thanks. For everything."

He stepped away from the doors and they immediately began to close. He held them with one hand, his eyes still watching her as she boarded the elevator. She stood facing him and saw more than heat and hunger in his gaze now. She saw all the regrets and the longing that he either couldn't put into words or didn't dare to.

As soon as he dropped his arm to his side, the doors started closing again. One more second, Claire told herself. Not even. Surely she could hold herself together for that long.

She was doing all right. Then, with the doors just inches apart, he suddenly shoved his hand in between. The automatic sensors immediately reversed their direction and Luke was reaching through the opening for her, grabbing her and dragging her against him.

His mouth came down on hers with a fierce hunger that washed away everything else, the pain and the worry and the fear of what tomorrow was going to be like. He caught her hips with his firm, strong hands and pulled her to him even more tightly, and all the while his tongue plundered her mouth, seeking, demanding, setting her senses on fire.

He kissed her as if he wanted to lose himself in her. *No,* she thought, *as if he already had.* It was a kiss that tasted of

Love in the First Degree 219

heat and honey and possibilities. Claire gave herself totally, unrestrainedly to the embrace, and for one brief, mad moment she forgot how things really were.

It wasn't until he pulled away and she looked into his eyes that she remembered there were no possibilities to be found there, only regrets.

"I really am sorry," he whispered.

Then the doors closed and she was alone.

She barely had time to compose herself before she reached the lobby and found herself surrounded by laughing, chattering hotel guests, some in a hurry to reach the casino, others looking as if they'd spent the night there.

Claire had planned to stop by Brad's office and thank him for his help, but she definitely wasn't up for that now. She would call him from home, she decided, along with Mona and Gerald.

She checked out and was halfway to the exit that led to the parking garage when she heard a woman's voice calling her name. She turned to see Sherry Wakefield hurrying across the lobby toward her and was ashamed of the wave of dismay she felt and the accompanying urge to keep walking. She just wanted to get away from there as fast as she could.

"I'm so glad I caught you," Sherry said. "They told me at the desk that you just checked out. Is that true?"

"Yes, it is."

She frowned in confusion. "But why? Where are you going?"

"Home."

"Home? How can you go home now? When Luke hasn't even gone to court or anything? When he needs you here?"

"Luke doesn't need me," Claire said, glancing impatiently at the exit a few feet away. As sympathetic as she was to Sherry, she didn't feel like discussing any of this with her right now. "He's made up his mind about what he's going to do and he doesn't need my help to do it."

"Maybe not," Sherry said, as Claire turned to go, "but I think maybe I do." She caught the sleeve of Claire's shirt. "Please, Ms. Mackenzie, can I talk with you?"

"I'm sorry, Sherry. I'm really in a hurry and—"

She broke off as the other woman's face crumbled with disappointment.

"I'm sorry," she said to Claire. "I didn't mean to bother you or anything. It's just that Ms. Kurtz told me some of the things you said to her and that you might be willing to help me if you could."

Claire peered at her with increased interest. "When did you speak with Mona Kurtz?"

"She called me first thing this morning. Ms. Kurtz knows I'm always up real early with the boys. I'm glad she did call, because I've been needing someone to talk with about this."

"You mean about your ex-husband's death?"

"Yes. I..." She glanced around nervously. "Do you think we could take a walk outside? This is sort of private. And besides, I don't want to run into Luke until I get to say what I have to say. I won't take too much of your time, I promise."

Claire nodded. "All right. Why don't you lead the way? I'm afraid I still get lost in this place unless I use the garage exit."

Sherry led her through the labyrinthine hotel to the boardwalk and then a short distance to a place where the boardwalk extended out over the beach. Dressed in neat, navy blue shorts and a white open-neck jersey, she looked more like a vacationer than a casino show girl. Claire had dressed for comfort on the long drive home and her turquoise T-shirt tucked into cream-colored denims blended equally well with the casually dressed tourists all around them. In spite of the crowd, there were only a few other people sitting on the nearby rows of benches, some old men feeding the sea gulls and a family taking a break from their walk along the shore. They found a private bench off to the side and sat.

"I guess I should just start at the beginning," Sherry said, "except sometimes I don't even know where that is anymore. So I'll just start with the hardest part to get out. Luke didn't kill Nick, Ms. Mackenzie." Her gaze had been skittering from Claire's face to the horizon and back. Now she looked directly into her eyes. "I did."

Claire had braced herself, knowing what was to come, and she managed to keep from her expression any trace of the emotions roiling within. Inside she was trembling, with relief for Luke's sake and anguish for Sherry and her sons. Outwardly, she was the epitome of professional control and reassurance as she briefly placed her hand on Sherry's.

"I know, Sherry," Claire told her. "As I questioned people on Luke's behalf, the pieces kept falling into place."

Sherry sighed deeply, some of the stiffness leaving her. "Ms. Kurtz said you might have it all figured out. She said she wasn't a hundred percent certain what you knew for sure and what you just surmised was true, but I'm glad I finally said it anyway." She sighed again and rubbed her fingertips along her breastbone. "I already feel like some of this knot here has been chipped away. Not that I think saying it changes anything," she explained hurriedly, as if she feared Claire might disapprove of her relief.

Claire smiled to reassure her. "I know you don't think that, Sherry. And I think I have some idea of how hard this has been for you. All of it."

"There's more," she said. She licked her lips and pressed them tightly together. Claire could guess what it was that she was finding even harder to confess than murder. "Nick wasn't my oldest son, Ben's, real father. Luke is."

"I know that, too," Claire said quietly.

The other woman gaped at her, clearly stunned by Claire's response to her second revelation. "Luke told you about that?"

"Yes. I hope you don't mind."

"Who am I to mind what anyone else says or does? Especially Luke. That man has saved me from my own stupidity—or tried to at least—more times than I care to count." She turned, resting one elbow on the bench back, and studied Claire for a few seconds. "I guess it just proves my hunch was right."

"Your hunch? About what?"

"About Luke being in love with you."

Claire shifted uneasily. "Let's get back to talking about you, shall we? You said you wanted my help?"

"I do. And in a way, what I just said about Luke being in love with you is about me." Seeing Claire's instinctive flinch, she quickly added, "Not in the way you must be thinking, though. There was never anything like that between Luke and me. We were friends...." She shrugged and stared at the toes of her white sneakers. "And we were lonely. Things just sort of happened. I'm not particularly proud of that time of my life, but having Luke for a friend—and having him be Ben's father—isn't one of the things I'm ashamed of." She slanted a quizzical look Claire's way. "Am I making any sense at all?"

"Yes," she replied uncertainly. "And no."

The fact that Sherry could smile through her obvious nervousness made Claire like her more than she was prepared to.

"What I'm trying to say is that I never wanted Luke to take the blame for something I did. And now, knowing that he's found you and has even more reason not to throw away his life by going to prison, there's no way I'm going to stand by and let him do what he's planned."

"Sherry, I admire your honesty, but I think this is something that you and Luke have to work out between you."

"No," she countered sharply, placing her hand on Claire's arm as she hitched her purse strap over her shoulder and prepared to rise. "You know Luke. He'll just try and steamroll over me so that he can have things his own way. I can't even blame him all that much. I haven't done such a great job of arranging things in the past. But that's going to change," she declared, determination sharpening her gaze.

"I'm through with secrets and lies and hiding so many different things from different people that I go crazy trying to keep straight in my head who knows what about me. I've made up my mind to wipe the slate clean and start fresh, for me and my kids. And for Luke, too. I'm going to tell the truth, all of it."

Her expression turned imploring. "That's why I need your help, Ms. Mackenzie. Ms. Kurtz promised that she'll stick right by me no matter what happens, but I need legal advice, and that she can't give. This is so hard for me, and after talking to you the other day, well, I trust you." She shrugged a little dejectedly. "I'm not even sure who I'm supposed to go see first, the police or a lawyer. I don't even know what to say and when to say it. Will you help me? Please, Ms. Mackenzie?"

Claire had no quick response to offer. Sherry's request put her in a very difficult position. The other woman was vulnerable and scared, and she was in a lot of trouble. Wasn't that why Claire had come to Atlantic City in the first place? To help someone who needed her help? Did it make such a difference that the someone who needed her was Sherry, instead of Luke?

It shouldn't. Every professional instinct she possessed told her that. If anything, she was even better prepared to assist Sherry. Her belief in Luke had been based on nothing more than a memory and a whim, while she had already discovered solid evidence and reasonable motive to defend what Sherry had done.

What's more, she felt a personal link to Sherry's cause. What Mona Kurtz had said about the patterns of abuse not being broken until every woman who was mistreated spoke up about it had struck home and left her with a new sense of personal responsibility. She hadn't had the courage it would have taken for her to speak out twelve years ago. Did she have the courage to help Sherry speak out now? Even if it meant incurring Luke's wrath, which she had a feeling was exactly what she would be doing by helping Sherry?

"I know this is sort of out of the blue," Sherry said, the desperation she was feeling was obvious in her tone and in the way her whole body was straining forward. "If you need to take some more time to think it over..."

Claire shook her head. "I don't need any more time to think about it, Sherry. I don't know how much help I can be. Technically, I don't practice law in this state." Technically. She smiled ruefully at the irony in that. Then, seeing that Sherry assumed she was backing her way into a refusal, she broadened her smile encouragingly. "But if you want an unofficial advocate, you've got one."

"Are you saying you'll stay and help me?"

"That's exactly what I'm saying. But before I can do anything to help, we have to figure out where the beginning is and you have to start there and tell me everything. Do you think you can do that?"

Sherry nodded, her own smile shaky, but tinged with hope in a way that left Claire with no doubt she was doing the right thing. No matter how Luke reacted when he heard about it.

This wasn't the first time she had found herself trapped between the ethical demands of the profession she loved and loyalty to a person whom she loved even more. Her father's hidden involvement in her most recent case had put her in a very similar position. Then, she had bowed to personal loyalty and walked away—no, *run* away—from the victory that resulted, with a sour taste that in some small, insidious way had forever changed her attitude toward everyone involved... including her own father. And herself.

Love in the First Degree

She wouldn't let that happen again. Maybe fate had intervened here to give her a chance to atone for her misjudgment in that case, she thought, recalling her thwarted attempt earlier to call her father and tell him she was on her way home. Sorry, Dad, plans have changed. She knew for sure that she'd been given a chance to recapture the feeling she had the very first time she walked into a law school classroom, as if she really could make a difference in people's lives. And the prospect excited her now as much as it had then.

She and Sherry sat outside, talking, for over an hour. When the heat became oppressive they moved indoors, to a quiet corner booth in a café a short distance from the Delta Queen and the threat of running into Luke.

At first, Sherry's answers to her questions were rambling and disjointed. Claire understood that was because there was so much built up inside her she had to get out that it was ridiculous to expect it to flow from her as neatly as a stream running downhill. This was more like watching a geyser that spewed forth in fits and stops.

She also had to consider the painful and embarrassing nature of so much of what Sherry had to say. Claire understood that it was sometimes hard to understand the things you were willing to do, and to endure, for love, much less share them with someone else.

The fact that she was a stranger might have made it easier for Sherry, at least in the beginning. It wasn't long before she stopped feeling like a stranger, however, and Claire had the sense that Sherry, too, was gradually lowering her innermost defenses. Maybe it was knowing that they each shared a special bond with Luke or simply a basic feminine drawing together in the face of a kind of brutality they couldn't fathom, for whatever reason, Sherry was able to open up to Claire about the details of her life with Nick Addison. She talked at length about Nick Addison's pledge to raise Ben as his own son and about her bright hopes at the start of their marriage. And about how, as it all fell apart, disappointment had turned to pain and fear and an endless cycle of cruelty and lies that she didn't know how to escape from.

She confirmed what Luke had told Claire about how Addison's attitude toward Ben had changed sharply after his own son was born. Sherry was able to supply horrifying firsthand details about his treatment of poor Ben that Claire was certain she wouldn't have dared reveal to Luke. Details that made Claire's heart ache for the little boy who hadn't asked to be caught in such a grown-up war of egos and hatred. She let Sherry proceed at her own pace and made a mental note to explore further the extent of the psychological abuse Addison might have inflicted on both the boys.

Sherry spoke of holidays that ended in trips to the emergency room, family outings that disintegrated into public shouting matches, and the private retaliation that always followed once Nick Addison had his family where he wanted them, behind closed doors.

It was all horrible and hard to listen to, but Claire sensed Sherry's agitation increasing sharply as she drew closer to talking about the actual night of the murder.

"I just wanted him to leave me alone," she said, her delicate chin quivering as she struggled with the tears that had fallen intermittently throughout their conversation. "I thought for sure after that scene at the shelter that things had changed. Nick agreed to the divorce and I just kept telling myself it was over, it was really over."

She looked down, pinching the bridge of her nose between her steepled fingertips.

"But it wasn't?" Claire prodded gently.

She shook her head. "It only got worse. Nick came around the very next day after the divorce became final and said he just wanted me to know that he might not have a legal right to me any longer, but he had other ways of getting what he wanted...the only thing he'd ever wanted from me, he said." She sniffed back tears.

"Do you know what he meant by that?"

"Oh yeah, I knew, all right. Sex. He was talking about sex."

"Do you mean he was threatening to rape you?" Claire asked, struggling to keep the anger that was churning inside from her voice. It wasn't going to help Sherry for her to succumb to emotion, too.

"He didn't need to rape me," Sherry replied, lifting her tear-streaked face, her expression full of self-loathing. "I had no choice but to go along with whatever he wanted me to do...whenever he wanted it, and Nick knew it."

"So Nick expected you to sleep with him even after the divorce?"

"He didn't just expect it, he made sure it happened. And there was no sleeping involved. It was..." She stopped and swallowed hard. "Sex for silence, he called it," she went on, with a broken attempt at a laugh that challenged Claire's effort to remain professional. "It was very simple. Unless I went along with whatever he wanted, he would tell Ben the truth—that he wasn't really his father."

"And you didn't want that?"

She shook her head, dragging in a couple of deep breaths. "As rotten a father as Nick was most of the time, he was the only father Ben knew. Nicky was young still, but the divorce and everything it entailed really bothered Ben. He's like that—sensitive to what I'm going through—and he keeps everything he's feeling inside. Luke's the same way." She glanced quickly at Claire. "But I'll bet you've already figured that out."

"Yes, I have," she replied. "So you thought it would upset Ben even more to know the truth?"

Sherry nodded, her expression grim. "I know now that I was wrong...wrong to ever lie about it in the first place and then doubly wrong to try to cover up the lie with more lies and more secrets. I guess I wasn't feeling all that great to begin with about then and I was worried... worried what my own kid would think of me if he knew the truth."

"I can easily understand why you might feel that way, and how easy it would be for someone to take advantage of your doubts and fears." Claire refrained from adding that she could especially understand it coming from someone who had battered and harangued her until she was driven from her own home, someone who had destroyed her hopes and broken her heart and still couldn't leave her alone. A bastard like Nick Addison.

"At first he said it would only be a few times," Sherry went on, almost talking to herself. "Just till he got me out of his system, he would say. But after a while, I knew... I knew it was never going to end."

"Is that why you went to Nick's room the night he was killed, Sherry? Because he'd told you he wanted to sleep—to have sex with you?"

"Yes," she said, averting her gaze. "He called me at home before I went to work."

"And did you have sex with him that night?"

She nodded. "Yes. It wasn't even that bad. Not as bad as—" she shuddered "—other times. I told him I was on break and it had to be real quick and it was. Then when I went to get dressed, he went to the other room and came back a minute later, all dressed himself and holding a camera." Her jaws snapped together and Claire saw the first hint that there was deep anger mixed with her pain and remorse. Everything inside Claire applauded her spirit.

"He said I could go back to work just as soon as he took a few pictures... for insurance purposes. He said he wanted some backup in case I ever got to thinking that maybe Ben was old enough to understand the truth about his real father and all. He said if that happened, then Ben would also be old enough to see the pictures he was going to take, see for himself exactly what a casino slut his mother was."

Love in the First Degree

Claire sat in silent horror while Sherry's shoulders heaved and she pressed the napkin against her closed eyes.

"Casino slut, that's what he called me all the time," she said when she could speak around her quiet sobs. "He said that's why he had to up the ante with pictures, because it was the only thing a casino slut would understand."

"What happened then, Sherry? Did he use the camera?"

"No." Her breath shuddered in and out. "I was so furious with him, so damn mad that I guess I attacked him. I know I knocked the camera from his hands and it broke. I took it with me when I left and threw it in a Dumpster out back. Right then, though, he was swearing at me and coming after me. I tried to grab the rest of my stuff and make it into the bathroom. I figured I could lock the door and stay there until he calmed down."

"Did you manage to do that?"

"No. I couldn't. He grabbed me and started slapping me and pushing me." She gritted her teeth and stared into her empty ice-tea glass. "He ripped my costume, over here near the strap," she added, demonstrating on her jersey. "I don't remember everything in order. I just remember my purse falling, and suddenly the gun was lying right there on the floor between us. I was sort of surprised to see it, really. Nick saw it, too, and the way he looked at it, then looked at me, I knew he really hated me. And I knew that he was madder than I'd ever seen him. And I was afraid if I didn't grab the gun first, he would get it and—and..."

She rested her elbows on the table and put her face in her cupped palms. Claire waited a minute or so.

"So you picked up the gun. Is that what happened next, Sherry?"

Sherry nodded without looking up. Again Claire waited. Finally Sherry lifted her gaze and met hers.

"I didn't mean to shoot him. I never meant to kill him.... I didn't even want to hurt him, really." Her voice grew soft, with a wistfulness Claire found hard to bear. "I just wanted him to leave me alone."

"I believe you, Sherry," Claire told her. She covered Sherry's hands with her own. "And so will whoever else listens to your story. If you're sure this is really what you want to do."

"It is what I want. I've never been more sure of anything in my life. I meant it when I said I'm through with letting lies and secrets run my life. Whatever happens has to be better than that."

"What about Ben and Nicky?"

"It will be better for them, too," she replied, her jaw tipped upward with determination. "After what they've been through, they can handle the truth." She smiled gently. "I want Ben to know what a wonderful man his father really is. In fact, knowing that he'll finally have a chance to really get to know Luke is sort of the silver lining in all this." She sighed, her smile sad. "I've wasted so much time, Ms. Mackenzie."

"Sherry, I have to be honest with you. I can't guarantee there won't be more wasted time ahead for you. What I'm trying to say is that although I think you have a very strong chance of being acquitted of all charges, stronger than ever after what you've told me today, it's still only that, a chance. There are no absolute sure bets in a courtroom."

"I understand that."

"And you still want to go ahead?"

"I still want to go ahead. Even if I didn't know it was the right thing to do, for me and for my boys, I would want to do it for Luke." She smiled at Claire across the table littered with tearstained napkins. "That man deserves a shot at real happiness and I think you're it, but he can hardly expect a lady like you to wait around while he spends twenty or so years in prison."

Love in the First Degree 231

Claire marveled that Sherry was able to even consider anyone else's feelings right now, much less let them influence her decision.

"Last night I told Luke that you were lucky to have him for a friend," she said to Sherry. "I think that works both ways."

"Thanks. All I know is that when I was pregnant with Ben, Luke did everything he could to try to help me. He wanted to do right by me and the baby, he really did. But he was a gambler and a little bit wild, and I was too stupid and too afraid to take a chance on him back then." She smiled at Claire. "I think I owe it to Luke to take a chance for him now."

Chapter 13

Claire checked back into the Delta Queen without requesting the suite next to Luke's. This time she was given a room on the third floor and in the opposite wing from his. Which was for the best. Something told her she was going to want to be able to put as much distance as possible between them when he found out why she'd decided to stay in Atlantic City a while longer.

She unpacked and then phoned Gerald Rancourt, arranging to meet with him in his office later in the afternoon. Once there, she discussed the changed situation with Gerald and left it to him to relay the news to Luke. After all, technically Luke wasn't her client. Or her anything else, for that matter.

From there she drove directly to St. Michael's and picked up Mona Kurtz. She had invited Mona to dinner hoping to get to know more about Sherry. She did, but she also got to know more about Mona Kurtz, as well, and ended up liking and admiring the other woman even more than she had at their first meeting.

She was surprised to discover that Mona had been a math professor before becoming involved in establishing the women's shelter at St. Michael's.

"Somehow teaching logarithms never energized me the way helping a woman find the courage to take charge of her own life has."

"I know what you mean," Claire agreed, taking a sip of coffee as they lingered at the small Italian restaurant Mona had recommended, enjoying their conversation too much to leave. "As sad as it is to think about what's happened to Sherry and her kids, and what the three of them still might have to go through before this is all over, there's also something wonderful about the way she's determined to turn her life around, starting right this minute."

"Why, Claire, I do believe I see a tear in your eye," Mona exclaimed, her own dark eyes flashing mischievously. "Are you sure you're happy being a financial lawyer?"

"No," Claire said, surprising both of them a little by admitting it so readily. "But right now I don't seem to have time to think about it."

"Well, when you do have time," Mona countered, "and if you decide to try following your heart, instead of your head for a change, think about following it back here. I promise to send you all the work you can handle. Maybe not much in the way of fancy fees," she teased, "but plenty of good hard work."

"Fees are always negotiable," Claire said, laughing. "And who knows? One of these days I just might take you up on the offer."

Once again she was late getting back to the hotel and went straight to her room. She wasn't exactly avoiding Luke; she just wasn't crazy enough to go out of her way looking for the confrontation she was sure they were going to have the next time they met.

There was a message waiting for her from Gerald. As promised, he'd arranged a meeting with the D.A. to discuss the new developments in the case and to make preliminary arrangements for Sherry to turn herself in to the police. Ordinarily such a meeting would take place in the D.A.'s office and would most likely be done in several stages, each one including only the parties immediately involved in that aspect of the discussion.

However, as Claire had discovered, there was very little ordinary about this case. The D.A. had agreed to Sherry's request that the meeting be held at St. Michael's, where she felt more comfortable. It was also agreed that she would have both Mona and Claire with her for moral support and that there be only one meeting with everyone present to hear what she had to say. Sherry was adamant that there be no more misunderstandings or half-truths to haunt her later.

The meeting was scheduled for the following morning. Claire wasn't sure what Gerald told Luke about the meeting beforehand, only that he definitely hadn't told him she would be there. He was the last to arrive, and he was noticeably jolted when he saw her sitting beside Sherry.

He wasn't alone in being jolted. After only one day apart, the sight of him in a dark suit, light blue shirt and subtly patterned silk tie was so seductive to Claire's senses that she was glad she was sitting down, with her shaking knees hidden beneath the shelter's sturdy dining room table.

The homey atmosphere made the gathering seem less ominous and probably less frightening to Sherry. She had arrived early with Ben and Nicky, who were now romping outside with the other children presently living there. The sound of their laughter and the roar of plastic tires streaking across pavement filtered through the open windows. Another time their youthful exuberance might have been infectious, but not today.

Standing just inside the room, Luke glanced around the table, taking note of everyone present.

"What's going on here?" he demanded, his tone already clipped enough for Claire to take warning. "Rancourt?" he

Love in the First Degree

said, the name alone a demand as his gaze honed in on the attorney seated at one end of the long table. "I assumed that this meeting was to include only ourselves, Sherry and Ms. Kurtz. What gives?"

"I'm sorry, Luke. I didn't mean to mislead you. Why don't you have a seat and I'll introduce everyone?"

Luke ignored the invitation to sit. His neck above his collar was dark red, his eyes so black with impending fury that Claire avoided looking into them.

"This is Terrence Dowling," Gerald said, indicating the attorney from the D.A.'s office who sat across from him. Dowling was a tall, rugged man with receding gray hair and a reassuring, almost paternal smile. Deceptively so, Claire was certain. "He represents—"

"I know who he is," Luke interrupted. "The question is, what is he doing here?"

Dowling looked at Gerald. Gerald looked at Mona, who looked at Claire. Claire took a deep breath, but it was Sherry who spoke.

"Sit down, Luke. Mr. Dowling is here because I'm going to do something I should have done two weeks ago. No, longer than that... years ago. But like they say, better late than never." She flashed Luke a brave smile.

Understanding flickered in Luke's eyes. He shook his head and leaned over the back of the chair, instead of sitting in it as Sherry had requested. Hands braced on the table, he stared at her with a desperation that was painful to see. "Don't do this, Sherry. You don't have to do this."

"Yes, I do," Sherry replied, patting his hand reassuringly. Claire felt a burning at the back of her eyelids. "I really do, Luke. You see, when you come right down to it, this isn't about you or Nick or the kids, it's about me, and me being able to live with myself. So please, sit down and let me do what I came here to do. Tell the truth."

Sherry told the truth. All of it, and there was no one in the room, even among those who had heard most of it before, who was not shaken by her story. It was humanly impossible not to be deeply affected by her simple telling of the horrors that had gone on just beneath the surface of her seemingly normal, everyday family life.

It was Dowling's role to remain detached and unmoved, but Claire saw the muscle that ticked convulsively in his cheek as he listened to the worst of it and observed him wipe his palms on the legs of his trousers a time or two. Damp palms were a very good sign, she thought.

She found Luke's responses, or lack of them, much less encouraging. He sat absolutely still, his expression unwavering throughout, even as he learned for the first time how depraved Addison really was, how despicably he had tried to use Sherry's love for her son—Luke's son—as a weapon against her.

Luke didn't speak. He didn't need to. It was clear from the start of the meeting that control of the matter had been taken out of his hands and returned to Sherry, where it rightfully belonged. Although Claire was quite certain that Luke didn't see it that way.

During the past two weeks she'd seen him hotheaded and short of patience. She'd seen him fight for control and she'd seen him lose it, but this was something else. Something much more alarming. He was too still, too cold, too controlled. Especially for a man whose eyes burned like twin coals. Any jury watching him and looking into those eyes would have no doubt that he was a man fully capable of murder and a great deal more.

The meeting ended. Dowling didn't officially commit his office to offering a reduced charge of manslaughter, but in all the trial conferences she'd attended, she'd never seen a prosecutor come so close. Even his demeanor toward Sherry during his brief questioning of her had been extremely encouraging, and Claire allowed herself to feel the first sweet stirring of success. The procedure for Sherry to turn herself

Love in the First Degree

in the following day was agreed upon and everyone began gathering their things to leave.

Luke stood first. Again he slapped his palms down at the center of the table, only this time his gaze locked on Claire.

"I hope to God you're happy," he growled at her.

He was gone before Claire could respond.

"Don't be upset, Claire. I'll talk to him," Sherry said.

"No," Claire said, seeing red. "I'll talk to him myself."

She caught up with him on the steps outside. He'd reached the bottom as the front door banged shut behind her.

"Just a minute, Luke Cabrio."

He stopped, then slowly turned back to her, his hands jammed into his pants pockets, a scowl on his face that Claire thought better suited to one of the children now playing baseball in the side yard.

"I have nothing to say to you," he told her.

"How convenient. That leaves more time for me to talk, and I have plenty to say to you."

"I'm listening," he drawled, while everything from his tough-guy stance to the sardonic twist of his lips declared the opposite.

"Oh, what's the use," she muttered. "You were right, your mind has been made up from the start." Frustrated, she shoved her own hands in the pockets of her yellow suit jacket and discovered what she'd done with the missing piece of his puzzle. "Here," she said, getting ready to toss it to him. "A going-away present for you."

He kept his hands hidden in his pockets. "Whatever it is, keep it. You gave me more than enough while you were here."

His sarcasm fueled the temper Claire was trying to be mature enough to control. "You're right, I gave you plenty, but you're too stubborn and shortsighted to know it. If you ever figure it out, give me a call."

She ran down the steps, but Luke stepped forward to block her path to her car.

"If you're talking about the night before last," he said, "that was something we both wanted to happen."

"Please," she retorted, raking him with a disparaging look that didn't seem to phase him, but definitely helped buoy her self-esteem at that moment. "I know exactly what that night meant...to both of us. Much better than you do, I'd venture."

She watched as his olive complexion was heated by a tinge of red. Apparently he wasn't comfortable talking about what that night meant to him. Shouldn't be any big surprise for her there, Claire realized.

"All right then, what do you figure you gave me that I don't know about? Legal advice? I already thanked you for that, in spite of the fact that I didn't ask for it and damn well don't like the end result. Send me a bill."

"You jerk," she snapped, throwing the puzzle piece at him. It hit his chest and dropped to the ground. "That's not the only piece you're missing, Cabrio. I'm not talking about legal advice, I'm talking about your son."

His gaze narrowed as if she'd struck him, then swung instinctively to where the little boy was pitching a softball to a bigger kid swinging a plastic bat. The look of anguish that filled his eyes almost made Claire sorry she'd snapped at him. Almost.

"Ben?" he queried softly. "You're talking about Ben?"

"That's right. Since as far as you're concerned I'm entirely to blame for how this turned out, I might as well take the credit for the good part."

"There's a good part?" he inquired, reverting to sarcasm. "Sorry, I must have blinked and missed it."

"Then take another look. If you weren't so busy feeling sorry for yourself for getting knocked off your white charger in the middle of the battle, you might realize that you haven't lost a prison sentence, you've gained a son."

"A son who needs his mother," he retorted, but his voice had lost some of its bitter edge and his gaze once again found Ben and lingered.

"He'll have his mother," Claire said firmly. "Even I would be willing to bet the ranch on that. But now maybe, just maybe, he'll have a father, too."

He flicked her a wary glance before returning his attention to Ben. "What do you mean... *maybe?*"

"It's up to you. You want to be a real hero, Luke? There's your chance." She nodded toward Ben as he got ready to hurl the ball again. "Or are you really still stuck in that same old rut, believing that if you don't try, you can't fail?"

The batter connected with the ball and knocked it in their direction. It rolled to a stop at Luke's feet. He bent and picked it up, but before he could toss it back, Ben had trotted over to retrieve it himself.

"Here you go," Luke said, his voice revealingly gruff.

"Thanks," Ben said, cupping his hand for the toss. His grin made Claire's heart clench. She could only imagine what it was doing to Luke. "I remember you. Luke, right? You're my mom's friend."

Luke froze with the ball still in his hand. "That's right. I'm... friends with your mom."

"I'm Ben."

"I know. I know who you are, Ben."

The boy shrugged. "I just thought I'd remind you, in case you forgot my name and were embarrassed or something."

Son rescues father, Claire thought, her throat tightening. *A noble family tradition continues.*

"No, I didn't forget." He turned the ball in his hand. "You know, Ben, you'd get more power on your pitch if you tightened your windup, closed the angle of your stance a little."

Ben looked bewildered, but interested. "Could you show me?"

Claire saw the cords in Luke's throat tighten as he fought for control before answering.

"Yeah," he said, a smile overpowering his face. "Yeah, I can show you. Come on."

Ben trotted to keep up with Luke's longer stride as they headed, side-by-side, toward the improvised pitcher's mound.

Luke didn't look back at her. Claire didn't expect him to.

She walked over to her car and watched as Luke demonstrated and Ben mimicked a series of arm and leg movements that all looked pretty silly to her. After a few minutes she slid behind the wheel, and after a few minutes more Sherry came outside with Nicky.

As Claire drove away, Nicky had charged the pitcher's mound, with his mom in hot pursuit. A real family moment.

She didn't envy any of them the long road of explanations and adjustments that lay ahead. But to her amazement, she sure envied the moment.

Chapter 14

It took several days for everything discussed at the meeting to be enacted. Claire surrendered to the police. Reduced charges of manslaughter were filed against her and she pleaded not guilty by reason of self-defense and was released on bail. So far, the press coverage had been both restrained and favorable. Mona had friends in all kinds of places, as it turned out. Everyone, including Sherry, was optimistic.

Ten years ago she wouldn't have stood much chance of finding a sympathetic jury or even one predisposed to listening with an open mind to the prolonged and complicated chain of events that had led her to be in Addison's hotel room, holding a gun, the night he was killed. Fortunately, times had changed. Public sentiment had changed.

Sherry was in a position to help teach people even more and she was eager to do it. She was already doing something she told Claire she had been thinking about doing for a long time, volunteering a few hours a week at the shelter.

Claire found the other woman's courage to be a tremendous inspiration.

Gerald Rancourt was officially assigned to defend Sherry, and they hit it off from the start. She seemed to genuinely appreciate Gerald's slick brand of humor, and Gerald went way up in Claire's estimation because he seemed to genuinely appreciate Sherry's sweet nature.

From Sherry she had heard that she and Luke together told Ben the truth about his father, wanting him to know about it before the trial began and it was reported by the press. He was taking it as well as a seven-year-old could be expected to.

From Luke she heard nothing. The charges against him had been dismissed. He was officially a free man. And an invisible one, it seemed to Claire. As she moved through the hotel, she was always braced to round a corner or step from an elevator and find him suddenly in front of her. She wasn't sure whether she was braced because she wanted to run into him or was dreading it, only that she was becoming a little paranoid waiting for it to happen.

Except it didn't happen. And after a while, she had to stop kidding herself or feigning confusion. She wanted to run into Luke. She wanted him to grab her and kiss her the way he had on the elevator and tell her that he was as madly in love with her as she was with him and that he couldn't live without her.

Barring that, she'd at least like a modicum of closure before she left town.

There was really no logical reason for her to stay any longer. She'd promised Sherry to keep in touch and return for the actual trial. If they needed her input as it drew closer, she could easily provide it from her office in Providence.

If she still had an office in Providence, she thought, sighing as she strolled along the boardwalk in the direction of the Delta Queen. It was hot and she was reduced to souvenir shopping as an excuse for sticking around an extra day or so. She hoped the sweatshirt emblazoned with neon dice would soothe her father's ruffled feathers. They had finally spoken and he had made it clear that he expected her back at her desk first thing Monday morning. Or else.

He had no way of knowing there was nothing he could threaten her with that could hurt her any more than she was already hurting.

Today was Friday. Not much room to maneuver between then and Monday. Especially when you considered that Mona had invited her to have lunch on Monday so that she could introduce Claire to a friend of hers, an attorney who did a great deal of *pro bono* work on behalf of abused women and had a thriving practice besides. The woman was, according to Mona, very interested in taking on a partner, the right partner. Mona insisted Claire was the right partner. Claire was ashamed to admit that she was too lovesick to give much serious thought to her own future. Career-wise, that is. She thought about the possibility of a future with Luke all the time.

She wanted him to call.

She wanted to see him.

She wanted him.

Returning to her room, she let herself in and tossed the bag containing the sweatshirt and a dozen postcards she didn't have the energy to send onto the bed. She turned to close the door and knew instantly that she wasn't alone.

She was intended to know. Luke's jacket hung on the inside doorknob. She turned slowly, purposely avoiding looking at the chair in the corner by the windows.

She noticed his shoes, lying where they had been kicked off by the foot of the bed. She stepped over them on her way to the phone. Lifting the receiver, she depressed the disconnect button with the index finger of her other hand and spoke into the dead receiver.

"Front desk? I'd like to report an intruder in my room."

"Can you describe him, ma'am?" Luke asked from behind her. She hadn't heard him get up from the chair, and his laconic tone suggested he wasn't about to do so in any hurry.

"Yes," she said, still speaking into the phone. "He's stubborn and pigheaded and utterly impossible to reason with."

"Stubborn, pigheaded and impossible, hmm? Could you be a little more specific, ma'am?"

"Yes. He also has an annoying habit of showing up where he's not wanted."

"Maybe he's hoping he is wanted there."

Claire's heart contracted. "Maybe he should have thought of that sooner."

"You have to be patient with the stubborn ones, ma'am. They can be a little slow figuring some things out."

"It's not always easy to be patient."

"Just because it's not easy doesn't mean it won't be fun."

She heard the chair springs squeak and then his footsteps, three soft thuds against the carpet, coming closer.

"So do you want me to send someone to remove this intruder from your room, or can you handle him yourself?"

She had pulled her hair up off her neck to stay cool and he was standing so close she could feel his warm breath on her skin. Her spine turned to water.

"Oh, I could handle him myself," she said. "If I chose to. I'm just not sure I'm in the mood right now."

"In that case I'll get the head of security right on it," Luke promised, leaning closer still, making her senses spin. "In the meantime, try and keep him occupied."

"How do you suggest I do that?"

"You really want to know, ma'am?"

Claire wet her lips. "If I didn't, I wouldn't have asked."

He took the phone from her hand and dropped it back into the cradle. "Turn around, Claire."

Claire slowly turned to face him.

Love in the First Degree

He looked so good to her. She had to fight to keep from tossing her pride and the memory of the past few days of silence aside and just throwing herself into his arms.

He held out his hand, palm up. In it rested a small box wrapped in silver paper. "A going-away present," he said. "I figured turnabout was fair play."

"A going-away present?" she asked, eyeing it with much less interest than she actually felt. "Who says I'm going anywhere?"

"I figured you'd have to get back to work one of these days."

"Maybe. Mona told me about a position here in Atlantic City and I'm considering it. It would probably mean a cut in pay, but I'd be a full partner, doing the kind of work I want to do."

"I hope you do take it," Luke said. "The present is yours, either way." He moved it closer to her.

"I'm not sure I'm in the mood for presents, either," she said, afraid of what was in the tiny, square box, afraid it would rush her toward a decision she wasn't ready to face. She needed to hear more from him first. Much more.

"You have to take it. I've been waiting two days for it to be ready, calling the jeweler every hour to check on it, nagging him to finish so that I could pick it up and bring it to you. I couldn't wait to see you, Claire."

"You couldn't wait to see me?" she countered, shaking her head. "Yet you waited until a jeweler finished whatever is in that box to come here? That doesn't make sense, Luke. Not that that should surprise me."

"I had to wait," he told her, his voice revealing nerves stretched taut over time. A few days' worth of time, at least. "I couldn't come here without it because I didn't know what to say to you. I'm hoping this says all the things I want to say, or at least helps me to get started. Open it, Claire."

She stared at the box. "No."

"No?"

"No," she repeated, putting her hands behind her back. "No. I don't want to open it. I don't want to give you even a smidgen of a reason to think you can hurl accusations and blame at me—unfairly, I might add—and then ignore me, leave me hanging this way for days, and think you can come in here with some stupid ring and—"

"It's not a stupid ring."

"I'm sorry, some wonderful, beautiful ring, the most beautiful ring in the whole world, and—"

"Claire, do yourself a favor before you say anything else. Open the box."

Claire might have ignored his warning, if not for the hint of amusement lurking beneath it. She took the box and opened it and felt like an idiot.

"See?" he said. "It's not a ring."

"No, it certainly isn't." She stared at it. "It's a puzzle piece."

"Eighteen karat gold-plated," Luke said.

"It's a gold-plated puzzle piece."

"Look familiar? It's the piece you threw at me outside the shelter."

"You had a jeweler make a copy?" she asked, lifting it from the box. A fine gold chain was threaded through a small loop at the top.

"It's not a copy. I told you, I had it gold-plated. He messed up the hole the first time and I had to wait an extra day. You can wear it around your neck, if you want."

She looked up and saw his face become shadowed and vulnerable and realized that the cool, sophisticated Luke Cabrio, gambler and rescue artist extraordinaire, was nervous. At that instant, the most beautiful ring in the world couldn't have meant as much to her as the gold piece in her hand.

"I love it," she told him. "But now there'll always be a piece missing from your puzzle."

Luke felt a surge of frustration. "Claire, I don't give a damn about the puzzle. I'm more concerned with the piece that's missing from my life." He took a deep breath and reached down deep for more courage than he'd ever needed to break up a fight in the casino or toss a drunk from one of the bars. "That missing piece is you," he told her. "I was sort of hoping that giving this to you would get the message across without me having to actually say it all."

"Say it, Luke."

"It's not easy."

"Just because it's not easy doesn't mean it can't be fun." She stretched to put her arms around his neck and sidled up against him. "Better?"

"Feels better. Doesn't make it any easier to come up with the words for what I want to say, though. So I'm just going to say it. You were right," he told her, his hands resting lightly on her hips. She was wearing some kind of soft, gauzy blouse over shorts and it felt great. Her nearness slowly slipped the leash off a craving that had been several long, lonely days in the making.

"Right about what?" she asked.

"About me being afraid. I *was* afraid. Afraid to let myself become too important in anyone else's life because I might screw up somehow, the way my old man always did, the way I've seen so many people do. I didn't want to be like him in any way."

"You're not," Claire insisted, moving her hand to his cheek, stroking him in a move as dangerous as waving a match near spilled gasoline. "From what you've told me, I know you could never be like him."

"In some ways, no," he said. He caught her hand and held it still against his cheek before her touch drove him crazy. "In others, we're more alike than I want to think. He was a great one for taking the easy way out, and so am I."

"The easy way out? Luke Cabrio, if there's one thing I will never accuse you of doing it's taking the easy way out."

"I do. It's just that the easy way for me is different from what it was for my father, different from most folks, I guess. The easiest thing for me to do is always to get involved physically to put a stop to anything I can't deal with emotionally. I'd try to stop my father from hitting my mother. I stopped those guys from hurting you when I really wanted you myself. I can take the heat for Sherry, but I can't face having Ben know I'm his father. You called it—I come riding in on my white charger and then get away fast, before I have to live up to anyone's expectations. Before I have to find out for sure if I can live up to my own."

She rested her head lightly on his chest, giving him all the time he needed to continue.

"This time I can't do that," he said finally. "I don't want to get away from Ben. Or from you." His tone reflected the amazement he still felt at that discovery. "I love you, Claire. I want you to stay here with me. I want you to marry me. If you don't, you'll always be the piece missing from my life."

"Oh, Luke..."

"I don't expect you to answer right now. I know I hurt you, left you hanging. I know I'm a poor risk—"

"Funny you should mention risk," she interrupted, gazing at him with a smile that lit up her face. "Did you know that even for us diehard nongambling types, there's always one particular risk we can never turn down?"

He shook his head, afraid to hope. Him, the hotshot gambler, afraid to risk it.

"You're my risk," she whispered.

"You mean it? You'll marry me? I know it will be a big adjustment for you to make."

"How big an adjustment can it be? I already have a job offer. You have a great suite here at the hotel," she teased.

"I don't expect you to live here. I'll tell Max it's regular hours for me from now on. I'll buy a house. With a big fenced yard."

"Where you can teach Ben and Nicky to play ball."

Love in the First Degree

"And where I can make love to you under the stars." His mouth dropped to cover hers, his tongue tracing the soft contours of her lips. "I've actually dreamed about that, you know. Over and over."

"What a coincidence."

"You've dreamed about making love with me under the stars?" His hands reached inside her shirt, touching, searching, inviting.

She swayed against him, accepting. "No. But I've dreamed a lot about making love with you in a gym. Does that count?"

"It counts. Under the stars, in a gym, underwater...it all counts."

His hands closed over her breasts.

She moaned softly and said, "Underwater?"

"Did I mention the yard also has to have a pool?" he asked, bringing his lips to her throat.

"I don't think so."

"And a Jacuzzi."

Her head fell back. "Mmm."

"A swing set."

"Strictly for the boys' use, of course," she whispered.

"Want to bet?"

"On you? Always, Luke, always."

* * * * *

Silhouette celebrates motherhood in May with...

**Debbie Macomber
Jill Marie Landis
Gina Ferris Wilkins**

in

Three Mothers & a Cradle

Join three award-winning authors in this beautiful collection you'll treasure forever. The same antique, hand-crafted cradle connects these three heartwarming romances, which celebrate the joys and excitement of motherhood. Makes the perfect gift for yourself or a loved one!

A special celebration of love,

Only from

Silhouette®

—where passion lives.

MD95

THE MACKADE BROTHERS

the exciting new series by
New York Times bestselling author

Nora Roberts

The MacKade Brothers—looking for trouble, and always finding it. Now they're on a collision course with love. And it all begins with

**THE RETURN OF RAFE MACKADE
(Intimate Moments #631, April 1995)**

The whole town was buzzing. Rafe MacKade was back in Antietam, and that meant only one thing—there was bound to be trouble....

Be on the lookout for the next book in the series, **THE PRIDE OF JARED MACKADE— Silhouette Special Edition's 1000th Book!** It's an extraspecial event not to be missed, coming your way in December 1995!

THE MACKADE BROTHERS—these sexy, trouble-loving men will be heading out to you in alternate books from Silhouette Intimate Moments and Silhouette Special Edition.
Watch out for them!

INTIMATE MOMENTS®
™ *Silhouette®*

NRTITLE

**UP IN THE SKY—IT'S A BIRD, IT'S A PLANE, IT'S...
THOMAS DUFFY'S BRIDE-TO-BE!**

SPELLBOUND ROMANCE

Years ago, a very young Thomas Duffy had found a lost girl from another planet crying in the woods. He dried her tears, helped her find her spaceship—and never saw her again.

Then one day Janella, now very much a woman, dropped from the sky into his Iowa backyard, in need of a husband.

But the last thing Thomas Duffy wanted was a wife—especially one from another planet.

**OUT-OF-THIS-WORLD MARRIAGE
by Maggie Shayne**

available in April, only from—

INTIMATE MOMENTS®
Silhouette®

SPELL7

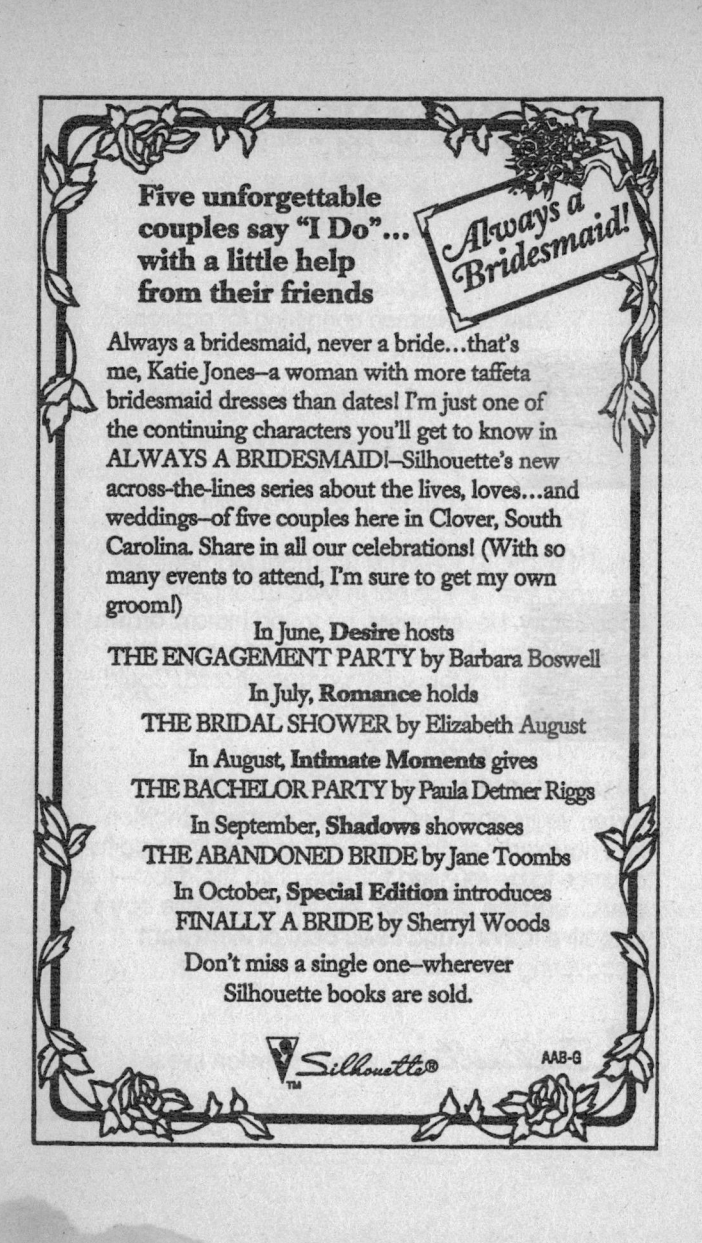

Five unforgettable couples say "I Do"... with a little help from their friends

Always a Bridesmaid!

Always a bridesmaid, never a bride...that's me, Katie Jones—a woman with more taffeta bridesmaid dresses than dates! I'm just one of the continuing characters you'll get to know in ALWAYS A BRIDESMAID!—Silhouette's new across-the-lines series about the lives, loves...and weddings—of five couples here in Clover, South Carolina. Share in all our celebrations! (With so many events to attend, I'm sure to get my own groom!)

In June, **Desire** hosts
THE ENGAGEMENT PARTY by Barbara Boswell

In July, **Romance** holds
THE BRIDAL SHOWER by Elizabeth August

In August, **Intimate Moments** gives
THE BACHELOR PARTY by Paula Detmer Riggs

In September, **Shadows** showcases
THE ABANDONED BRIDE by Jane Toombs

In October, **Special Edition** introduces
FINALLY A BRIDE by Sherryl Woods

Don't miss a single one—wherever Silhouette books are sold.

Silhouette®

AAB-G

INTIMATE MOMENTS®
Silhouette

WOUNDED WARRIORS

Men and women hungering for passion
to soothe their lonely souls.

The new Intimate Moments miniseries by

Beverly Bird

continues in May 1995 with

A MAN WITHOUT A HAVEN (Intimate Moments #641)
The word *forever* was not in Mac Tshongely's
vocabulary. Nevertheless, he found himself drawn
to headstrong Shadow Bedonie and the promise
of tomorrow that this sultry woman offered. Could
home really be where the heart is?

Coming in July 1995

A MAN WITHOUT A WIFE (Intimate Moments #652)
Seven years ago Ellen Lonetree made a decision
that haunted her days and nights. Now she had the
chance to be reunited with the child she'd lost—if she
could resist the attraction she felt for the little boy's
adoptive father...and keep both of them from
discovering her secret.

Silhouette® ...where passion lives.

BBWW-2